The Fine Colour of Rust

P.A. O'Reilly

W F HOWES LTD

This large print edition published in 2012 by
W F Howes Ltd
Unit 4, Rearsby Business Park, Gaddesby Lane,
Rearsby, Leicester LE7 4YH

1 3 5 7 9 10 8 6 4 2

First published in the United Kingdom in 2012
by Blue Door

A CIP catalogue record for this book is available
from the British Library

ISBN 978 1 40749 628 3

Typeset by Palimpsest Book Production Limited,
Falkirk, Stirlingshire
Printed and bound in Great Britain
by MPG Books Ltd, Bodmin, Cornwall

The Fine Colour of Rust

R

The Japanese have a word, *sabi*, which
connotes the simple beauty of worn and
imperfect and impermanent things:
a weathered fence; an old cracking bough
in a tree; a silver bowl mottled with tarnish;
the fine colour of rust.

CHAPTER 1

Norm Stevens Senior tells me I'll never get that truck off my land. He says it's too old, been there too long, the hoist will try to lift the thing and it will break apart into red stones of rust.

'Leave it,' he says. 'Let it rust away. One day you'll look and it won't be there anymore.' He gives me a sideways glance. 'Like husbands. You look away and when you look back they're gone, right?'

'Right.'

'So have you heard from the bastard?'

'Nope.'

'And you're getting by all right? For money?'

'I've got more money now than when he was here.'

We both laugh.

'Now, Loretta, you know I can take the kids for a night if you need some time off.'

'I might take you up on that. I've got a prospect. A biker, but a nice one, not a loser. On a Harley, no less.'

'A Harley?' He raises his eyebrows. Whenever he

does that, a pink scaly half-moon of skin above his left eyebrow wrinkles. He reaches up to touch it.

'You should have that looked at, Norm.'

'Yeah, yeah, and I should give up the spare parts work and get out of the sun too.'

He gestures around his junkyard. There are tractor parts, rolls of wire, tyres, motor mowers, corrugated iron sheets all rusted and folded, bits of cars and engines, pots and pans, gas bottles, tools, toys, bed frames, oil drums, the chipped blades of threshers and harvesters. Some of the machinery is so bent and broken you can't even tell what it was meant for. In the centre of the yard is a lemon tree, the only greenery in sight. It always has lemons. I'm sure I know what Norm does to help it along, but I don't ask. He's got four guard dogs too, tied up around the yard, vicious snarling things. As if anyone would want to steal any of this crap.

'Well, I'd better pick up the kids,' I say. I don't want to pick up the kids. I want to send them to an orphanage and buy myself a nice dress and learn to live the way I used to, before I turned into the old scrag I am now.

'Don't you worry about that truck.' Norm stretches out his long skinny arm and pats me on the back. 'It'll go back into the land.'

I get into the car, pump the accelerator like I'm at the gym and turn the key three times before the engine fires. I should have that looked at, I think. There's half a kilo of sausages on the seat beside me, and I realize they've been sitting in the sun for half an hour. When I unwrap the paper and have a sniff I get a funny sulphur smell. They'll cook up all right, I tell myself, and I gun the Holden and screech in a U-turn on to the road. I can't get used to this huge engine – every time I take off I sound like a pack of hoons at Bathurst.

It's three thirty already and Jake and Melissa will be waiting at the school gate, ready to jump in and whine about how everyone else's mum always gets there before I do. Maybe I will drop them off at the orphanage.

When I get to the school gate the kids are both standing with their hands on their hips. I wonder if they got that from me; old scrag standing with her hands on her hips, pursing her thin lips, squinting into the sun. You could make a statue of that. It would look like half the women in this town. Dust and a few plastic bags swirling around its feet, the tail lights of the husband's car receding into the distance. They should cast it in bronze and put it in the foyer of Social Security.

'Mum, we have to have four sheets of coloured cardboard for the project tomorrow.'

'All right.'

'And me too, Mum, I have to have a lead pencil and I don't want bananas in my lunch anymore because they stink.'

'All right.'

As I steer the great car down the highway

towards home I have a little dream. I'll swing into the driveway and sitting next to the veranda will be a shiny maroon Harley Davidson. I won't dare to look, but out of the corner of my eye I'll see a boot resting on the step, maybe with spurs on it. Then I'll slowly lift my head and he'll be staring at me the way George Clooney stared into J. Lo's eyes in *Out of Sight* and I'll take a deep breath and say to him, 'Can you hang on five minutes while I drop the kids at the orphanage?'

What I actually find when we get home is a bag of lemons sitting on the veranda. Norm must have left them while we were at the newsagent.

'Who are these from?' Jake asks.

'Norm.'

'How do you know?'

'Oil on the bag.'

I bought Norm a cake of Solvol once. Delivered it to the junkyard wrapped in pretty pink paper with a bow. He rang to thank me. 'I think you're insulting me.'

'It's for your own good, Norm.'

'You're a minx. If I was thirty years younger . . .'

'Fifty more like,' I told him, 'before you'd get those paws on me.'

That night, when the kids are finally settled in their rooms doing their homework, I get on the phone for the usual round of begging.

'Are you coming to the meeting tomorrow?'

'Oh, Loretta, I'm sorry, I completely forgot. I've made other plans.'

I can imagine Helen's plans. They'll involve a cask of white and six changes of clothes before she collapses on the bed in tears and starts ringing her friends – me – asking why she can't find a man. Is she too old, has she lost her looks? It helps to leave the house occasionally, I have to remind her. She certainly hasn't lost her looks. Auburn hair without a single grey strand. Straight white teeth. A country tan. Unlike mousey-haired skinny scragwoman me, she even has a cleavage.

'The grade-three teacher's coming,' I tell her, certain this will change her mind. 'And Brianna's offered to mind all the kids at her place. She must have hired a bouncer.'

'He's told you he's coming?'

'Yeah, he left a message on my machine,' I lie.

So Helen's in. After I herd up seven others with more lies and false promises, I put the sausages on. Sure enough, the sulphur smell fades once they start to burn. I used to enjoy cooking quiche and fancy fried rice and mud cake. Gourmet, like on the telly, the boyfriend would boast to his mates. Then we get married and it's, 'Listen, darl, I wouldn't mind a chop for a change.' Now the kids think gourmet is pickles on your sandwich. They won't even look at a sundried tomato. Last time I tried that, Jake picked them out of the spaghetti sauce and left them lined up like red bits of chewed meat on the side of the plate. 'Gross,' he said, and I had to agree, seeing them like that.

★   ★   ★

5

The meeting's in the small room at the Neighbourhood House because the Church of Goodwill had already booked the large room by the time I got round to organizing tonight's meeting. We're sitting pretty much on top of each other, trying to balance cups of tea and Scotch Finger biscuits on our knees. Maxine is supposed to be taking the minutes.

I thought I'd made it up, but the grade-three teacher has come, and Helen's paralysed with excitement and terror. She's wearing enough perfume to spontaneously combust and the smell's so overwhelming that Maxine has to swing the door open. Two minutes later the noise from the meeting next door starts up.

'Yes!' they all shout. 'Yes! I do, I do!'

'Well, I don't.' Maxine swings the door half-shut so that we're dizzy with perfume but still having to shout over the frantic clapping of people being saved next door.

I give the list of apologies and welcome everyone who's come, introducing the grade-three teacher in case the others don't know him. Helen's gone as pink and glistening as a baby fresh out of the bath. She'll have a seizure if she's not careful. I can't see the attraction. The teacher's five foot four, stocky, and always says, 'At the end of the day.'

'At the end of the day,' he says when I introduce him, 'I am totally committed to this cause. Our jobs are at risk too.'

Just in case, I look down at his feet, but no spurs.

I read out the list of agenda items. Brenda sighs loudly.

'Do we have to do all this agenda crap? And the motions? I motion, you motion. My Mark's doing motions you wouldn't believe and I have to be home by nine in case I need to take him to Emergency.'

'Yes, we do. Because we're trying to be bloody official. And as you well know, an emergency department that closes at ten in a town half an hour away is one of the reasons we're here. Soon this town will have no services for a hundred kilometres.'

'Oh, yes, ma'am.'

I roll my eyes. Maxine rolls her eyes. For a moment I think of us all rolling our eyes like a bunch of lunatics in the asylum and I almost cheer up.

'Item one. I've written a letter to the member for our local constituency about the closure of the school.' I pause for the inevitable joke about members which, to my amazement, doesn't come. 'We need everyone who has kids in the school to sign.'

'It'll never work.' Brenda is the optimist of the committee.

'Does anyone know how to drain the oil from a sump?' Kyleen pipes up.

Only another half an hour, I think, and I can pick up the kids from Brianna's, drop them at the orphanage and drive straight down to Melbourne. With the experience I've got, I'll land a good job in a centre for adults with attention deficit disorder.

When I pull up at Brianna's, the kids run to the front door, looking pleased to see me. They're way too quiet in the back seat. They must have done something horrible.

'So did you have a good time?' I ask. I speed up to catch the amber light and the Holden roars with the might of a drunken trucker. I can't make out exactly what Melissa says, but I might have heard the word *fight*. I think back. Were they limping when they got into the car? Was there blood? I can't remember anything like that so I turn on the radio and keep driving along the dark highway, listening to the soothing sound of a voice calling race seven of the trots, something I've learned to love since the radio got stuck on this station.

'Mum?' Melissa says, as we pull into the unsurprisingly Harley-free driveway.

'Yes, sweetie?'

'I don't ever want to leave this house.'

'I thought you wanted to live in a hundred-room mansion with ten servants and a personal home-work attendant?'

'Nup.'

'I know what it is – you love what I've done with the place.' My children were so impressed when I fixed the damp patch beside the stove with a hairdryer, a bottle of glue paste and three of Jake's artworks. I had been calling the agent about it for months, but my house is clearly outside the real estate zone of care and responsibility.

'Mum, I'm serious. If Dad sends a letter and we've moved we won't get it.'

I want to believe he'll send a letter – to his children, at least.

'Well, that's settled. We're staying.'

When we get inside, the kids brush their teeth without a single protest and climb into bed.

'You OK, Jakie?' I lean down to kiss him goodnight.

'Brianna and her boyfriend had a fight,' he whispers. 'I think he hit her.'

I kiss him twice, then again.

'I'm sure she's all right. I'll call her tomorrow. You go to sleep now.'

'I don't want bananas in my lunch.'

'I wouldn't dream of it. Bananas stink,' I say as I turn out the light.

Next morning, as I'm packing bananas into their lunch boxes, I realize I forgot to thank Norm for the lemons.

I drop into the yard on the way back from the shops. He's down the back of the block with three other blokes, all of them standing in a line with their arms folded, staring at the body of an old tractor. This would be the matching statue to mine: bloke standing, feet apart, arms folded, staring at a piece of broken machinery. No idea how to fix it. We could put Him and Her statues either side of the highway coming into Gunapan.

I wait beside the shed while the delicate sales negotiations go on. I've never understood exactly how the communication works. Perhaps the meaning is in the number of head nods, or the volume of the grunt as the customer shifts from one leg to the other. After they've stared at the tractor body in apparent silence for five minutes, Norm sees me and ambles up.

'Don't tell me you're going to sell something, Norm?'

'Not bloody likely. Every month these three clowns are here with some new scheme for making money.'

'None of them happens to ride a Harley?'

He doesn't even bother answering, just nods his head at their ute on the road. We step inside the shed for a cuppa. The radio's on the racing station.

'Harlequin Dancer made a good run from fourth in race seven last night,' I remark.

'You need a new car. I'm working on it, love. Shouldn't be too much longer.' Norm hands me a cup, covered in grease, and a paper towel to wipe it with.

There are enough parts in Norm's yard for him to put together ten perfectly good cars, and he has been trying to build me a new one for years. But his speciality is disassembly rather than assembly. As soon as the collection of engine parts and panels begins to bear a resemblance to an actual car, he decides it's not right and has to pull it apart and start again.

He takes a noisy slurp of his tea before he speaks again. 'Sorry I didn't get to the meeting.'

'The school's not your problem.'

'Course it's my problem. It's everybody's bloody problem.'

We drink our tea. The three blokes wave as they pass the shed. There's a protest at Randwick in race two. The jockey on the second-placed horse is alleging interference from the winner at the final turn.

'I've got money on that horse.' Norm turns up the volume.

'Which one?'

'The one that'll buy you a bottle of bubbly if it wins the protest. Long odds. Very long odds. Bring me luck, Loretta.'

The day's starting to heat up and blowies are banging against the tin roof of the shed. Norm picks up the trannie and holds it to his ear. I look out at the heat shimmering over the piles of junk. Norm's touching his crusty forehead as he listens for the outcome of the protest. He must win against the odds sometimes, I think – otherwise why bother betting?

CHAPTER 2

Thank you for your letter of 9 January. I fully understand the concerns you have expressed and would like to take this opportunity to explain how these concerns are being addressed by your government.

When I show the committee members the letter at the next meeting they hoot like owls. 'Fully understand!' 'Take this opportunity!' It's as good as a party, they laugh so much.

'I told you it wouldn't work.' Brenda nods sagely.

'It's a step.' I'm not letting her get away with *I told you so.* 'The first step. It's a game. We make a bid, they try to negotiate us down.'

'Sure.' She's still doing that nod. 'Like we've got real negotiating power.'

'Shut up, Brenda,' Norm says.

Helen is here again but the grade-three teacher is missing so Helen is downcast. No, she's more than downcast. Her high hair has flagged. Perhaps the heat in the air has melted the gel. Whatever

12

happened, the fluffy creation that brushed the architrave when she walked in has flattened out to match her spirit and she's slumped in the orange plastic chair beside me, motionless bar the occasional crackle as she winkles another Kool Mint from her open bag, pretending no one can hear the sighs and crunches of her working her way through the packet.

'I've written another letter,' I tell them. 'This time, I've copied it to our shire councillors, the local member, the prime minister, the headmaster, the school board, all the teachers and all of the parents at the school.'

Silence. Kyleen opens her mouth and closes it when Maxine jabs her in the ribs. Norm flips through the pages of minutes in his hands. The air is close and still and next door at the Church of Goodwill meeting someone is talking loud and long in a deep voice.

'I spent our whole budget on photocopying and postage,' I go on. 'You'll get the letter in the mail tomorrow.'

'Is that why we haven't got biscuits?' Trust Kyleen to ask. I've always wondered how many of them only came for the biscuits.

'I buy the biscuits,' Maxine answers. 'I didn't have time, that's all.'

We fall back into silence.

Eventually I speak. 'We could give up. Let them close the school – we can carpool to get the kids to Halstead Primary.'

13

No one moves. Brenda's staring at the floor. I'm expecting her to jump in and agree with me. Her house is painted a dull army green and her clothes are beige and puce and brown and her kids stay out on the streets till eight or nine at night as Brenda turns on light after light and stands silhouetted in the doorway with her cardigan pulled tight around her, waiting for them to come home. She turns up to my meetings as if she is only here to make sure nothing good happens from them. But tonight she reaches over to pat me on the knee.

'Loretta, I know it won't work, and you probably know deep down it won't work, but you can't give up now,' she says.

Kyleen stands up and punches the air, as if she's at a footie match. 'That's right! Don't give up, Loretta. Like they said in *Dead Poets Society*, "Nil bastardum",' she pauses, then trails off, '"carburettorum" . . .'

'"Grindem down"?' Norm finishes.

Next day, Norm's cleaning motor parts with kerosene when I knock on the tin frame of his shed.

'Knew it was you. You should try braking a little earlier, Loretta.' He doesn't even have to look up.

'Norm, what happened to your forehead?'

'Bloody doctor chopped off half my face.'

'Oh, God, I knew it. I knew something was wrong with that patch of skin. Not skin cancer?' My heart is banging in my chest.

'Not anymore.' He reaches up to touch the white

14

bandage, which is already covered in oily fingerprints. 'They think they got it all.'

He dunks the engine part into the tin of kerosene and scrapes at it with a screwdriver. I want to hug him, but he and I don't do that sort of thing. I'm going to buy him sunscreen and make him wear it, especially on those sticking-out ears of his. I'll buy him a hat and long-sleeved shirts. I can't imagine life without him.

'Mum, I found some flat tin.' Melissa is in the doorway, shading her eyes with her hand and watching Jake teetering on top of a beaten-up caravan, his arms whirling like propellers.

'Jake, don't move,' I scream.

My toe stubs a railway sleeper as I bolt towards the caravan.

He was probably fine until I panicked. His eyes widen when he looks down and realizes how high he is. His first howl sets off the guard dogs. His second howl sets off car alarms across town. By the time Norm and I coax him down we've both sustained permanent hearing loss. I hold him against me and his howls ease to sobbing.

'Come on, mate, it wasn't that bad.' Norm lifts Jake from my grasp and swings him down to the ground. 'I'll get you a can of lemonade.'

Jake takes a long, hiccupping breath followed by a cat-in-heat kind of moan as he lets out the air.

'Mum! I told you, I found some.' Melissa pulls me, limping, to the back of the yard.

My toe is throbbing and I'm sweating and cross.

15

I wonder why I don't buy a couple of puce cardigans and sink back into the land myself, like Brenda or that truck.

We drag the bits of tin to the shed where Jake is sitting on the counter listening to the golden oldies radio station while Norm scans *Best Bets*.

'Have you got any paint for this tin? I'm going to make signs for the school.'

Norm shakes his head. 'You're a battler, Loretta. And I suppose I'm expected to put them up?'

'On the fence.'

One of my best dreams is Beamer Man. Beamer Man powers his BMW up to the front of the house and snaps off the engine. He swings open his door, jumps out and strides up my path holding expensive wine in one hand and two tickets to Kiddieland in the other.

'We'll need the children out of the way for a week or so,' he explains, 'while I explore every inch of your gorgeous body.'

'Taxi's here. Have a lovely week.' I can feel his eyes on my effortlessly acquired size-ten torso as I give the kids a gentle push out the door.

They run happily to the taxi, clutching their all-you-can-eat-ride-and-destroy Kiddieland tickets, then Beamer Man closes the front door and presses me against the wall.

'Mum, you've painted "Save Our Schol". And you've got paint on your face,' Melissa interrupts to tell me before I get to the good part.

Why did I decide to do this in the front yard? My arms are smeared to the elbows with marine paint, and I'm in the saggy old shorts I swore I'd never wear outside the house. Imagine if Harley Man or Beamer Man went by.

I have a terrible thought. Did Norm mean battler or battleaxe? The school had better be worth all this.

CHAPTER 3

Norm's come by to drop off more lemons and pick up a few of my lemon tarts. He leans in an old-man-at-the-pub kind of way on the mantelpiece and picks up a postcard I've propped against the candlestick.

'Who's this from?' he asks, turning it over without waiting for an answer.

'My sister, Patsy, the one who works at the uni in Melbourne. She's on a research trip to Paris.'

'She works at the uni?' He props the card back after he's read it.

'Yep, she's a lecturer there.'

'She must be pretty smart. What happened to you?' Norm winks at Jake, who giggles and scratches his face the way he's been doing since he got up. I know what's wrong but I'm trying to pretend it's not true. Even though the kids in his grade have all had the vaccine, some have still come down with a mild case of chickenpox.

'Dropped on my head as a baby. So did you get the windscreen?'

'Didn't get it, but tracked one down. A new bloke is doing car repairs out the end of the Bolton

Road. Set up the other week. Actually, he's about your age. Not bad looking either. Good business. Nice and polite.'

'Beautiful wife, six well-behaved children,' I add.

Norm leans back and frowns. 'Really?'

'No, but probably.'

'I don't think so. He smelled of bachelor to me. Divorced maybe. Anyway, he quoted me a good price, said to bring the car and he'd put in the windscreen straight away. So you can take it down whenever you like.'

'What's his name?' I ask Norm.

'Merv Bull.'

I shake my head. Only in Gunapan. Merv Bull sounds like an old farmer with black teeth and hay in his hair who scoops yellow gobs from his ear and stares at them for minutes on end like they'll forecast the weather. The image keeps replaying in my mind as I finish wrapping the lemon tarts in waxed paper.

'You can't judge people by their names, Loretta, or you'd be able to carry a tune.'

'That's unkind, Norm. I may not have turned out to be the talented country-singing daughter my mother was hoping for, but then, neither did Patsy or Tammy. We haven't got the genes for it. I don't know why Mum keeps up these crazy fantasies.'

A week and a half later, after having been held hostage in the house by a child even more itchy and irritable than normal, I set out to get the new windscreen.

It's years since I've driven down the Bolton Road. I remember when we first moved to Gunapan I got lost down here. I was heading for the Maternal Health Centre. My first pregnancy. My face was so puffed up with heat and water retention I looked like I had the mumps. I took a left turn at the ghost gum past the stockfeed store as the nurse had advised on the phone, and suddenly I was in another world. Later, of course, after I'd found my way back into town, I realized I'd turned left at the wattle tree past the Pet Emporium, but anyway, it was as if I'd magically slipped out of Gunapan and into fairyland. The bush came right up to the roadside, and in the blazing heat of the day the shade from the eucalypts dropped the temperature at least five degrees. I got out of the car, waddled to a picnic bench in a clearing and sat drinking water for twenty minutes. Hope bubbled up in me. The baby would be fine, my husband Tony would turn out not to be a nong, we would definitely win the lottery that Saturday.

Only one of those things came true, but I've always loved that bit of bush. I'd come out here with the kids sometimes in the early days and walk the tracks, listening to the sound of the bush, when I could hear it above their endless chatter, and smelling the minty eucalypts.

We've just swung into the Bolton Road when

Jake asks if he can have a Mooma Bar from the supermarket. His chickenpox has dwindled to a few annoying itchy spots, but they won't let him back into school yet, no matter how much I beg. He's bored and tailing me like a debt collector. Any excuse to get out is good.

'There's no supermarket out here.' The moment I speak I see a shopping trolley on the side of the road. Someone must have walked that trolley five kilometres. Unless it was tossed in the back of a ute and driven here. Further along the road is one of those orange hats they use to steer drivers away from roadworks. A couple of minutes on we see a load of rubbish dumped a few metres off the road. A dozen beer bottles lie around the charcoal of an old fire with what looks like bits of an old picnic bench sticking out of it. A heap of lawn clippings moulders beside a brown hoodie and a pair of torn-up jeans. I slow down, pull the Holden over to the side of the road. The trees still come right up to the roadside, but behind them is light, as if someone is shining a torch through the forest.

'We came here on my birthday,' Jake reminds me.

He's right. We came out two years ago with green lemonade and presents and a birthday cake in the shape of a swimming pool. Kyleen and Maxine and their kids came, and we played hidey at the old shearers' hut. Three kangaroos burst out from behind the hut when we arrived and crashed off through the bush. We called them 'shearing kangaroos' and Jake thought that was a real kind of 'roo till Norm put him right. But now I can't make sense of where that hut might be. The face of the forest is completely different. Ahead of us, a wide dusty dirt road leads in through the trees. I can't see the picnic area. And that light through the trees is wrong.

I drive along the bitumen to where the dirt road enters the bushland.

'I don't want to go in there,' Jake says.

More rubbish litters the side of the track – plastic bags and bottles, juice containers, old clothes, building materials – as if this piece of bushland has become the local tip. I peer along the track. It seems to lead into a big clearing that wasn't there before. The bush used to stretch way back. I would never let the kids run too far in case they got lost. Now if they ran off they'd end up standing in a flat empty paddock the size of a footy field.

'Footy field,' I mutter. 'Maybe they're building a new footy field.'

That can't be right, because even the old footy field is in trouble. The footy club has a sausage sizzle every Saturday morning outside the supermarket to raise money to buy in water. All the sports clubs around here are desperate for water. Some have had to close down because the ground is so hard it can crack the shins of anyone landing awkwardly on the surface.

'Let's go. I'm bored.'

'Hey, Jake, open your mouth again and show

me your teeth. I think it might be time for a trip to the dentist.'

That always shuts him up. We climb back into the Holden and reverse into the Bolton Road to continue the journey to our new windscreen.

CHAPTER 4

'Look at all these cars, Jake.' We pull in with a mighty shriek of brakes at Merv Bull's Motor and Machinery Maintenance and Repairs. 'Why don't you hop out and have a look around while I talk to the man. Look at that one – a Monaro from the seventies! You don't see those much anymore. Especially in that dazzling aqua.'

Jake purses his lips and rolls his eyes and waggles his head all at once. He keeps doing this lately. I wonder if he's seen a Bollywood film on the diet of daytime television that filled up chickenpox week.

'Are you trying to get rid of me, Mum?'

'Yes.'

He sighs and swings open the car door. He slouches his way to the shade at the side of the shed while I quickly pat down my hair in the rear-view mirror before I step out of the car. I can't see any sign of Merv Bull. A panting blue heeler stares at me from the doorway of the shed as if I'm a piece of meat.

'Hello?' I call. 'Mr Bull?'

The blue heeler slumps to the ground and lays

its head on its front paws, still staring at me. The sign on the side of the shed says *Nine to Five, Monday to Friday*. I look at my watch. Ten fifteen, Tuesday morning.

Jake scuffs his way over to my side. 'There's no one here, Mum, let's go. Let's go to the milk bar. You promised that if I . . . you would . . . and then I . . . and then . . .'

As Jake goes on with his extended thesis on why I should buy him a Violet Crumble, I shout 'Mr Bull!' one last time. A man emerges from the darkness of the shed. The first thing I notice is that he's hitching up his pants. He strides forwards to greet me and stretches out his hand, but I'm not shaking anything I can't be sure was washed. When my hand fails to arrive he pulls back his arm and wipes both hands down the sides of his shirt. He's standing between me and the sun. I can't see his face let alone its expression.

Jake's jaw has dropped and he's staring at Merv Bull as if he's seen a vision. He's this way with any man who's around the age of his father when he left.

'Hi,' Jake whispers.

'Hello.' Merv Bull leans down to shake Jake's hand. 'I'm Merv. Who are you, then?'

'Jake.'

'Pardon me?'

Jake's awestruck voice has soared into a register that only the blue heeler and I can hear.

'This is Jake,' I step in, 'and I'm Loretta. I think Norm Stevens told you I was coming?'

'Ah, you're the windscreen.'

'That's me.'

'Can't do it till this afternoon, sorry. But you could leave the car here and pick it up at five.'

'Sure.' I put on a bright fake smile. 'Jake and I'll walk the five kilometres back into town in this thirty-degree heat and have a pedicure while we wait.'

'We could stay here and look at the cars,' Jake whispers.

Merv Bull shades his eyes with his hand and looks down at me. I can see him better now. Norm was right, he's handsome in a parched rural bloke kind of way. Blue eyes and dark eyelashes. Looks as if he squints a lot, but who doesn't around here. He's frowning at me like a schoolteacher frowns at the kid with the smart mouth.

'I do have a loan car you can use while yours is in the shop. To get you to your pedicure, that is.'

'Ha, sorry, only joking.' I'm turning into a bitter old hag. I'm reminding myself of Brenda. Soon I'll become strangely attracted to beige. 'That would be great. Any old car will do. I mean, hey, we are used to the Rolls Royce here.'

'Mum! That's not a Rolls Royce. It's a Holden!' Jake beams proudly at Merv.

'You certainly do know your cars, mate.' Merv pats Jake on the shoulder.

Now I'll never get Jake out of here. Merv, to be addressed hereafter as God, goes back into the shed to get the keys for the exchange car, and Jake and the blue heeler trot faithfully after him. I watch his long lanky walk. My husband never walked that way, even though he was about the same size as Merv Bull. My husband Tony – God love him wherever he may be and keep him there and never let him come back into my life – was a stomper. He stomped through the house as though he was trying to keep down unruly carpet; he stomped in and out of shops and pubs letting doors slam around him; he stomped to work at the delivery company and stomped home stinking of his own fug after eight hours in the truck; and one day he stomped out to the good car and drove off and never stomped back.

We'd been married ten years. I never dreamed he'd leave me. After the second year of marriage, when I fell pregnant with Melissa, I settled down and stopped fretting that I'd married the wrong man. It was too late, so I decided to try to enjoy my life and not spend all my time thinking about what could have been. I thought he had decided that too.

A month after he'd gone a postcard arrived. By that time I'd already finished making a fool of myself telling the police he must have run his car off the road somewhere and insisting they find him. The postcard said he was sorry, he needed to get away. *I'll be in touch. Cheque coming soon.*

Still waiting for that cheque.

'It's the red Mazda with the sheepskin seat covers over by the fence.' Merv Bull hands me a set of car keys on a key ring in the shape of a beer stubby. 'She's a bit stiff in the clutch, but otherwise she drives pretty easy.'

'Been getting a lot of business?' As I speak I take Jake's hand in mine and edge him quietly towards the Mazda before he realizes that we're about to leave his new hero.

'It's been good. They told me it'd take a while to get the ordinary car business going again, especially since no one's worked here for a few years, but I guess I've been lucky. I'll probably have to get an apprentice when the big machinery starts arriving.'

'Big machinery?'

'For the development. Whenever it starts. I thought it was supposed to be in Phase One already. That's what they promised me when I bought the place.'

'Right.' I've lived in this town for years and I still haven't got a clue what's going on. 'So that big hole in the bush on the Bolton Road is the development?'

'Yep. But for the moment what I've got is cars, and there seems to be no shortage.'

I look at him again. I want to ask if it's been mainly women customers but I don't. I will have to tell Helen about Merv Bull. If Merv is single and if he doesn't hook up with anyone in a hurry, he'll be a rich man in this town. He'll be mystified at how many parts appear to have simply fallen off cars. I inch closer to our loan car, still not letting on to Jake what I'm doing.

I stop as my arm is yanked backwards. Jake has caught on and he's trying to pull his hand out of mine.

'Can I stay here, Mum? Please!'

'No, Jakie. Mr Bull has to do his work.'

'I'll be quiet, I promise. I'll look at the cars. You go and I'll wait here.'

Merv Bull looks at me.

'He can't bear to spend a minute without me,' I say.

'I can see that,' Merv answers.

Finally we manoeuvre Jake into the car with a promise of a workshop tour when we return.

'How much will it cost?' I remember to ask as I pump the accelerator and turn the key the way I would in the Holden. The tiny Mazda lets out a roar of protest. 'Sorry, sorry!'

'Might drive a bit differently to your car.' Merv calmly waves the exhaust smoke away from his face. 'Should cost about a hundred dollars. Maybe a hundred and twenty, but no more.'

While the magically vanishing husband was not good for much, he did know how to change the oil in the car and do a few odd jobs. He probably could have managed fitting a second-hand

29

windscreen. Now I have to pay for everything. And with Jake sick I'm taking time off work, and I have even less money than usual.

'Feeling better today? Ready to go back to school?' I ask Jake with a frisson of desperation as we drive along in the Mazda. The ride is so smooth we don't even have the sensation of movement.

'Can we have a car like this?' Jake asks. 'When's Auntie Patsy coming to visit? How long will we be in town?'

'No. Soon. Until I've finished photocopying the Save Our School flyers and it's time to pick up Liss.'

Helen's waiting to pick up her neighbour's boy at the school when Jake and I zip down the road to collect Melissa. I execute a neat U-turn, a feat impossible in the Holden, and pull up at the gate. Helen almost falls out of her car.

'Oh my God! A new car! Where'd you steal it?'

'It's a loaner from the mechanic.'

'Oh.' She screws up her face in sympathy. 'Hey, a letter arrived for you at the school. Melissa's probably got it. Another one from the minister about the school.'

I don't ask how she knows. I never ask how she knows what we watched on television the night before and what brand of hair dye I use and how Melissa's grades are going. But now I know something she doesn't. I decide I'll wait and see how long it takes her to find out about the new mechanic.

'Do you know what the letter says?'

'Loretta! As if we'd open your mail! But we've all guessed. It says, "Thank you for your recent letter. I'd like to take this opportunity" . . . da de da de da.'

Melissa appears at the car door holding out the minister's envelope as if it's a bad report card. I take it and fling it on the front seat and Melissa leans through the passenger side window and peers inside the car. 'Is it ours?' she asks.

'Nope.'

'Actually,' Helen calls out on the way back to her car, 'I've booked in to that new mechanic for a service, too. I've heard he's very good.' She waggles her bottom and kicks up a heel. Of course she knew.

Poor Giorgio, I think. Giorgio is the old town mechanic, pushing eighty, bald and bowlegged. We've all used him for years to keep our cars running with bits of string and glue. I decide I'll keep going to him for my servicing, even if he is getting so absent-minded that last time he forgot to put the oil back in the engine. Luckily Norm noticed the car hadn't leaked its normal drips on to his driveway.

When I get back to the garage I'm devastated at having to return the keys to the Mazda. We've been around town ten times playing the royal family, waving at everyone we know.

'That'll be eighty dollars. Didn't take as long as I thought.'

Jake's rigid beside me as I hand over the cash. Melissa stands next to him chewing her thumb. I've had words with Jake in the car about not nagging Merv for a tour.

'Mr Bull's a busy man,' I said. 'He doesn't want to be bothered by little boys. You don't want him to think you're a whining little boy, do you? So you wait and see if he offers again.'

'Anyway, mate, bit of bad news.' Merv crouches down in front of Jake. 'I'm sorry, but I have to get away early tonight. Can we do our tour another time?'

'Yes, please,' Jake whispers. Melissa puts her arm around his shoulders and they turn away and scramble on to the bench seat in the back of the Holden.

'I mean it,' Merv says to me. 'I'd love to give the little bloke a tour. Another day. Give me a call anytime.' He reaches into his back pocket. 'Here's my card.'

Something's odd when I drive off: my vision. Through the new windscreen I can actually see the white line in the middle of the road. The Holden throbs and rattles down the Bolton Road and I find myself humming to an old song that I can hear clearly in my head. I can hear it so clearly that I'm singing along with lyrics I didn't realize I knew. Even Jake seems happier. He and

Melissa are bopping their heads along to the beat. Melissa leans over and turns up the volume on the radio and the tune bursts out of the speakers. We look at each other. Merv has fixed the radio. No more race calls, no more protests, no more ads for haemorrhoid cream.

'I love this car,' I sing.

'Me too!' Jake shouts over the pumping beat. By the time we've reached the supermarket, we're all singing along at top volume, windows rolled down, faces pushed out of the car like excited Labradors. Brenda, who happens to be getting out of her car in the supermarket car park, hears us roar up, turns, frowns and purses her lips. I'm convinced it's because we're exhibiting signs of happiness, until I pull into a parking bay and Brenda comes over to commiserate.

'I heard there was a letter from the minister. Never mind, Loretta. We knew it wouldn't work.'

Once we're inside the supermarket, I tear open the envelope while the kids do their usual wistful lingering in the snack foods aisle. The letter doesn't say I've saved the school. No surprise there. But there is another big surprise. On the way home we drop into Norm's.

'Guess what?'

Norm's running his hand over my smooth windscreen.

'Nice. The old one had as many craters as the

surface of the moon. It was a wonder you didn't run into a truck.'

'I got a letter. The education minister's coming to Gunapan.'

'Whoa. Here comes trouble.' He reaches up and fingers the ridge of scar on his forehead. 'I can feel it in my engine.'

CHAPTER 5

Over the next week, the heat builds until at eight thirty on Monday morning it's already so hot that the birds are sitting on the fence with their beaks open. I walk out of the house with the children in tow and pull open the driver's door. It squeals as usual.

'Bush pig!' Jake shrieks. He opens the back passenger door, which also squeals.

'Bush pig!' Melissa's shriek is even louder. They fall about laughing, swinging their doors open and shut and imitating the squeals of metal against metal.

'Get in the car.' No one should be laughing in this kind of heat.

The road to town is flat and empty. As we bump over the pitted tarmac, sprays of pink-and-grey galahs explode into the sky from the fields beside us. On a low hill to the north I can see Les on his tractor, motoring along in the leisurely fashion of a man on a Sunday drive. The sun picks out a shiny spot on one of his wheels and it flashes in a radiant signal each rotation.

'Mum, what's the collective noun for bush pigs?' Melissa asks and Jake bursts into giggles that he tries to smother with his hand.

'I don't know. The same as domestic pigs, I suppose. What is that? Is that a herd?'

'A herd of bush pigs,' Jake shouts.

'A pog of pigs!' Melissa says.

'A swog!'

'A swig! A swig of pigs!'

I wind down my window and push my arm out, leave it there for a moment so Les can see my wave.

'Is that Les?' Jake asks.

'Mr Garrison to you.'

'All the other kids call—'

'I don't care.'

We pull up at the school gates. Melissa and Jake sit silently in the back seat as if they're hoping I'll turn around and announce a once-in-a-lifetime no-school day.

'What's all this about bush pigs anyway?' I look in the rear-view mirror and see Melissa shaking her head vigorously at Jake.

'Nothing.' She catches me watching her and blushes. She has her father's colouring, pale skin that stays freckly no matter how much suncream I slather on her, and sandy red hair. When she blushes her face blooms like a scarlet rose.

They jostle their way out of the car, mutter a goodbye, and run through the school gate, separating at the scraggly hedge and bolting away to their respective groups of friends.

Bush pigs, I think and head off to work.

Gabrielle, the Chair of the Management Committee at the Neighbourhood House where I work, can't answer when I ask her the collective noun for bush pigs. She has dropped in un-expectedly. The Management Committee consists of volunteers from the local community, most of them women from the larger, more wealthy prop-erties outside Gunapan. Supposedly their role is to steer the direction of the Neighbourhood House, to use their skills and contacts in developing the profile of the house in the community, to oversee the efficient management of the house finances and so on and so forth. In reality, they meet once a month to hear the report of the House Managers and drink a glass of wine before they start talking about land values and the inter-national wool and beef markets.

'Flock?' she guesses. 'Herd? Posse?'

'Herd, that's what I said.'

'Darling, I really haven't got time to chat about this. I'm on the trail of a wonderful opportunity. Very hush-hush, from my sources.'

A thought occurs to me. 'Are you talking about that development thing?'

'No, not the development. I'm talking about wool. The finest merino. I have access to a flock that these people need to sell immediatcly at a very nice price. Buy, agist, shear and sell in a month. A business proposition that could make someone a lot of money.'

'I'll do it.' A lot of money – exactly what I need.

'Oh, darling, if only you could. Except it will take about twenty thousand to get this thing off the ground.'

'Ah.' I am not surprised.

'So you carry on and I'll pop on to the computer for a moment. We have the contact details of the committee members here, don't we?'

'About that development—' I start to say, but Gabrielle waves me away.

'Sorry, darling, I must get on with this.'

Gabrielle logs on to the computer and I go back to my work of sorting the donations for our book exchange. The covers are embossed in the silvers and royal blues with scarlet blood spatters that attract the average literary type here. Everyone in Gunapan obviously loves horror. Perhaps that's why they live in this fine town.

Norm has knocked us up a bookcase from the old floorboards of the Memorial Hall and each time I slide a book on to the shelf a cream-coloured puff of powder drifts from below the shelving. He said the insects are long gone. Powder post beetles, he called them. They sound exotic, like tiny rare insects making dust fine as talc, flitting away when they are grown. I told him I could imagine them with transparent iridescent wings, perhaps a glow like fireflies in the forest. 'Nah, love,' he said, 'they're borers.'

I shelve *Prey* and *The Dark Rider* and *Coma* and *Pet Sematary* and soon I can't bear to see another cover promising supernatural thrills and chills. As I am about to check the spelling of *cemetery* in the dictionary – was all that schooling wasted? – I see a different kind of book in the pile. The cover has small writing and a picture of a woman in a dark red dress. She's lying on a couch. But when I look closer, because the picture is also small, I see she's not, in fact, lying on a couch. She's from a different world. Her world has divans, not couches. And she isn't lying on the divan. She's reclining on the divan. Her dress is draped in elegant folds across her slender thighs. Her high-heeled shoe dangles from her foot. I bet she never wears knickers with stretched elastic that slither down and end up in a smiley under each bum cheek.

After I've wiggled my hands down inside my jeans and hauled my undies back up to their rightful position, I open the cover. Inside is an inscription:

To my dear M, remember Paris. With love from Veronica.

I've never met a Veronica in Gunapan. I know a Vera, who makes the best ham sandwiches at the CWA but wants to sniff everyone's breath before they go into the hall because she's the last standing member of the Gunapan Temperance Union. But no Veronica. Maybe the 'M' lives here.

Could it be Merv Bull? He doesn't seem the type to recline on a divan in Paris. I flip the book over and read the reviews on the back.

An elegiac work that brilliantly explores the chiaroscuro of love. Hmm, I think. Elegiac. Exactly what I would have said. The dictionary is on the upper shelf of the bookcase and I pull it down.

'Gabrielle,' I call into the office. 'Have you read *The Paper Teacup*?'

'No, darling. Why?'

'Oh, well, it's absolutely marvellous, Gabrielle, you must read it. I found it rather elegiac.'

Gabrielle doesn't answer. I wonder if I pronounced the word correctly. I tiptoe over and peer around the doorjamb to see if she's doubled over with laughter at this idiot who can't pronounce *elegiac*. Over her shoulder I see her typing *elliejayack* into the computer's search engine. I creep back to the bookshelf and start shelving more *Night of the Beast* and *Death Visitor* books.

Ten minutes later Gabrielle leans out through the doorway. 'I don't like sad books. Give me a good thriller any day.'

Once she's left with the information she needs, I finish up my work and make a phone call to the office of the Minister for Education, Elderly Care and Gaming. The night after I got the letter, I rang the SOS committee members to tell them that the minister was coming to Gunapan. It took a while to convince some of them.

'Is he coming for the BnS Ball?' Kyleen asked. She's been talking about the Lewisford Bachelors and Spinsters Ball for a while, usually bringing it up during completely irrelevant conversations. It's not the biggest BnS ball in the state, but it is known as the one with the lowest dress standard. A frock from the opportunity shop and a pair of boots is acceptable attire, which suits Kyleen well because that's what she wears a lot of the time anyway. I'm sure she mentioned the ball because she can't find anyone to drive her the hundred kilometres to Lewisford, but I doubt the minister would give her a lift, even if he was a bachelor and on the lookout for a country spinster.

The letter had said to ring the minister's office to arrange a date for his visit. I organized an emergency SOS meeting where we got through two packets of Jam Jamboree biscuits and four pots of tea and argued about the merits of an earlier visit or a later visit, as if we'd have any say in the matter anyway, and didn't decide anything except that there was less jam in a Jam Jamboree than there used to be.

Maxine had the answer. 'Give him a call. Sort it out over the phone.' As if calling government ministers is an everyday chore of mine.

The minister's assistant answers the phone.

'Gunapan,' he repeats slowly, as if he is running his finger down a long list.

Surely not that many people write letters to the minister every second week?

41

'OK, here we are. Correspondence Item 6,752/11. Yes, action required. Schedule a ministerial visit. So, how many minutes do you want him to speak for?'

'I don't want him to speak. I want him to save our school.'

'Ah, you're that lady.'

'Yes, I am.' It's good to take a firm stand, even though I suspect 'that lady' is ministerial office code for raving lunatic.

'And he'll need a half-day to get there and back . . .'

I can hear him flipping through pages.

'All right. It could be either June 27th or July 19th.'

'But you've threatened to close the school by the end of the second term in April. Not much point in visiting a school that's already closed.'

I hope he's blushing. He reluctantly suggests a day in March, complaining all the while that he'll have to reschedule appointments to make it happen. I complain back that we all have commitments and it's not so easy for us in Gunapan to rearrange things either. I don't mention that he's proposed the visit for a pension day, when the whole town is aflurry with shopping and bill-paying. It's very hard to get anyone to do anything else. But since there's no other possibility we agree to set the date.

By mid-afternoon even more birds are sitting stupidly in the trees with their beaks open. This is one of those days when they might fall stone dead to the ground, heatstruck. On the horizon a thin column of grey smoke rises and forms a wispy cloud in the pale sky. The start of a bushfire. Or some farmer trying to burn off on a day when leaving your specs lying on a newspaper could make it burst into flame. There's no way to be in a good mood on a day like this. No way, when the air conditioning in the car is broken and the steering wheel leaves heat welts on your palms. Days like this it seems as if summer will never end. We'll go on sweltering and we'll cook from the inside out, like meat in the microwave. They'll cut us open at the morgue and find us filled with steak and kidney pudding. On the outside we'll be nicely pink.

Days like this I think about picking up Melissa and Jake from school and I can see everything before it happens. They'll fall into the car and yelp at the heat on the vinyl seats. They'll ask for icy poles from the shop, or ice creams, or they'll want to go down to the waterhole for a swim. The council swimming pool's shut for renovations. All winter it was open, the heated pool empty except for five or six people who have moved here from the city and who put on their designer goggles and churn up and down the pool thirty or forty times every morning before they purr back to their farmlets in huge recreational vehicles.

One time I decided to get fit and I went along at six thirty in the dark with the kids. After they got tired of messing around in the free lane, the kids sat on the edge of the pool dangling their feet in the water and shouting, 'Go Mum!' as if I was in the Olympics. The other swimmers lapped me four times to my one and by lap five I was dangerously close to going under for the third time.

'Never mind, Mum,' Melissa reassured me. 'We love you even if you are fat.'

Then during the third month of spring this year, the council announces the swimming pool will close for renovations. Right over summer. What renovations? we ask. What can you do to a swimming pool? It either holds the water or it doesn't. And in summer, after years of drought, when we save the water we use to wash vegetables and time our showers, the pool is our one indulgence in this town. No, they say, we're putting in a sauna and a spa and we're building a café. You'll be glad when it's done, they tell us. We've tendered it out. It will only take five months. Why? we ask again, but no one answers. Truly something stinks at that council.

'Don't say a word,' I tell the kids when they stagger past the wilted gum trees of the schoolyard and into the car. 'We're going to buy icy poles and we're going to the waterhole.'

If they had any energy left they'd cheer, I'm sure, but Jake has dark circles under his eyes from not sleeping in the heat and Melissa turns and looks out through the open window, lifting her face to catch the breeze.

'Mrs Herbert said we don't have to do any homework tonight because it's too hot and I got a gold star for reading,' Jake shouts above the hurricane of the wind rushing through the car.

I never bother locking the house in this kind of heat. If we shut the windows we'll never sleep. It's become a habit to walk through each room when I come home, counting off the valuables. While Jake and Melissa head off to their bedrooms I mentally mark off the computer, the DVD player, the change jar. The telly's not worth stealing. Melissa shuts her door while she changes. She's eleven now, but she reminds me of me when I was fifteen. One night not long ago she shaved her legs in the shower. I saw the blood from a cut seeping through her pyjama leg.

'What on earth are you doing?' I sounded louder than I'd meant to. 'Once you start you can't stop. The hair grows back all thick and black and soon you'll look like an orang-utan. Then you'll have to shave all the time.'

'You do it! Anyway, the other girls were laughing at me.' She was looking down at her hands and sitting rigidly still, the way she does when she lies.

'They were not. I bet you saw it in a magazine. Or on TV.'

Melissa arched her head in the kind of movie star huff it took me years to master and stamped off to her room.

Now Jake and I wait ten minutes, fifteen, while she changes into her bathers.

'Come on, Liss,' Jake calls, 'we're boiling. Let's go.'

Melissa's room is silent. I knock on the door.

'Sweetie, don't you want to cool down?'

'I'm not going.' The door stays firmly shut.

Jake does an exaggerated sigh and collapses on to a chair. I can feel the sweat on my face, running down between my breasts, soaking into my bathers under my dress. Three flies are circling me, landing whenever I let my attention drift.

'You go.' Her voice is muffled behind the door. 'I'll have a shower.'

'Please, let's go, Mum.' Jake reaches out to take my hand and pull me towards the front door.

Melissa's a mature eleven-year-old, but I am convinced that if I leave her alone in the house for more than twenty minutes a spectacular disaster will happen and she'll die and I'll be tortured by guilt for the rest of my life. I've pictured the LP gas tanks exploding, the blue gum tree in the yard toppling on to the house, a brown snake slithering out of a kitchen cupboard. Of course, any of those things could happen while I'm at home too, but I would have no guilt factor. The guilt factor means I may never have sex again, because attractive men looking for a good time rarely drop in spontaneously at my house. On the other hand, it has saved me from many of Helen's girls' nights, involving outings to pubs that the same attractive men looking for a good time never visit. I was also lucky enough to miss Helen's ladies-only party where an enthusiastic twenty-year-old tried to sell dildoes and crotchless panties to astonished Gunapan farm wives.

'Melissa, either you come or we don't go at all, you know that.'

'Noooooo!' Jake's cry of anguish echoes on and on in a yodelling crow call.

Finally Melissa agrees to come and wait on the bank while we take a dip. I tell her that I'm going in even though I have thighs as thick as tree stumps.

'It doesn't worry me.' My bright voice makes my lie obvious.

'That'd be right,' Melissa mutters from the back seat.

'Young lady,' I start, but it's too hot to argue so I swing the car backwards out of the driveway and set off.

It's been three years since Tony left us. Three years in real time, and more like thirty years in looking-after-children time. I'm sure mothering years go even faster than dog years. I can feel my back turning into a question mark. Sometimes I catch myself hunched over the steering wheel or sagging in a kitchen chair, and I can imagine myself after a few more mothering years, drooling into my porridge in the retirement home. Come on luvvie, they'll say to me, sit up straight now, after all, you're only forty.

The road leading into the gully swings around the bend and we can see the whole town, or at least as many people as would normally be at the swimming pool, clustered around the small waterhole like ants at a droplet of sugar water. Bush pigs at a billabong, maybe. The waterhole's half the size it used to be because we get no rain, but it's still deep enough to swim.

'What were you two talking about this morning? Bush pigs was it?'

'Yeah.'

'No.'

With the ground near the edge of the water trampled to mud, we find a spot further back underneath a stringybark tree and lay down our towels and unpack the iced cordial and biscuits. Melissa goes off to sit next to her friend Taylah. Jake and I make our way down to the water, saying hello to everyone on the way. Some of the mothers who have caught sight of me pretend to be reading the messages on their children's T-shirts or searching for something in their bags. I know they're afraid I'm going to ask them to do something for the Save Our School Committee, but I don't have to now because the minister's coming to Gunapan.

'The minister's coming to Gunapan,' I call out cheerily, making a fist of victory, and they nod and smile anxiously as you do when a lunatic has decided to talk to you.

Further up on the hill I can see a family sitting apart from everyone else. Four children and a woman. They lean in together, talking.

'Who's that up there?' I ask Jake.

'Dunno.' He doesn't even glance up, as if he knows without looking who I'm talking about.

I keep squinting at them as I wade in, but I can't make out their faces. Then I feel an eddy of water around my knees and before I can move someone has grabbed my ankles and I'm under, flailing around in the murky water, trying not to swallow any. I make it to the surface for a breath before Jake sits on my head. Even underwater I can hear his shrieks and Kyleen's unmistakable snorting laugh. I finally manage to stand up straight, my feet anchoring themselves on the squelchy bottom where the silt oozes in silky bands between my toes.

'Very funny.'

'Yep,' she says between snorts.

Further out, the bottom of the waterhole falls away and the water is dark and deep. Even on a day like this when half the town has swum here, water from the depths still swirls in cold ribbons to the surface. I leave Jake playing with Kyleen and her little girl near the edge of the waterhole and I swim out and roll on to my back where the water is cooler. The sun seems to have less power here.

Up on the hill I can see the lonely family still huddled together. They're moving about now, gathering their things and putting them into plastic bags. They start making their way back to the road, but instead of walking down through the people bunched around the banks of the water-hole, they skirt the long way around the top of the hill until they reach the bus stop further down the ridge. I close my eyes and float for a while, trying to block out the sounds of kids screaming and parents bellowing and the rustle and crackle of the grass and leaves in the heat.

Melissa is waiting when Jake and I clamber back up to dry ourselves with our dusty hot towels. She's wearing jeans and a long-sleeved top and her face is scarlet with the heat. I wonder if she's nicked herself shaving again. It would be typical of a child of mine to decide that self-mutilation of the legs wasn't enough. Why not shave your arms as well? And your stomach and neck while you're at it?

'Where's Taylah?' Jake asks her.

'Gone home.'

'Sweetie, I've got a spare T-shirt in the boot, why don't you put that on.'

'I want to go home. You said you were only going in for a dip.'

I stretch out my hand to help her up. She ignores it and pulls herself up with the aid of a tree branch, then winces and brushes her dirty hand on her jeans. I can see that nothing will make her happy today. Melissa was always Tony's little girl. When he left I didn't know how to make it up to her. She's grown old in the time he's been gone. I offered her a puppy for her last birthday and she refused it.

'Why?' I asked her.

'Because it'll die. And you never know when.'

At home Melissa goes off to her room and Jake hangs around the kitchen while I boil the water for frankfurts. I get him buttering the bread and I lean out of the kitchen window, trying to catch some air on my face. Across from our block is a small farm. Fancy clean white sheep appear in the paddock one day and are gone the next. The farm owners don't speak to us. A few times a week I see the wife driving past in her Range Rover with the windows closed. She wears sunglasses and dark red lipstick. I can't imagine her crutching a sheep, much as I try.

I've spent some of my great fantasy moments being that woman, usually on days like this when I'm hanging out of the window and moving my face around like a ping-pong clown to try to catch a breeze. In my imagination I've sat in her air-conditioned dining room, laughing gaily, my manicured hands and painted nails flitting about like coloured birds as I discuss the latest in day spas. I've waved goodbyc to my tiresome yet fabulously wealthy and doting husband, and changed into a negligee to welcome my lover, the Latin horse whisperer who lives above the stables and takes me bareback riding in the moonlight. In this dream, my boobs are so firm that even the thundering gallop of the stallion cannot shake them.

'Mum,' Jake interrupts as I'm about to drift into my other world.

51

'Mmm?'

'Melissa's crying.'

'Don't touch the saucepan,' I say, turning off the gas. 'And butter four more pieces of bread for your lunches tomorrow.'

She doesn't want to open the door when I knock, but I can hear the phlegm in her voice, so I push the door open anyway. Melissa's sitting on the carpet beside her bed. I go and sit beside her, my bones creaking as I lower myself to the floor. It's a little cooler down here, but I'm still sweating. Melissa's face is all splotchy and snot is coming out her nose. I pull one of my endless supply of tissues out of my pocket and wipe her face. She tries to push my hand away.

'I'm not a baby,' she sniffles.

'I know.'

We sit quietly for a few minutes and eventually I slip my arm around her shoulders and kiss her forehead. She leans in to me and sighs a big shuddering sigh.

'What's up, kiddo?'

'Nothing.'

We sit for a while longer. Her breathing gets easier and slower. She's not going to tell me anything, that's obvious, so I decide to finish making tea. When I get to the kitchen, Jake's so hungry he's ripped open the packet of frankfurters and is gnawing on a cold one.

'Did you do girl talk?'

52

'Where did you hear that line?' I'm trying not to laugh.

'Norm told me that's what girls say they do, but really they're gossiping about how to get boys.'

'Well, Norm's wrong. And I'll be letting him know that next time I see him.'

'Why don't you marry Norm?'

'Because he's a hundred years old and smells of tractor. Why don't you marry Kimberley? You play with her at school every day.'

'Yuk!'

'Yeah!'

At least that's sorted.

When she finally emerges from her room, Melissa eats two frankfurts in bread, dripping with butter and tomato sauce, and a few forks of salad. After we've washed up she drifts back to her room to do her homework. I've pulled all the flywire screens shut and I make the kids hold their breath while I go around the house spraying the mozzies. In Melissa's room I glance over her shoulder. She's on the internet, looking at a page about the United Nations.

'Mum, were you around when the United Nations started?'

'Possibly, if I'm as old as I feel. But no, I don't think so. Are you doing a project?'

She nods. She switches screens to show me her essay and I see that at the top of the page she has made a typing mistake and it says *The Untied*

Nations. I like that title. It makes me think of Gunapan, a town lost in the scrubby bush, untied from the big cities and the important people and the TV stations and the government. Gunapan keeps struggling on the way it always has and no one takes any notice at all except to cut a few more services. There are probably thousands of towns like us around the country. The untied nations.

'Why don't you look up the collective noun for bush pigs?' I must learn to use the computer better myself.

'I did – it's a sounder,' Melissa says.

'What a great word! Sounder. Sounder.'

'It's not that good, Mum.'

'Sounder, sounder, sounder. A sounder of bush pigs.'

'Mum, I have to do my homework.' She heaves an exasperated sigh that would do a shop assistant in a toffy dress emporium proud. 'Please, I need some peace and quiet.'

CHAPTER 6

A good mother would be culturing organic yoghurt or studying nutritional tables at this time of night, when the kids are asleep and the evening stretches out ahead, empty and lonely. I've checked every channel on the TV and tried to read a magazine, but it's all rubbish. I'm too hot to concentrate on a book. I should be planning spectacular entertainments for the visit from the education minister, but that seems too much like hard work. Now I'm bored. I sound like Jake. Bored, bored, bored. If I was a bloke, I'd wheel the computer out of Melissa's room and look at porn for a while.

The only trouble with the second-hand computer stand I bought is that it squeaks whenever you move it. Melissa half-wakes and moans, and I shush her and hurry the computer out of the room. I'm not interested in porn, but Helen's promised me a whole other world of fun on the internet and I think it's time I found out more about it, as research of course, to protect my children. Last time I played around on the computer, Melissa, through child technomagic, tracked what I'd been looking at the night before. 'Are you going to buy a motorbike, Mum?' she asked. 'What are spurs, anyway?' Now I've learned how to clear the history of what I've been browsing, so I'm feeling daring. I pull down the ancient bottle of Johnny Walker from the top of the cupboard, pour a shot, add a splash of water and realize the only ice I have is lemon flavoured. What the hell, I think, and drop the homemade icy pole upside down into the glass.

Outside the flywire screens, the night noise of the bush carries on. It's not the white noise of the city where I grew up – the drone of cars and the rattle of trams, the hum of streetlights and televisions muttering early into the morning. It is an uproar. When we first moved out here I was terrified by the racket. It sounded as if the bunyips and the banshees had gone to war: screaming, howling, grunting, crashing through the bush, tearing trees apart and scraping their claws along the boards of the house. Soon enough I realized that the noises were frogs and cicadas and night birds. Kangaroos thumping along their tracks; rutting koalas sending out bellows you'd never imagine their cute little bodies could produce; the hissing throat rattle of territorial possums and an occasional growling feral cat. Against all that the whirring of the computer is like the purr of a house pet.

Once I'm connected to the internet I do a search on myself, in case I've become famous while I wasn't paying attention. I'm not there, so I try my maiden name, Loretta O'Brien. Someone with my name is a judge in North Carolina, and another person called me died recently and her grandchildren have put up pictures of her. She has a touch of the old scrag about her. I wonder if it's the first name that does it to us. All that unfulfilled singing potential.

The lemon icy pole sure adds a distinctive tang to Johnny Walker. I top up the glass with water and take another sip, shards of melting ice sticking to my lips as I type in *Gunapan*. We're part of a geological survey. The Department of Lands has posted a topographical map of the region. Gunapan is an Aboriginal place name. Well, der, I think, tossing back more of the tasty lemon whisky and adding a touch more water. The next hit is an online diary of a backpacker from Llanfairfechan in Wales who stayed for a night in a room above the Gunapan pub. *One night is plenty enough in this place*, she writes. *I had very bad dreams.*

Jake calls out in his sleep. He does this – occasionally shrieks in the night – but it means nothing. Bush pig, I think, refilling my glass and pulling a strawberry icy pole from the freezer. It's weeks since I've been tempted to drop the kids at the orphanage and drive to Melbourne to take up my new life of glamour with a hairless odourless body. The little bush pigs have been behaving quite well. Now I realize that was the calm. Something's coming, but I don't know what.

I lean back and sip my drink – Johnny and a strawberry icy pole, it's a Gunapan cocktail – and click away until I'm looking at the guest login for online dating in Victoria. I hesitate on that page a while.

'It's not only weirdos,' Helen told me once. 'Some blokes look quite handsome. Although that does seem to be mainly the shorter ones. Anyway, you don't have to do anything. It's soft-core girl porn.'

I select *Rural south west* and *Male* and *Over six feet* and *Doesn't matter* about children. Then *Go*. The screen comes up with five photos on the first page and a big list of other hits. One hundred and forty-two single men in rural south-west Victoria? This deserves a green icy pole and another shot of Johnny.

I read about Jim, who likes long walks on the beach and romantic dinners. Jim lives in Shepparton in central Victoria, many hours' drive from the beach. Giuseppe has two grown children and likes working out. Mel loves movies and romantic dinners and golf, and would like to share his wonderful life with a special lady. Joe's looking for a happy busty lady with no issues. Good luck, Joe.

As I scroll down the list I start finding these people funnier and funnier. Matthew's spent a lot of time working on his spirituality and he'd like to meet a woman with the same interests so they can grow together. Like a fungus, I think. Shelby would like a petite Asian lady with large breasts who's open-minded and looking for a good time. Hey Shelby, most of the men in this town pay good money for that. I open up my password-protected email and send Helen a message. *Looking for a handsome wealthy man with no issues and a Beamer. Must love slumming it, buying expensive presents for the lady in his life, and have no objections to feral children.*

I slump back into the kitchen chair, which is a few inches too short for the computer table. My neck hurts. The screen in front of me has ads all over it. Casinos, jobs, real estate. Maybe I should look for a new house to rent, one that doesn't heat up to 400 degrees. Thinking about real estate reminds me of the hole in the bush on the Bolton Road.

I type *Gunapan development* into the search bar. You get thousands and thousands of answers in these searches and none of them are what you want. The council minutes are online. That should send me off to sleep. The local super-market's car park resurfacing process is described in glorious detail. I cannot understand why these things would be on the internet. I find the council's forms for applying for a building permit. I try another search, this time on *Gunapan bush*. Then I type in more place names from the local region combined with *development* and then I try *bush clearing* and then something else and by this time I'm pretty tired of it but I click through to one more page and that's where I find the article.

It doesn't have Gunapan in the title, or even in the article, which is from a newspaper in Western Australia, and which is talking about a resort development to take place on twelve hectares outside Halstead. Outside Halstead? The map in the article shows where the development will take place and I can see that it's the old bush reserve in Gunapan, but our town isn't mentioned. Only a few lines about how the development may help to *revive the depressed small community nearby.* Depressed! The only depressed person here is Brenda, and even she picks up during the Gunapan Fair.

The company building the resort is a Western Australian developer *with successful resorts in Queensland, WA and the Territory, as well as significant investment in plantation forestry and logging.* I want to print this page out but the printer's still in Melissa's room.

'Mum?'

The cry comes from down the hall. Jake's awake.

'Mummy.'

He only calls me Mummy when he's frightened. I clean up the browser and close it down, then hurry to Jake's room, taking deep breaths to expel the smell of Johnny from my mouth. Jake's nightlight is on, a rotating globe with fish painted on the outside and a static seascape behind. The mechanical rotation of the outer plastic globe makes a reassuring grinding sound once each cycle like the slow purr of a contented cat.

'What is it, Jakie?' I whisper from the doorway.

'I'm not a bush pig,' he whispers.

'Of course you're not,' I say firmly. I sit down beside him on the bed and rest my hand on his hot, sweaty chest. 'Why would you think that?'

'They said so.'

'Who said so?' Anger starts to rise inside me. I remember I started thinking about bush pigs after Melissa and Jake began joking about them. 'Where did this come from, anyway?'

He doesn't answer. His steady breathing makes my hand rise and fall as he drifts back to sleep.

Next morning I'm waiting for them at the breakfast table with a pile of bacon on a plate and the spatula jutting from my hand. Melissa and Jake both sit down at the table without speaking, without looking at the bacon. I dish the crispy strips onto buttered toast, slop on scrambled eggs from the frying pan and hand them a plate each.

'What's going on?' I ask. 'What's this bush pig business?'

'Nothing.' Melissa has her stubborn face on.

Jake's eyes begin to redden. The circles under his eyes are even darker today. The heat went on and on all night until even the bugs got exhausted and stopped making noise at about four in the morning. There was an occasional crack as the tin roof shucked off the heat of the day and the house settled and sighed. Not only did no one sleep properly, I'm also feeling the effects of my romantic night with Johnny Walker, and I'm in no mood to be messed with.

'I don't want silence or sulking or tantrums. Tell me what it's about. Who called you a bush pig, Jake?'

Silence. My throbbing head. Jake and Melissa stare at their plates. The crispy bacon is wilting, the eggs are getting cold, the toast is going soggy. The urge to shout is rising in me and I want to smother it – I must not become a shrieking single mother.

'So . . .' I lighten my tone of voice. My back is still to the children. 'I'm not cross. I want to know, that's all.'

'I had a project on bush pigs,' Melissa says.

'Then why would Jake be upset?' I turn around to face them, my expression a mask of control and calm.

'I called him a bush pig.' Melissa shoves a blackened curl of bacon into her mouth as if that will stop me asking her questions.

'Is that it, Jake? Did your sister call you a bush pig?'

Melissa's staring so hard at Jake he'll start sending off smoke in a minute. He crosses his hands over his lap.

'I need to go to the toilet,' he says. Little liar.

'It's true! It is, Mum. I did call him a bush pig. I'm sorry.'

Something smells here. I'm sure she's lying. But she's as stubborn as her father. I turn to Jake.

'Lies come back to bite you on the bum. You know that, don't you, Jake?'

'I want to go to school now,' he says for the first and probably last time in his life. 'Did you put a banana in my lunch?'

The boy is obsessive. I take the banana out of his lunch box and open Melissa's.

'I'm not having it!' she yelps.

'What is it with bananas and this family?' I say. 'They're good nutritious food and they're cheap.'

'They stink!' Jake and Melissa say together.

By the time I've finished the washing-up, Melissa and Jake are ready to head off. I drop them at school and drive on to the Neighbourhood House, sweating in the hot morning sun.

At ten thirty my sister Tammy calls to let me know Mum's in hospital in Melbourne.

CHAPTER 7

'What's that noise?' Jake has an unerring knack for asking awkward questions. He leans down and peers under the seat between his legs, sits up and cranes his neck, looking around the corridor. I reach over and poke him to be quiet.

'Mum, your bra is creaking again,' Melissa whispers crossly.

'Sshh,' I tell her.

'It's creepy, Mum. You should throw it out.'

'I'm sure you'd be very happy to have me arriving at school to pick you up with my breasts flopping around.'

'Oh, disgusting.' Melissa looks as if she's about to faint.

'You'll have these troubles soon enough, my girl.'

'No, I won't, because I'm never buying underwear at the two-dollar shop.'

I was sure I'd never told anyone about buying that bra at the two-dollar shop. It seemed such a bargain until the creaking started. Even with that, I thought it was a waste to throw it away.

'You can go in now, she's decent,' the nurse calls from the doorway of Mum's room.

Jake runs in first, calling out, 'Hi Nanna!' Melissa and I follow more slowly. Jake stops as soon as he gets in the doorway and sees his nanna tiny and yellowish in the big hospital bed. He backs up and presses against me. Melissa stands rigid at our side. Their nanna's bed is one of four in the room. Two are empty. An ancient man with a liver-spotted head is snoring in the one diagonally opposite.

'Hi Mum. How are you feeling?'

She turns her gaunt sallow face to me and frowns. 'Did you bring me a Milk Tray?'

I produce the box of chocolates with a flourish from my handbag and pass it to Melissa. 'Give these to your grandmother, sweetie.'

'My name is Melissa,' my gracious daughter answers.

'Give me the chocolates, girl,' my even more gracious mother says. 'I've been waiting for them since eleven o'clock.'

'Are you sure you can eat those, with your liver?'

My mother reaches for the nurse alarm button.

'OK,' I say, taking the box from Melissa and tossing it on to the bed. 'So how are you feeling?'

I send Jake to the vending machine next to the ward for a packet of chips while Mum tells me about my sisters, Tammy and Patsy. Tammy visited yesterday with her three immaculate children. Tammy brought a hand-knitted bedjacket, five novels, a basket of fruit and best wishes from her husband Rob, who is smarter than Einstein and a better businessman than Bill Gates – apparently Bill could learn a thing or two from Rob about point-of-sale software. One of the children had written a poem for her nanna.

'Melissa, do you want to read your cousin's poem?' I ask sweetly.

Melissa smirks into the magazine she's picked up.

My other sister, Patsy, visited with her friend. Mum thinks that Patsy's friend would look so much nicer if she lost some weight and started wearing more feminine clothing. And took care of that facial hair, for God's sake. Then she might be able to get a man.

'Speaking of which, have you heard from thingo?' she asks.

'Nope,' I say. 'So when do you get out of here?'

'Where are you staying?'

'We're in a motel.'

'It's horrible,' Melissa says. 'The bedspreads smell of cigarettes. And they're baby-shit yellow.'

'Melissa!' I protest, but she gives me the as-if-you've-never-said-it-yourself look.

'You could always stay with Tammy. They have a six-bedroom house.'

They do have plenty of room at the house and we did try staying once, but Tammy and I discovered that these days we can only tolerate two hours of each other's company before sisterly love turns sour. It became clear that she thinks her wealthy lifestyle exemplifies cultured good taste and mine has degenerated into hillbilly destitution, while I think Tammy is living a nouveau riche nightmare while I represent a dignified insufficiency.

Tammy's husband rarely comes home because he's so busy being successful. When he does arrive he's late, and Tammy's favourite nickname for him is 'my late husband'. 'Allow me to introduce "my late husband",' she announces to startled guests. Her husband smiles distantly and gives her a shoulder squeeze like she's an athlete. Last time the kids and I came down we ate luncheon – not the meat but the meal – at their place on the Sunday. Jake swallowed a mouthful of the smoked trout and dill pasta and before it even reached his stomach he had puked it back into the plate. It looked much the same as before he had chewed it, but the sight of the regurgitation had Tammy's delicate children heaving and shrieking. 'Haven't they ever seen anyone chunder before?' Melissa remarked scornfully on the way home.

My mother turns her attention to Melissa. 'And you, young lady, are you doing well at school?'

Melissa looks at her grandmother with an arched eyebrow.

'Yes, Grandmother,' she answers.

'I won't have any granddaughter of mine being a dunce.'

Melissa turns her head and gives me a dead stare. I can't believe she's only eleven.

'All right,' I intervene briskly, 'let's talk about you, Mum. How are you feeling? When do you get out?'

'I'm yellow, in case you hadn't noticed.'

'Can I get a packet of chips too?' Melissa says, so I give her some money and tell her to find Jake while she's at it.

'Good.' My mother pushes herself upright in the bed as soon as Melissa has left the ward. 'Now the children are gone we can talk. I'm going to sell up and move to Queensland, the Gold Coast. Albert's bought a house on the canals with a swimming pool and a sauna. My liver's packing up. I don't know how I got this hepatitis thing, but I can only guess it was from your father all those years ago. That lying cheat. Apparently it's contagious. You and the kids had the test like I told you?'

'Yes, we're fine. Who's Albert?' I am incredulous.

'He's from the bingo. He's no great catch, I admit that, but who else is offering me a house in the sunshine?'

'Not the one with the five Chihuahuas? The one you used to make jokes about?'

'Having those dogs doesn't actually mean he's

homosexual. He's quite virile for an older gentleman.'

'Oh, Mum, enough detail. And why can't you say this in front of the kids?'

'You need to tell them in your own time. I know they'll be upset I'm leaving, but when they get older they'll understand.'

'I'll break it to them gently.' I don't want to point out that we only come down to Melbourne at Christmas and her birthday anyway.

'Tammy and Patsy'll miss you,' I say. 'And the junior poets.'

My mother almost smiles before she says, 'I love Tammy's children dearly, you know that, Loretta.'

'I know.'

'Anyway, when I sell, I'm giving you a few thousand dollars. Don't tell Tammy or Patsy. You need it, they don't.'

From down the corridor comes a long howl, followed by grievous sobbing.

'They torture people in here, you know,' Mum says. 'The nights are hell. The screaming and moaning, it's like being inside a horror film.'

I have a bad feeling that I recognize that howl. But rather than spoil the moment, I think about the good things.

'A few thousand dollars?' I say.

'Depending on the price I get for the flat. You'll get something, anyway. Five or six thousand maybe.'

A holiday for one – or two? – in Bali, I think. Or an air conditioner. Or both! A proper haircut and blonde tips! A bra that doesn't creak! Champagne and sloppy French cheese and pâté! Silk knickers!

'I expect you'll want to spend it on the kids, but keep a couple of dollars for yourself, won't you. You could use a bit of smartening up. Any men on the horizon?'

'Actually,' I say, 'there's a rather good-looking mechanic who definitely has eyes for me. He keeps himself quite clean, too.'

'As opposed to that grubby old junk man you hang around with?'

'Yes, as opposed to Norm, who has his own special standard of hygiene.'

'And has this bloke asked you out?'

'Not yet.' Needless to say, he hasn't recognized yet that he has eyes for me. I wonder if I am talking about Merv Bull? Have I developed a crush? Am I becoming Helen?

From down the corridor, the howling and sobbing is growing louder. I can't avoid it now.

'You need to look for your mother,' I can hear a woman telling Jake. 'Open your eyes, dear.'

'Loretta, you should give up that political hocus-pocus you've got yourself into. Put your energy into finding a partner and a father for those children.'

'The Save Our School Committee is precisely for "those children". Anyway, we've had a win.

The minister for education's coming to Gunapan in a few weeks. We've got a chance to change his mind about closing the school.'

'Is he married?'

Jake's sobbing, very close now, startles awake the man in the bed across from Mum. He raises his spotty head and shouts, 'You buggers! You buggers! Get out of it, you buggers!'

'Shut up,' my mother calls over at him and he stops immediately.

'Nutcase,' she says to me. 'Every time he wakes up he thinks the Germans are coming for him.' Mum lets her head drop back on to the pillow and stares at the ceiling. 'The Gold Coast. I can't wait.'

'So when do you go?'

'Mummeeeeeeee,' Jake screams as he runs into the room and flings his round little body on to my lap. He buries his face in my shirt, covering me in snot and tears. Melissa strolls in behind him eating a chocolate bar.

'The lady says she's going to clean up Jake's chips.'

With Jake in my arms I stagger out to the corridor and call out thanks to his rescuer, a woman in a blue cleaner's uniform who is hurrying back towards the lift.

'What were you doing on the second floor, Jakie?'

'Idroppedmychipsntheysaidicouldn'teatthem-offthefloorndicouldn'tfindyoooooooo.' His sobbing is

71

slowing now. 'So, so so Itriedtofindyouand, hic, Icouldn'tfindyouandIwent, hm, downthestairsand, ugh, theladysawmeand . . .'

'Ssh, ssh.' I squeeze him tightly to me.

'I'm tired now,' my mother says from the bed. 'Thanks for visiting, darlings.'

On the way back to the motel I ask the kids what they'd buy if they had a thousand dollars.

'A motel!' Jake screams.

'What would you buy, Liss?' I can see her in the rear-view mirror. She looks out through the window for a while, down at her hands, back out through the window.

'I dunno.'

'Go on, a thousand dollars. What would you get?'

She sighs a great heaving sigh and writes something on the car window with her fingertip.

'Some proper clothes. From a proper shop so I'm not the world's biggest dag.'

'Don't be silly, you look beautiful. You could wear a sack and you'd look beautiful.'

We pull into the motel car park to pick up our bags from reception and have a toilet break before the long drive back to Gunapan. Once we're on the highway I drive for an hour, and when it gets dark we stop at a roadhouse. We order the lamb stew with chips and milkshakes and sit down at a table beside a man who resembles a side of beef and who appears to be eating a side of beef. At the far end of the roadhouse

72

café is another family. They seem to be trying to stay away from everyone else, like that family at the waterhole.

'Who are those people we saw up on the hill at the waterhole the other day?' I ask Melissa, who's leafing through an ancient women's magazine she found on the table. She shrugs. 'I don't think I've seen them before,' I go on talking to myself.

'Can I watch TV when we get home tonight?' Jake asks.

'No.'

'Miss Claffy had an engagement ring on yesterday,' Melissa says. The magazine is open at the page of a starlet wearing an engagement ring that could sink the *Titanic*. The food arrives at the table. I can tell immediately that I've made a mistake ordering the stew. I thought it would be healthier than hamburgers.

'Is this lamb?' Jake asks.

'I think it was lamb a few years ago,' I tell him through a mouthful of gristle. Grinding this meat down to a consistency I can swallow is a full-body workout.

'Can we have pizza tomorrow night?'

'The ring had a diamond on it. Miss Claffy said diamond can cut a hole in glass.'

'You must have seen those kids at school. Isn't one of them in a class with you?'

'I don't want anchovies on my pizza tomorrow. I want double cheese.'

'Someone should welcome them. You kids have no idea how hard it is for a new family in a small town.'

'Why don't you have an engagement ring, Mum?'

'What?'

'Didn't Dad give you an engagement ring?'

'I don't want olives either. I hate olives.'

'We didn't really have an engagement. We just got married.'

'Miss Claffy said her fiancé asked her to marry him in a restaurant and everyone heard and they all clapped.'

'We had a lovely wedding though. I can show you the pictures.'

'We've seen them,' they both say quickly.

Melissa and Jake have pushed aside their stew. They dip their chips in the stew sauce and suck on their milkshakes. I wish I'd ordered myself a milkshake. The side of beef beside us finishes his meal, burps ferociously and sways his bulk out to the car park where his rig is waiting for him like a tame T-Rex. Jake wants to go out and have a better look, but I hold him back.

'Is Nanna going to die?' Melissa asks.

'Oh, Lissie girl, of course she's not. It's worse. She's moving to the Gold Coast.'

'Really?'

'Really. With her new boyfriend.'

'She's an old lady! She can't have a boyfriend.'

'And what about your poor mother? Am I too old to have a boyfriend?'

'You're married.' Melissa's disapproving frown would qualify her instantly as a headmistress. 'To Dad,' she adds, in case I'd forgotten.

CHAPTER 8

My sister Patsy has only been in the house for five minutes and she is already enthusiastically embracing the joys of country life.

'When are you going to leave this dump and come back to Melbourne?' she says.

She's parked her brand-new Peugeot on the street in front of the house, and I think nervously of Les, the farmer further down the road. On a hot day Les sometimes drives the tractor straight off the field and heads to the pub. His Kelpie sits beside him on the wheel hub, barking madly at cars overtaking them. Late at night, Les will steer the tractor back home down the road, singing and laughing and nattering to himself, the dog still barking. No one worries because the worst that can happen is him driving the tractor off the road somewhere and him and the dog sleeping in a field. But no one ever parks on this road at night.

'So Patsy, let's move that beautiful car of yours into the driveway and swap with mine. Wouldn't want anyone to steal it!'

'You've got no reason to stay here,' Patsy goes on. 'That bastard's not coming back and the kids are young enough to move schools. Mum's gone to the Gold Coast, so she won't bother you. Come back to the real world.'

I have thought about going back to Melbourne. A part of me believes that being in Melbourne would magically make me more sophisticated and capable. My hair, cut by a hairdresser to the stars, would curve flatteringly around my face and my kids' teeth would straighten out of their own accord.

'Can't take the kids away from the clean country air,' I tell Patsy. When Tony and I first moved to the country for a better-paid driving job he'd been offered, we shifted from an outer western suburb, treeless, grey and smelling of diesel, the only place we could afford a flat. Everyone there was miserable and angry and even our neighbours tried to rip us off. For the same money as that poky flat we rented a three-bedroom house with a yard in Gunapan, only forty minutes' drive from his work in Halstead, and still had enough money for dinner out once a week. Now I'm a single mother with two kids, I could never survive back in the city. I've developed a vision of a life where I, deserted mother scrag, can't get a job in the city, don't know anyone, spiral down the poverty gurgler until I become an over-the-counter pill junkie watching *Judge Judy* in my rented house in a suburb so

77

far from the centre of Melbourne it has its own moon. I can't feed the kids because I've spent all our money on an Absetciser off the telly and the chemist keeps asking me has my cold cleared up yet.

'Loretta!' Patsy shouts. 'I said, are you a member of the golf club? George is getting into golf in a big way, so I thought we could play a round when she gets here. Apparently the local course isn't too bad.'

'No,' I mutter, still feeling queasy from my Melbourne vision. 'I think you can buy a day pass. It's a bit yellow, though. They're using recycled water on the greens.'

The next evening, when Norm drops in, George has arrived. She's sitting on the couch with her arm around Patsy. I've wondered how Norm will react when he finally meets Patsy and George. I haven't told him a lot about my sisters and their families.

'Unbloodybelievable,' Norm announces from the doorway, before he's even put a foot in the room.

'What's that?'

He's got something under his arm. Something green, with wheels.

Norm looks down as if he's forgotten he was carrying anything. 'Oh, a trike for Jake. Found it when I was rearranging the junk in the yard. It must have been hidden in that tractor rim for years. No, what's unbloodybelievable,' he puts the

78

tricycle on the floor and waves a sheet of paper in my direction, 'is this.'

'You'd better meet my sister and her friend first.'

I introduce them all and Norm stuffs the paper in his pocket before shaking Patsy's hand, then George's. He looks George in the eye and says, 'Welcome to Gunapan.'

'Thanks,' George says, wiping her hand on her jeans. 'Into cars?'

'Nah, love, I'm a recycler. Salvage and parts for all things man made,' Norm says. He splays his hands in front of him. They're spectacularly dirty today.

'Norm, didn't I buy you some soap?'

'Don't want to strip the natural oils from my sensitive skin,' he says turning his hands over to examine the palms, which are equally filthy.

In the old cars and house lots that turn up at Norm's junkyard, he finds women's magazines and house-and-garden magazines and reads them cover to cover. Then at unexpected moments he'll give you a beauty tip. 'Your hair could do with a lift, Loretta,' he'll say. 'Have you tried lemon juice to bring out the blonde highlights?' Sometimes he puts on a camp voice to do it. Other times, like today, he'll be completely deadpan. Most people don't know how to react, but George looks back at him, equally deadpan.

'Very wise. That must be how you've maintained that remarkable complexion.'

Norm's fingers reach up and play gently across his stubble. 'Exactly. And I'm very careful about my diet. Not too many colourful foods.'

'Like vegetables?' George suggests.

'Exactly,' Norm answers.

I'm thrilled that George and Norm are getting on so well. I've never seen Norm be rude to anyone who didn't deserve it, but I was wondering last night how well I actually know him. Sure, Norm's looked out for us like a grandfather since Tony left, but I hardly hear anything about his life before we met him. For all I know he might have been a member of the Ku Klux Klan or the anti-lesbian league of Gunapan.

Norm stays for tea and we cram around the kitchen table with our plates of wild-mushroom risotto. Having George, a two-star chef, in the house, I decided to have a go at something more adventurous than my usual Tuesday night chops and salad, but the anxiety of cooking for a professional was too much for me. I'm shattered. Now I've drunk a glass of the wine Patsy brought and all my anxiety is gone. The light around the table is glowing golden and everyone is charming and attractive, even Norm. I look at my darling children, full of wonder at their beauty and intelligence.

'Mum, is the rice supposed to be crunchy?' Jake comes in once again with the wrong question at the wrong time.

Patsy leans over and whispers in Jake's ear. The

wild mushrooms cost a fortune so I keep chewing, trying to ignore the gritty bits grinding against my teeth. George is telling Norm all about Paris.

'Patsy was writing notes for her book and I was shopping for meals and washing the clothes. Very Gertrude and Alice.'

'Right, Gertrude and Alice,' Norm says. He looks at me and I smile a knowing smile. George is obviously talking about a fashion label.

'Anyway, Paris has the most amazing charcuteries full of cured meat. I wish my French was better. I pointed at things in the display cabinet and took them home to try and figure out what they were. The most amazing flavours! I never realized you could get so much out of a pig.'

Patsy groans. 'Here we go. Now we've been to Paris she's obsessed. She's threatening to build a meat-curing shed in the backyard in Carlton. She'll be wanting a piggery next.'

'I might have a few odds and ends at the yard to help out with a shed. You could even knock up a smokehouse,' Norm remarks. He lifts Jake's books and pencils off the dresser and he and George start sketching smokehouse plans on the back page of an exercise book.

'What was unbloodybelievable?' I finally remember to ask Norm.

He colours a watermelon pink under his stubble. A pink of righteous outrage by the tone of his voice.

81

'That bloody council has sent me a bloody notice telling me that the yard is "unsightly" and has to be tidied up.' He pulls the crumpled letter from his pocket and hands it to me. 'Unsightly? If you call Picasso unsightly! That yard is an abstract interpretation of the changing face of Gunapan, I'll have you know. It's art. And they want me to clean it up before May.'

'Why?' I scan the letter, but it has no explanation of why anyone would care about whether Norm's yard is unsightly or not.

'It's got to be the development.'

At last, someone who knows about the development. I should have asked Norm in the first place. He knows everything about this town.

'What's going on, Norm? I saw a big hole in the forest.'

'The development,' Norm says again, as if he's talking to himself. He's like me – we spend far too much time talking to ourselves, even when people are in the room with us. 'What else could it be but the development trying to smarten up the town for when the tourists drive through? That council has got a lot to answer for.'

'Sorry.' I turn to Patsy and George. 'This must be boring for you, but I want to find out about this development thing. They've trashed the forest down on the Bolton Road and—'

'Mike from the council's waste department said he'd seen that councillor, Samantha Patterson, with a whole lot of blokes in suits, poking around

82

the bushland, and next thing they've got a licence to pump water from a spring underneath,' Norm butts in.

'Pump water? But this town's desperate for water! If there's water, it should be coming into the town.'

'I'll do the dishes,' Patsy says, standing and stretching.

'You help Aunty Patsy with the dishes, Liss.' I've already worded up Patsy on the bush-pig question, hoping Melissa might feel more inclined to talk to a more glamorous relative. I tow Norm off to the lounge room to interrogate him about what's going on while George takes Jake outside in the last of the evening light to teach him about riding a trike.

By the time Norm's told me everything he knows about the development, which is only that some big corporation bought the land and the council approved the building plans and the pumping of the spring, I'm spent. With Patsy here for two full days already and George for one, I've run out of words. Adult conversation takes so much more work than telling someone to brush their teeth. After Norm heads off to the pub to show his unsightly letter around, I decide to take a catnap before dessert.

CHAPTER 9

The next morning at seven o'clock, mouth gluey, skirt rucked up around my waist, blouse twisted into an armlock, I struggle off the bed, calling out that the kids should be getting up now. Melissa pops her head around the door.

'Aunty George is making homemade crumpets for breakfast.' She shakes her head reproachfully at me. 'You slept in your clothes last night!'

Jake races into the room and throws himself on the bed. 'Aunty Patsy says I'm probably the smartest boy she's met in her whole life!'

We're eating crumpets with butter and jam when the doorbell rings. It's too early for anyone I know to visit so I decide to ignore it. Everyone looks at me.

'It's seven thirty! Who could it be? The Queen? Someone's probably asking for money for charity.'

The doorbell rings again. I keep chewing my crumpet. I had no idea homemade crumpets were so muscular.

A head passes the kitchen window and a minute later something clatters on the back veranda.

'Wait,' I hear Norm say.

George opens the back door. Patsy screams. Jake jumps up from the table and starts running.

'Meet your lawnmower,' Norm declares.

The goat stands as high as his waist. It's rubbing its stubby horns up and down the veranda post and pawing at the floorboards.

'Good God.' George steps closer to inspect the goat. 'Look at the size of that thing. Is it, is it . . .?'

'It's a goat, George,' Norm replies calmly. 'Loretta keeps complaining about mowing the lawn. Here's a free lawnmower.'

'No,' I protest.

'She's a beautiful goat. A lovely nature. She'll be a good family pet as well.'

'No.'

To my amazement, while Jake is cowering behind the kitchen door – there, he does take after his father – Melissa gets up from her chair and goes over to the goat. She leans down and presses her face into the goat's neck and sniffs. Then she moves around in front of it and looks into its eyes.

'Hello goat,' she says.

The goat pushes its head forwards and gently butts her shoulder. I feel Patsy's hand take mine and squeeze it under the table. Melissa has her arms around the goat's neck and she's leaning her face against its creamy curly coat.

'I hope that goat's clean,' I say to Norm. Norm shrugs, picking something black and crumbly off

85

his pants and flicking it into the yard before he speaks.

'Animals have their own kind of clean.'

We're all mesmerized by Melissa, who seems to have turned into a goat whisperer. The goat's nuzzling her right hand, and with her other hand she's stroking its chest.

'Is it a male or a female?' I ask Norm.

'Female,' he answers. 'You don't want a buck. Very smelly, bucks.'

'Can I give it some crumpet?' Melissa asks George, who graciously agrees that Melissa can feed her two-star crumpet to an animal of a species known to eat clothes and the clothes line they came on.

The goat nibbles the crumpet from Melissa's hand. Without my noticing, Norm, Melissa and the goat seem to have edged further and further forwards so that now they are in the kitchen. As if it can hear my thoughts the goat turns to me and burps loudly.

'No,' I protest again.

Melissa swings around from goat adoration to give me her well-practised 'evil mother' look.

'No goats in the kitchen.' I have to take a stand. Norm and Melissa and the goat start backing out the door. They jam up halfway and have to wriggle around. It's the goat that clatters out backwards first.

'It has to have a wash.'

'I'll help Melissa with that,' Patsy the traitor says.

'Never in the house.'

Everyone nods. I realize they're all against me.

'We don't know how to look after it.'

'Nothing to it.' His jolly tone says that Norm knows he's won. 'Let it eat the lawn and give it some feed from the livestock feed shop. A bit of water, and you're right. My mate who owns goats'll drop by now and again to check it's OK.'

'I'm not picking up its poo.'

Strangely, no one jumps in to solve that problem.

'I said, I'm not picking up its poo. If you want to keep it, Liss, you have to clean up after it.'

'I will,' she calls out from the veranda, where she's still busy having a goat love-in.

Norm leans in and whispers to her. At least, he thinks he's whispering. Norm's slowly going deaf, but he hasn't realized yet.

'Don't worry about the poo,' he whispers to Melissa so loudly that the lightshades rattle. 'It'll just go back into the land.'

Melissa rushes into the kitchen to give me five sloppy kisses on the cheek. 'Thanks, Mum. Thanks for letting us have her.' Then she's back outside. Who could have guessed my daughter would fall in love with a goat? Staying in the country was a mistake, I knew it.

'How about you, Jake?' George asks. 'What do you think of the goat?'

Like a grown man, Jake is reluctant to admit to being afraid of anything. Instead, he'll wait till the final minute of terror when he can't take it any longer and he'll burst into tears and start blubbering for his mummy. I recognize that quivering underlip and stiff upper lip look.

'Terror,' I say to George, at exactly the same time as Patsy asks, 'What are you going to call it, Liss?'

'Yeah, that's great.' Melissa is only half-listening.

'Terror's an unusual name,' Patsy says, looking at me with her eyes wide.

Terror the goat? This could be some kind of warning from the universe.

'What about Daisy?' I suggest. 'Or Olive? Or Jodie or Julia or Kim?'

'I like Terror,' Melissa says firmly.

'You mean Terra as in earth, right?' My wonderful, wonderful sister.

'I guess so,' Melissa answers, mumbling because she has her face mashed into the goat's coat.

That will do. Terra. Although I know from now on I'll always think of the goat as Terror.

'Take Terror down to the yard and introduce her to her new home while I have a word with Norm,' I tell Melissa.

Norm turns hurriedly. He's halfway down the veranda steps before I can even point the finger of blame.

'See you tomorrow, Loretta,' he calls over his shoulder. We head to the front of the house to watch him from the front door. He's made it to his truck in record time. That old gammy leg doesn't seem to be playing up this morning. 'I'll bring

88

some stuff for Terror. Bye George, bye Patsy. Let me know if you need any materials for that smoke-house!' His last words are drifting off into the distance because he's already backed out of the drive and turned into the road.

After I've dropped Jake and Melissa at school, I come back and sit on the veranda with Patsy and George. We sip cups of tea, watching Terror munching her way through every speck of green in the yard.

'It adds a nice pastoral touch, having the goat.' Patsy must be warming to our rural paradise where children fall in love with goats. 'Of course, it's you who'll be picking up the poo.'

'I know. So did Melissa tell you anything about the bush-pig business?'

Patsy rubs her forehead. 'She said school was no fun anymore, but she didn't mention a bush pig. She mentioned some new girl.'

Terror clops up the veranda steps and looks menacingly at Patsy, who hands over her biscuit.

'Don't do that, darling,' George says. 'You'll encourage it.'

'I'm not saying no to that brute.' Patsy hands Terror the last biscuit off the plate. Terror swallows and burps, noses the plate, jumps off the veranda and returns to stripping the trees in the yard.

'What about the new girl?'

'It was hard to make out what she was on about. You know how kids tell a story as if you already know half of it? She was talking about a war, how the girl had been in a war.'

I knew there was something odd about the family I saw sitting away from everyone at the waterhole. They seemed so alone up on the ridge, five silhouettes against the white-blue sky of late afternoon. They probably never even made it to the water, what with the whole town watching them take every step down that hill. I remember when I first came here with Tony, how people stopped their conversations and turned and stared when I walked by. Mind you, that was probably because they were wondering what kind of birdbrain had hooked up with Tony. If only someone had said something . . .

'When are you going to send the kids down to stay with us?' George asks.

My neck cracks with the speed of my head turning.

'You want to look after Melissa and Jake?'

'For a few days,' George answers quickly. 'We wouldn't want them to get homesick.'

Patsy's looking dubious. She's told me about the time they had Tammy's children to stay. James, twelve years old, suggested that George should have put a little more pesto in the lamb crust. Eliza, nine, tripped the power overload switch in the house one night by using a hairdryer, a hair straightener, electric tweezers, an electric footbath for softening feet before a pedicure, and a neck

90

massager all at once. When the power came back on, Eliza wanted to go home because her hair had gone frizzy and she needed the gel she'd left in her bathroom.

'*Her* bathroom?' I asked.

'The new house,' Patsy said. 'They each have a bathroom. They're using enough water to irrigate the Mallee.'

'I suppose I could let the kids go for a couple of weeks,' I say, giddy with excitement.

'Days, Loretta, a couple of days.'

'Five days?' I offer. 'Six?'

If I could have a holiday from the children I love so much I sometimes want to smother them, who knows how my life would improve. I might take up gardening and cake decorating. I might discover a talent for painting watercolours or writing poetry. Brilliant small-business ideas would pop into my head as I worked up a sweat jogging around the Wilson Dam, knocking one more centimetre off my tiny waist and toning my long slender thighs.

'Oops, hang on a tick,' I tell Patsy and George, putting down my chipped mug. 'Got to get the chicken fillets out of the freezer for tonight.'

When I get back the tea party is over. Patsy and George are packing their things inside, and Terror is nosing around the plates, checking for crumbs.

'Shoo! Off the veranda, Terror,' I say. Terror stares at me without budging. She has pale green eyes and black horizontal pupils. 'People sacrifice your type to the devil,' I tell her. 'Shoo.' I point down the stairs, but Terror bends her head towards my hand. Her top lip stretches out and, like a hand in a mitten, her lips probe all over my fingers and the back of my palm. 'You are one spooky goat,' I tell her, drawing my hand away and stroking her side. Her coat is softer than it looks. She pushes her head against my belly.

'Sucked in,' George says from the doorway. 'I guess I won't be making goat curry out of that one.'

'It's not a pet, George. It's a lawnmower.'

'Sure. Next time we come I bet the lawnmower has its own place set at the table.'

Terror nudges me once more before she heads back down into the yard.

'How about Easter?' Patsy says from behind George. 'The kids can come and stay for a few days. I'll take a break from uni. We can do the aquarium, things like that.'

'Great.' That's all I have to say. Otherwise, I'm speechless. This will be my first holiday from the children in eleven years. I can see myself trans-formed. The pudge has magically fallen from my hips and I'm wearing a long, slinky silk dress. I'm in the function room of the golf course, tossing my newly blond-streaked hair and full of ennui or some other French feeling at these boring rich men crowding around me. I'm certain something like this will happen when I'm child-free. All I need to do is to stop eating immediately.

In the meantime, it's only a week until the minister comes to Gunapan. We have to get organized.

CHAPTER 10

At ten thirty-four on the day chosen for his Gunapan tour, the minister arrives in the manner of royalty, chauffered inside a big white car that glides soundlessly to a stop in front of us. He steps out of the car, unplugs the mobile earpiece from his ear and tucks it into his suit pocket, smooths back his hair with the heel of his palm and clears his throat.

We're standing in a line along the school fence like a bunch of schoolkids. The headmaster steps out of the welcoming committee line to thrust a hand in the minister's direction.

'Welcome to Gunapan, Minister.'

The minister gives a regal nod.

I remember the day I first heard they were going to close the primary school. My whole pathetic do-as-you're-told life reared up in front of me and I said, 'No, I'm not going to be walked over again. I'm going to stop this.'

Helen, always supportive, suggested, 'Can you end world poverty and bring peace to the Middle East while you're at it?'

Norm asked how my four-year-old découpage project was going.

They were both right. I've never finished anything in my life. The ghost of some radical from the sixties must have taken over my body. I started using words like 'mobilize' and 'comrade'. Norm nicknamed me the Gunna Panther. I wrote letters and painted signs and demonstrated in front of the school to a crowd of mothers picking up their children while Melissa hid, humiliated, on the floor of the car. Jake did a protest war dance – one of the mothers thought he was busking and threw him a dollar.

Now, finally, the Minister for Education, Elderly Care and Gaming is here to visit Gunapan Primary School on his way to open a new agricultural campus further up the highway, and I'm struck dumb. The radical spirit has deserted me and all I can think about is how to ruff up my blouse to hide the butter stain from Jake's greasy breakfast fingers.

In front of the school, the minister, the mayor and the headmaster shake hands vigorously, nodding and looking around, frowning and smiling in turn, as if they're having a whole conversation without words. After a moment I realize the minister's flummoxed because no one's taking his picture. I pull my old Kodak from my handbag and aim it. The flash lights up the gathering and the minister, obviously relieved, lets go of the headmaster's hand. I meant to get film yesterday, but the chemist told me it's cheaper to buy a new digital camera than to process three rolls of film so I didn't bother.

We've planned a tight half-day's entertainment for the minister – primary school, Country Women's Association, local industry and lunch at the pub, where he can see his portfolios of elderly care and gaming taken care of simultaneously in the pokies room.

Last week we had a meeting about the visit. The first thirty minutes was spent discussing what we're supposed to call the minister. The headmaster is convinced we should address him as 'Minister'. Norm wants to call him 'mate'. I preferred Mr Deguilio, but in the vote I lost because half the people in the room couldn't pronounce it.

'And if we mess it up we'll sound like a bunch of hicks,' Helen said, as if that would be a surprise.

First stop is morning tea at the Country Women's Association Hall. The minister tells his driver to wait because he'd like to walk and see a bit of the town so we follow the mayor and the minister in file down the street. Bowden, our very own local hooligan, drives past in his hotted-up Torana, leaning on the horn the whole way to the milk bar where he screams to a stop with a flourish of smoking tyres.

'Membership of the CWA is very strong in Gunapan,' the mayor tells the minister on the way into the hall. We crowd inside and jostle for a place near the food. 'We're a tight-knit community, working together, and the CWA has a proud history in this town. If we have an emergency such as a bushfire, the CWA ladies make tea and sandwiches for the volunteer firefighters and prepare bedding for anyone who's had to abandon their home.'

'Homemade country scones.' The minister breathes a sigh of pleasure as he sits in front of the mound of freshly baked scones Kyleen bought first thing this morning at the supermarket. 'You don't get food like this in the city anymore. It's all focaccias and squid-ink pasta.'

'We have focaccias too, Mr Minister,' Kyleen says, 'but I've never heard of skidding pasta.' She pulls out the chair beside the minister and the headmaster dances around behind them in a panic. I don't think Kyleen's his first choice for Ambassador of Gunapan.

'I always thought black pasta looked odd anyway,' the minister replies. He takes the cup of tea Kyleen has poured for him and helps himself to a scone.

On that signal, the rest of us launch ourselves in rugby team fashion at the two trestle tables, load up with the scones and jam and cream and settle down on the seats around the walls for our free feed.

I'm stuffing the last scone into my mouth when the headmaster sidles up. He's gripping his saucer so tightly the cup is rattling.

97

'You've got to do something about Kyleen,' he hisses.

I look over and Kyleen waves to me. She's sporting a cream moustache. So's the minister. Kyleen's laughing. She leans in and whispers in his ear, leans back and laughs again.

'What? They seem to be having a great time.'

'Kyleen's telling him the story of last year's power blackout.'

I scuttle over, still chewing my scone, and stand beside Kyleen, grinning like an idiot.

'That's so funny, Kyleen. Maybe . . .' I interrupt as she gets to the part where Norm's stripping the copper wire from the old electricity substation while further down the road the newly privatized power company is preparing to run a test surge on the safety equipment they've installed.

'Norm's never had a lot of hair,' Kyleen goes on, ignoring me. 'Well not that anyone can remember.'

She explains to the minister how she happened to be driving backwards past the old substation at the time because every other gear in her car had stopped working and it was the only way she could get to the mechanic.

'Jeez, I got a crick in my neck. And as I'm passing the substation—'

The minister's smile is so rigid it's as though someone sprayed his face with quickset cement. I imagine this is one of the skills a politician needs.

'Minister!' I shout. 'We're running behind schedule. It's time to visit Morelli's Meats.'

'Oh, we'd better be off. Terribly sorry to miss the end of your story.' The minister puts out his hand to shake with Kyleen, who offers to ride in the government car with him so she can finish. But the headmaster has placed his hands affectionately on her shoulders and when she tries to stand she finds herself clamped to the seat. The mayor waves at me to hurry the minister away.

So I'm stuck with him. I rush him outside and take another pretend photo in front of the CWA Hall before racing him back to the car. Kyleen's in the background of the shot, struggling to get away from the headmaster.

'Can you send copies of those photos to my office?' He's panting as we charge along the footpath.

'No problem, Mr Deluglo.'

The emails we got from his staff before this visit requested a tour of local industry. We thought hard. The Social Security office is the obvious centre of industry in this town. Most of us spend at least half a day a week in there trying to sort out missed payments or overpayments or underpayments or having a chat because it's the one place you know you'll find certain people on a Thursday morning. But that portfolio belongs to another minister.

Gabrielle from the Neighbourhood House Committee was eager to entertain the minister at her property, but we voted against letting him go to the big farms because they're the ones with money and he'd never believe how the rest of us live.

It was Norm who thought of Morelli's Meats.

'He can take a side of beef home for the barbie. And you've got to admit, they have a mighty presence in the town.'

It's true. The monthly tallow and glue melt on a day with a north wind is something visitors never forget.

Mario Morelli was thrilled to be selected to represent the town's industry.

'We'll give him the full tour! I'll make sure everyone's got clean smocks.' He patted Heck on the back. 'I hope he comes on a butchery day. Youse people don't understand the skills Hector's got with a cleaver. He's a bloody artist.'

When the minister and I arrive back at his car the driver is sprawled in the passenger seat reading the newspaper.

'Do you know how to get to the next stop?' the minister asks him and the driver puffs scorn out through his nose.

'My charioteer,' the minister says. 'Honestly, you are a marvel, Nick. I don't . . .'

He's talking to no one because Nick's already in the driver's seat fondling the steering wheel and gently revving the engine. Gunapan hasn't seen a car this shiny since my husband Tony did a runner in Delilah, the CRX.

The mayor's waiting for us outside Morelli's Meats. The pens in the slaughter yard are empty, so we're lucky. After he lost his first driving job in Halstead Tony did a stint here, which is how I know that slaughter day's the one to avoid. The staff turnover is very high, and we don't want the minister chatting to a trainee with a bolt gun.

Mario hurries out, pulling off his plastic apron and flinging it back to his son who is hurrying behind. He wipes his hands on his trousers and steps up, arm outstretched, to the minister who takes the hand and pumps.

'Mario Morelli, Morelli's Meats, Minister.'

'Looking forward to seeing your men at work, Mr Morelli.'

Not to be left out, the mayor steps up. I sigh and drag out the empty Kodak, but luckily the cadet reporter from the *Shire Herald* is pulling up at the kerb. He lifts a camera with a paparazzi-sized lens from a bag over his shoulder, and the minister's smile widens.

'Minister, could we have you shaking hands with Mario again? And the mayor?' the reporter says.

After they've finished the handshaking fiesta, Mario escorts us on the tour. The abattoir is white and clean – and empty. Mario hurries us through the killing room, the freezer filled with carcasses on hooks, the penning yard, the loading dock and the staffroom. When we reach a door we've already passed three times as we zigzagged through the building, Mario pauses, his hand on the knob.

101

'Minister, you are about to see art in motion. It's unusual to be doing this work at an abattoir, but when we found out what Hector could do, we couldn't let him go. So we run our own butcher shop as well as the abattoir.' He swings open the door, the minister steps inside and applause breaks out.

Half the town is inside the room. They must have sneaked in the back during our tour. They're sitting in rows facing a stainless-steel cutting bench where Hector stands, cleaver in one hand, ribcage of the pink and white fatty carcass of an enormous cow being massaged by the other. I'd never realized how tiny Hector is. He gives off an air of being a big man, but now I see that two and a half Hectors would fit inside that cow.

Norm waves to me from the front row. Kyleen's sitting next to the headmaster at the back. The staff of the abattoir take up the middle row. They are wearing glaringly white smocks and hats that remind me of shower caps, and their arms are folded to show off their tattoos to best advantage.

'Oh God,' the reporter moans with pleasure, 'I've got a great headline for this. Meat the Minister.'

The minister and the mayor get the seats directly in front of the bench. I move to the side and stand beside Mario and the reporter, who's scribbling fast and giggling to himself.

'Heck, you ready?' Mario calls.

Hector cracks his knuckles and flexes his arms, reaches over and flicks the switch to start the

102

bandsaw at one end of the long bench. A selection of cleavers and knives hangs from hooks above him.

'We had this bench made up specially for Hector after he won the state championship,' Mario tells the reporter.

Hector steps away from the cutting bench, rolls his neck and touches his toes twice. He moves back up to the bench and wrangles the monstrous carcass into his arms.

'Ready.'

Mario holds the stopwatch up for the audience to see. As he presses the button he shouts, 'Go.'

In the next thirteen minutes and twenty-four seconds, Hector slices the carcass down the middle, leaps up on the bench and wrestles the legs off, hammers the meat with a mallet that he seems to have pulled out of his T-shirt, carves slabs of meat from every part of the carcass, zooms more sections through the bandsaw and thrusts his arm up to the shoulder into parts of the cow that magically fall apart into cuts of meat. The air gets thick with minute particles of meat and bone and gristle and all the while Hector's grunting and shouting.

'Round!' he calls as he flings a fan-shaped selection of rump cuts to the front of the bench. 'Rib-eye! Brisket!'

'Done!' he screams, dropping his knife on the bench and raising his hands into the air. We turn to Mario, who's staring at the stopwatch.

'Holy Jesus,' Mario whispers. 'He's broken his own record.'

It takes ten minutes for the applause and cheering to die down. The abattoir blokes crowd around Hector, slapping him on the back and punching him and hugging him.

'It's not official because we didn't have an independent timekeeper,' Mario's telling the reporter, 'but it shows you – Heck hasn't even reached his peak. We're going to take out the Australia-wide. Youse people don't understand the talent we've got in this town.'

'Mario, you've been hiding this bloke away!' the mayor says. 'We could get him on TV.'

'He's got a big future. He's only nineteen.'

We all look at Heck. I would have picked him as thirty-five.

'Outdoor work,' Mario says, shaking his head.

The mayor keeps brushing at his robe. It's an odd mottled colour. I reach over to pick a bone chip from his gold chain.

'Don't worry, that'll clean up. It was worth it to see Heck perform. He's a champion.'

'The minister?' I ask.

Out in the yard Norm's got hold of a wet cloth and he's wiping the minister down while Nick, the charioteer, leans against the car, watching.

'Bit of a dry-clean and the suit'll be fine. There, that feels better, doesn't it?' Norm's talking all cheery, like he's pacifying a child. The minister stands with his arms out. He raises his face to

Norm to have it wiped. I think he's regressed. We can't send him back to Melbourne like this.

'School's next!' I say. 'Let's get cleaned up before the choir.'

The driver holds open the door while Norm and I help the minister into the car. Halfway to the school he snaps back to his old self, plugs himself into the mobile and talks gobbledegook to someone about outcomes and competencies. When he pulls out the earplug he's got the concrete smile back, festooned with a morsel of raw steak glued to his upper lip.

'Fascinating. What an experience,' he says. 'So next it's the school?'

This would be the denial stage.

'Maybe we'll freshen up first at the Neighbourhood House,' I suggest. We don't want him to go frightening the children.

'Good idea,' he replies cheerfully.

In the front of the car Nick swats a fly away from the windscreen.

CHAPTER 11

The headmaster's taken my signs off the school fence. I was happy with the misspelled one. It looked like one of the kids had made it. Now the schoolyard's back to its usual self. Waist-high cyclone wire fence, a few bedraggled trees, adventure equipment that stopped having adventures years ago. The education department seems to have forgotten the school already. Heat rises from the asphalt in the yard and cicadas make attempts at calls that peter out after a few strokes like a chainsaw that won't catch. I wonder if everyone arrived here before us, or if they've gone to the pub to celebrate Heck's record.

The door of the school opens and the grade-three teacher bounds down the steps and pitter-patters towards us, his hands waving and his little belly bouncing. I must remember to tell Helen I think he's gay.

'Minister, welcome to Gunapan Primary. We've prepared a tour for you, nothing too boring or too long. I understand you must see the same thing over and over again so we won't keep you, but we want you to know that you won't find a more dedicated staff or a better-run school than this. At the end of the day, what you're getting here is value for money, Minister, value for money.'

The minister nods. He's still a little dazed, but back at the Neighbourhood House a brisk rub with a washcloth brought him back to reality. After I'd twisted the washcloth corner into a bud and cleaned out his ears he'd asked if he could go to the toilet.

'Yes, but hurry up, we haven't got all day,' I told him. 'And don't forget to wash your hands.'

The Basic Ed kids were coming out of the Neighbourhood House classroom and two Down's syndrome boys rushed into the toilet after the minister. I knew they'd be staring at him in that unnerving intent way they have, but I could hardly follow them into the men's toilet. Sure enough, after a few seconds I heard one boy shriek and giggle. Damien ran out of the toilet, his big flat feet slapping on the tiles, and his hands flapping.

'The man farted!' he screamed, and laughed until he began to snort.

Tina, the Basic Ed teacher, came and stood beside me. She draped her arm around her giggling son for whom the funniest thing in the world always has been, and always will be, farting. 'Shut up, Damien. Who's in the toilet?' she asked.

'The Minister for Education, Elderly Care and Gaming,' I told her.

'Oh, ha ha. Come on kids, let's go,' she called, and the boys tumbled off after her. A few seconds later the minister walked out.

'Ready, Mr Degugulo?' I asked.

'Yes, thank you,' he'd answered in a high-pitched voice and walked unsteadily to the car.

Now I'm following the grade-three teacher, who is ushering the minister up the steps of the school and gabbling as if he's snorted speed.

'One hundred and twenty-three children, four teachers and three teachers' aides, you can't complain about that for efficiency, Minister. Productivity up eleven per cent in the last two years. All local children. We have a need, oh yes, we have a real need in the community. Where would they go, you ask? They'd have to go to a school forty kilometres away, a one-hour bus ride with all the pickups along the way, that's two hours' travel a day, into a school that already has seven hundred children. We run a sports program, oh no, you won't find an obesity problem in this school population . . .' He pauses, looks down and pats his paunch. 'Well, maybe the teachers could use a little work, but the children are fit and healthy and the grades they're getting, Minister, we're in the top twenty in the state for that even though . . .'

I drop back discreetly as he leads the minister into the headmaster's office, where the headmaster has appeared in a clean suit and spectacles, sitting behind his desk and shuffling papers.

'Where are you?' I ask Helen on the mobile. 'I'm alone here with a traumatized member of parliament and a grade-three teacher who's taken mind-altering drugs. Did I tell you I think he's gay?'

'Figures. I'm on my way. We had an emergency at the surgery and I had to stay an extra half-hour while the doc fixed the guy up. Some idiot from the abattoir with a bone splinter in his eye.'

I'm standing on the school steps when she pulls up.

'What do you want me to do?' she asks.

'I don't know. We've had a couple of hiccups. Heck dismembered a cow and spattered the minister with gore.'

'Oh.'

'And Kyleen told him all about Norm stripping the copper wire from the old substation.'

'Oh.'

'That's probably OK. I think that's all wiped from his memory. But now what? I didn't think this through, Helen. A visit to the school isn't going to change his mind. Every school can trot out a choir.'

'I'm not so sure they all have a fire-eating team.'

'Oh, God. I thought that teacher ran off to learn the lute in Nimbin.'

'He left the gift of the grade-four circus club. They can all swallow fire. But I think it's only a demo with three girls today.'

I close my eyes. If I believed in a compassionate

God I'd pray. Please, Your Benevolence, don't let the minister catch fire. I'm sure all that fat from the abattoir is flammable. I can see it now. We're on track to send the minister back emotionally shattered, smeared with blood and bone and barbequed. Of course you can keep your school, they'll say. Gunapan's an example to us all.

'We have to do something to convince him,' I say. 'What? What?'

The strains of 'I Still Call Australia Home' are drifting from the classroom window. Helen winces.

'I knew they'd never hit that high note. Well, look over there. Who might that be?' Helen nods at Nick, the driver, who is still reading the paper. He must be memorizing it.

'The charioteer. At least that's what the minister calls him. Ministerial driver.'

'So maybe Ben Hur will have an idea. He probably knows this minister fella better than anyone.' Helen turns away from me and pokes around in her handbag for what seems like only a moment. When she turns back, her face is fully made-up and she's dabbing at her fresh lipstick with a tissue.

Nick watches us warily as we approach the gleaming chariot. He pulls a chamois from his back pocket and erases a fingerprint smudge from the passenger door. The performance reminds me of the way dogs sniff around the grass with feigned nonchalance when another dog approaches. He's a big man with thick upper arms and a sumo-wrestler kind of sway to his body when he walks.

'The car looks beautiful,' Helen says to him. 'Must be hard work keeping it so—'

'Ladies, no need to beat about the bush. How can I help you?' Nick's voice is deep and throaty. He flicks a mote of dust off the windscreen with the corner of his chamois before he leans back against the driver's door and folds his arms across his chest. I can tell Helen has taken a fancy to him by the way she's clutching my arm so tightly gangrene is setting in. He's a good-looking bloke, all right, but I don't think she should get her hopes up – after all, he's leaving town in one hour and fourteen minutes. That's even faster than your average Gunapan husband.

'Well, it's just that . . . well, you know, the minister is here because my friend, Loretta,' she gestures back at me, even though I have become nothing to her in the presence of this shining knight, 'organized all these petitions and letters and everything and got the headmaster and the mayor to sign and all that to try and stop them closing Gunapan Primary School.' She pauses to take a deep breath. 'And now the minister's here and we want to get him to change his mind but he's had some bad experiences and we don't know what to do.' Another breath. 'And we thought that since you drive him around you must know lots about him and stuff and maybe you could, you know, give us some hints on how to—'

Nick raises his hand, which I notice is muscular also.

'I'd love to help. Especially when I'm asked for assistance by a stunning lady like yourself . . .'

I'm sure I hear Helen simper. I never knew how a simper sounded before today. She's going to start fanning herself and talking in a *Gone with the Wind* accent next.

'What can you do?' I ask. 'I've been on the case for seven months and all I've got is a visit.'

'Leave it to me. I'll have a word with the big man.'

Right. While Helen continues her flirting I sigh and turn to watch the minister being herded down the steps of the school by the headmaster and the grade-three teacher, who's still talking at an incredible speed. I want to cry. All those months writing letters and calling people and chairing meetings that hardly anyone came to. And for nothing except a chance to see Hector disassemble a cow in record time. Which actually was amazing, but doesn't help my kids.

The minister folds back into his car and reappears at his final destination, the Criterion, which used to be all green tiles and ancient toothless farmers propping up the bar, but has been renovated and is now pink and lemon with a new menu that includes confit of duck as well as some old favourites like surf and turf. The ancient toothless farmers have moved to the pokies room out the back.

112

We're having a set lunch in the dining lounge, paid for by my fundraising efforts with the chocolate drive back in November, but I don't have any appetite. Helen's in the bar with Nick. I can see her through the servery hatch, simpering and fanning herself with a beer coaster. Nick notices me watching and gives a thumbs up. I wonder if he's indicating his chances with Helen. He'd better get a move on. The minister's schedule has him out of here in eleven minutes.

When the minister stands up to give a speech, which he promises will only take a few minutes, I keep poking at my chicken parma. I think about what will happen to the school grounds when the school closes. Maybe they'll build a housing estate on the site. Couples will move in. They'll grow vegetable gardens and paint their houses and have babies. The mothers will start a campaign. A school for Gunapan! They'll paint signs and write letters and one day the Education Department will send a portable classroom and a teacher. Meanwhile, because it's Gunapan, the husbands will have mysteriously disappeared.

I only notice the minister's gone when Helen claps me on the back and sighs.

'That chauffeur! What a man. I'm in love.'

I sniff and poke a little harder at the parma sauce.

'Aren't you excited?' she asks.

The headmaster and the mayor come back inside and order beers. It's the middle of the day. I've never seen the headmaster drink, even at night.

'To Loretta!' they shout and raise their glasses.

'And to Nick!' Helen calls out and swigs from her wine glass.

'Who?' the headmaster says.

They're crowded around me, laughing and talking about Heck's show and making plans for the biggest fete in the history of the school.

'It's not closing?' I say.

'Didn't you hear the minister? Changing demographics, supporting the country constituency, the last meeting of the education advisory committee, blah blah blah. You did it, Loretta!'

The grade-three teacher bounds into the pub's dining room, brandishing a letter.

'They're not closing us down! This arrived today!'

'Old news, mate,' Mario Morelli says. 'Have a beer.'

'That must be why the minister kept staring at me with this meaningful look,' the grade-three teacher says musingly. 'I'd finish saying something and he'd stare as though I was supposed to add something else, and it made me prattle away as if I was on speed. He must have been expecting me to say thank you.'

Helen looks longingly through the open door at the puff of dust left by Nick's chariot. Even though the decision must have been made weeks ago, she clearly believes Nick rode in to save us.

'What's the catch?' I look around. I've lived in

Gunapan for thirteen years. I know things aren't this easy.

'Catch? What catch?' the headmaster says, stretching his mouth in an unconvincing smile. 'Drink up, Loretta.'

'You'll have to tell me sometime.'

'Let's have a nice drink and enjoy your victory.'

Usually the headmaster enjoys the job of predicting dire consequences. Usually you can't stop him spreading bad news like jam on toast.

Something else occurs to me. 'What's this about the development and Samantha Patterson?' I turn and ask Vaughan, the mayor. 'What's going on?'

'Samantha Patterson? She's not involved with the development. That portfolio belongs to Chris Dunn. By all accounts the development is going to be great for this town. So don't start on that, Loretta. Look! Here's Hector, the other man of the moment.'

The headmaster pours champagne into my glass and it froths over the rim like the lacy dress of a Southern belle.

'To us,' I say to Helen, raising my glass.

'To Gunapan,' she answers, and we skol.

Don't start on that, the mayor says. But I can't help myself. I'm the Gunna Panther.

CHAPTER 12

'He's got a bloody cheek.' Tina's talking on the phone when I walk into the Neighbourhood House office. She glances over her shoulder at me and smiles, then says, 'OK, gotta go, talk to you soon,' and hangs up the phone.

'Getting cooler at last,' I remark as I hang my jacket on the peg behind the door. 'How come you're still here?'

'Have to get this stuff out to the parents.'

With five teachers and three part-time staff in the tiny office of the Neighbourhood House you'd think we'd be falling over each other, but our schedules rarely cross. Apart from running into her when I was dragging the minister around town, I haven't spoken to Tina for a month. She comes in to teach the Basic Education students who arrive by bus once a week to learn cooking and housekeeping skills. They race up to the office counter and push their round grinning faces in through the window. They are always laughing and joking except when they throw a tantrum and Tina has to physically restrain them.

Her son, Damien, sits beside her now, stuffing envelopes and licking the flaps with his sloppy tongue.

'Hi, Loretta,' he says, smiling with drool running down his chin.

'Damien, clean up your face for heaven's sake.' Tina holds out a tissue to him.

'Do you ever go to shire meetings?' I ask Tina.

'God no, why?'

'Just wondering. I'm trying to find out about this development and no one knows anything but gossip.'

'I heard there's some commercial secrecy thing.'

'See? I bet you don't even know what it is.'

'It's a resort with a golf course and a spa and accommodation. Everyone knows that.'

'But we've got a golf course!'

'It's not for us, Loretta. It's a resort for rich people. From outside, you know, who come to the resort and stay a few days and get pampered and go home.'

'That's crazy. Gunapan's an ordinary town in a dry country on a dry road that's been in drought for seven years. Why would anyone want to come here?'

'Loretta, stop being dense. I told you, they won't come to Gunapan. They'll probably come by helicopter or limousine or something. We'll never see them. Don't worry about it.'

'But the water!' I'm almost shouting now. 'They're taking the water!'

'No, they've got their own spring,' Tina says, sounding as cross as me. 'They're not touching our water.'

'But . . .' There's no point shouting at Tina. Doesn't anyone understand that the water under the ground should be ours? For Gunapan people and the farmers around us, water is life: water is crops, it's native animals surviving drought, it's one swimming pool for a thousand people. It's community. Those wealthy people will pour the water into perfumed spa baths and carve it into ice sculptures for parties. They'll use it to wash their already pristine recreational vehicles and hose stray leaves off the driveways of the resort.

'They say it'll generate twenty jobs for locals.' Tina nods. 'That bush land was a tip anyway. People dumped their rubbish there. It stank.'

'Not before, it didn't. It used to be beautiful. It was green and quiet and cool.' Of course, I get it now. It was green and cool when everywhere else was dry and hot because it had water underneath – the spring. Smart developers.

'Oh my God, he's back,' Damien says to me in a monotone, still with a goofy grin. He's obviously repeating what he's heard, and Tina flushes a deep red.

'Did I tell you to clean up your face?' she says sharply.

'Who's back?' I ask.

'I can't bear it, I'll have to do it myself.' She stands up and grasps Damien's hand to pull him towards the bathroom.

The phone starts ringing as soon as I sit down at the desk.

'Do you have patchwork classes?'

'I can't pay my power bill and they say they're going to cut me off next Monday.'

I wander out to the kitchen for a cup of tea and stand by the window while the kettle boils. Sometimes this job wears you down. Everyone wants something. Outside the window a horse is straining over the barbed-wire fence of the paddock next door trying to reach a clump of green grass. The fence is decorated with shredded plastic bags that have been caught there in the wind. The earth of the paddock is baked like the brown dry top of a burned pie.

Back in the office, the phone rings again.

'Is that you, Loretta?' Helen asks.

'Mmm,' I answer, my mouth full of teddy bear biscuit.

'He's back.'

'Mwah? Phoo?'

'Him! The bastard!'

'Phoo oo meem?' I don't want to believe her. Why would he come back?

'I saw him. He was driving down past the supermarket towards the bridge. He's cut his hair, but it was him. Same car, the CRX.'

For a moment there is silence on the line.

'I'm coming to the House. Don't move.' Helen hangs up.

I can't move. I can't even swallow the teddy bear biscuit that's turned to dry crumbs in my mouth. What will happen when Jake and Melissa see their father? Does he want to take them? Would they go with him? Does he want to come back to us?

By the time Helen arrives I'm moulded to the orange plastic office chair. My husband's return has flipped me back into the old Loretta, the Loretta who fretted and chewed her fingernails and smoked a packet of Winfields a day and rang around people's houses trying to track down her husband to ask him to bring back some milk, but in reality to find out where he was. The Loretta who nagged her children and let her hair go lank and was too nervous to even try to find a job because she knew she was too stupid to keep one. Just like that, the old Loretta is back because her husband is.

'Whatever you're thinking, you're wrong.' Helen plonks a second strong cup of tea on the desk in front of me.

The tea is too hot to drink, but I take a scalding sip anyway to loosen the biscuit clag welded to the roof of my mouth.

'I'm not thinking anything. I can't think,' I tell her. My scalp is so tight I feel like a ballerina.

'Do you want me to follow him, find out what he's doing?'

120

I shake my head.

'Do you want me to kill him?'

I nod. Then laugh a little. 'And trash the CRX. Have you got any idea how much money he spent on that car?'

'I kind of guessed when I saw him licking the trim one time.'

I choke on my tea.

'Good to laugh in times of crisis,' she says, thumping me on the back.

After Helen heads off, I work hard for the rest of the day, trying not to think of him. His name barely crosses my mind. After all this time and after hearing everyone else call him 'that bastard' and 'whatshisname' and 'the ex' so often, he has become those things to me. Even though the children and I carry his surname, Boskovic. What a surname for someone called Loretta. He turned my name into a tongue-twister. I try not to think of him and I spend half the day running to the toilet because I think I'm going to throw up and the other half having flashbacks of our life together, the stomping angry life made for us by that bastard.

In the evening, as I'm dishing up macaroni cheese with bits of vegetable cunningly hidden inside, I tell the kids that their father has been seen around town.

'Is he coming to visit?' Jake asks, as if this is some distant friend of the family.

'Of course he is.' Melissa is so excited she drops

a spoonful of macaroni in her lap. 'He's come back for us. I knew he'd come back.'

I make another slice through the crusty breadcrumb top of the macaroni cheese and serve myself a massive helping.

'I'm sure he'll call soon,' I say finally.

But he doesn't. Three days pass. Every day I think this will be the day he calls. People ring to tell me what he's doing. He drank at the pub Wednesday and Thursday nights. He played pool. He visited this bloke and that bloke, he took his car to Merv Bull to have the injectors cleaned, he bought four hubcaps from Norm. He met a woman who got off the bus late on Friday night and kissed her, then went back to his pub room with her.

Melissa's mood is black by the end of the week.

'It's you,' she accuses me. 'He doesn't want to see you so he won't come around.'

She's only eleven years old, I keep telling myself. 'He's busy, that's all. He'll be around soon.'

Meanwhile, all I can do is go on doing what I always do. At the Neighbourhood House I sit in on the creative-writing class. Ruth, the teacher, asks one of the students to read her list aloud to us.

'The List of Pleasing Things. Looking out from my window on a moonlit night and seeing the silhouette of a kangaroo and her joey beyond the trees in the yard. Getting a handmade card from my granddaughter with the r in "Christmas" written backwards. The scent of the sea on the breeze of a cool change, even though the coast is hundreds of miles away. Finding my photograph in the local paper after an event. The sound of the door closing after the last guest has left the house.'

Ruth has her hands pressed hard to her lips when we look up. Whenever someone reads aloud in the class, we stare at the floor or our feet or our pens and paper on the grey Laminex table. Ruth had suggested we close our eyes to listen, but we all seem to prefer to keep some vision. I'm not sure why the others do it. I keep my eyes open but my face down so no one can read what I'm thinking. I'm a plant, a spy, an espionage agent for the committee. They sent me in undercover to find out why three women insist that Ruth's class in creative writing at the Neighbourhood House continue term after term while everyone else who joins the class drops out after a couple of weeks.

Today we're writing lists. Earlier Ruth read out some lists from the *Pillow Book* by Sei Shonagon, a lady-in-waiting at the Japanese court in the eleventh century. The members of the Imperial Court were supported by the taxes on the population and their only job was to be royal. Ruth told us that poetry flourished, and art and calligraphy. The days of the people at court were spent in the pursuit of beauty. Moon-viewing parties were common. The ladies caught fireflies in the sleeves of their kimonos.

'Did you hear the detail in what Shonagon writes?' Ruth had said. 'And the honesty? How many of us will admit to being pleased when we're chosen above the rest, the way Shonagon does when the Empress calls her to her side before any of the other ladies. And the wickedness! The one where she talks about finding a letter that is torn up but not so torn up that you can't piece it back together again – delicious.'

Now Ruth takes her hands away from her mouth. She reaches out as if she is about to hug the woman who read out her list.

'Perfect, Eleanor,' Ruth says. 'You have found exactly the right tone, the right spirit.'

Eleanor blushes and laughs. I can imagine members of our committee enjoying this class. After all, they are our own landed gentry.

'Can you see how the ordinary is also full of beauty?' Ruth asks us and we nod.

Next it's my turn to read aloud. 'I don't think I've done it right. Maybe someone else should read theirs.'

'Now, Loretta,' Ruth says, shaking her head. 'In this class, we don't judge each other. We're learning together.'

I shrug my shoulders and pick up my piece of paper. I take a deep breath. Reading out my work makes me feel like I'm in primary school.

'OK,' I say and I look around at the four nodding faces of the teacher and my classmates. 'OK, I wrote a few things. The List of Pleasing Things.

Wednesday night comedy on the TV. A Kmart undies sale. The smell of the Scouts' sausage sizzle outside the supermarket on a Saturday. Reading my daughter's diary and not finding anything horrible about me. The jingle of spurs.'

Ruth wipes her forehead with her hand. It's warm in here, all right, but not that hot.

'That's lovely, Loretta,' she says. 'Now, who's next?'

Everyone who hasn't read yet shoots their hand in the air. I remember this moment from school. It's when someone gives a dumb answer to the teacher's question and the others all realize immediately that they can do better. My career as a writer is over in thirty minutes. The other class members read out their lists and not one of them has anything as ordinary as Kmart in it. Roses, moonlight, the smell of mangoes, the swish of silk against your skin. Is this why my life turned out the way it did? Perhaps I should work on developing refined taste and lofty thoughts.

While they're reading I try to imagine what Norm's list of pleasing things might be. Finding an abandoned car on the side of the road and the tyres still have tread? Or Melissa's. I think and think but I can't imagine what my own daughter's list of pleasing things might be. What kind of mother am I?

That night at tea I ask Melissa, 'If you had to write a list of things that pleased you, what would they be?'

'Things that please me?'

'Things that make you feel good.'

'Why?'

'I wondered, that's all. I had to do it today in writing class.'

'Are you learning to write?' Jake says, and giggles.

'Very funny, Mr Top of the Class in Spelling.'

'I got a hundred per cent.'

'And that's the hundredth time you've told us,' Melissa says.

'So what would they be, Lissie?'

'Dad coming back to live with us.'

'I guessed that might be one. What else?'

'A pair of Manolo Blahnik shoes.'

I stare at her. 'I thought I told you that show was off limits. That's American rubbish for grown-ups, not for children.'

Melissa looks up at the ceiling and sighs.

'Didn't I?'

'No.'

'I think I did, young lady.'

'You told me I could never watch that show in this house.'

I hate children. One minute they don't know which shoe goes on which foot, the next they're using logic that would make Aristotle proud.

'Who let you watch it?'

'Helen. She says I'll learn how to deal with men.'

'And Helen's the champion of dealing with men, of course. Well, I'm telling you now – you are not allowed to watch that rubbish. Life's not like that. And it's certainly not like that around here. You go ask for Blahniks at the shoe shop in Halstead and they'll send you to the delicatessen.'

'I'm going to Melbourne the minute I leave school.'

'Don't think Melbourne's some great centre of sophistication. Remember, I'm from there.'

That came out all wrong. Melissa's sniggering. I hate children.

CHAPTER 13

The next day I'm on the phone first thing. 'Helen, how could you let Melissa watch *Sex and the City*?'

'She loved it. And I didn't explain what fellatio is. I told her you'd talk to her about that kind of thing.'

'Oh God.'

'She did ask if it was the same as a blow job, but I said to talk to you.'

'Oh double God. Where did she learn that? She's eleven!'

'It's a new world, Loretta. They know everything. Anyway, I found out. The girlfriend's only twenty-four.'

'What?'

'Tony's new girlfriend. The one staying with him at the pub. She's a child bride. Secretary at the place where he was working up in Mildura.'

'They're married? They can't do that. We're not even divorced yet.'

'A figure of speech, Loretta. Gee, relax.'

Now I'm angry. He's brought his new girlfriend to town, he's paraded her around, he's been

128

spending money and hanging out with his mates, and he hasn't even said hello to his children. I get off the phone from Helen, who's urging me not to do anything silly, and I ring the House and tell them I can't come in today.

First I visit the police station.

'Have you applied to the Family Court for maintenance?' Bill says.

'It's a bit hard to get money from someone who's disappeared. I mean, I know you can apply, but it didn't seem worth the trouble.'

Bill taps his report sheet with his biro. 'Not a lot I can do here. I feel for you, love. It's a common problem in this town.'

At the Social Security office in Halstead I run into Brenda. She offers me a squashed tomato sandwich from her handbag. She's brought a blow-up neck pillow.

'What number are you?' I ask. She shows me her ticket, which says forty-three, and I look at mine, which says sixty-eight. At the counter a man's getting all steamed up and piling papers on the desk in front of the receptionist.

'This isn't a rates notice,' she says flatly. 'It's a title. We need the rates notice.' She leans forwards and rubs her forehead. 'I'm sorry, Mr O'Hagan. It's the rules. We're stuck with them too. If we don't follow the rules the whole process goes back to scratch and it takes even longer.'

'Fuck!' he shouts. He scrunches the papers in his fist and turns to the queue. 'Fuck them. Fuck youse. All this for a measly two hundred bucks. Fuck youse all.'

Back at the Gunapan pub, the barmaid says my husband's gone out. 'With his lady friend. Sorry, Loretta,' she adds.

For an hour I drive aimlessly around town, then it's time to pick up the kids from school.

Tony's waiting at the school gate with his child bride.

It's so hard to walk I feel as if my legs have pins in them. They won't bend. I swing them around in half circles so I can move forwards.

'Hey Loretta,' the bastard says. 'What have you done to yourself? Been playing footy?'

'Hello Tony,' I whisper.

The child bride thrusts a hand at me. 'Nice to meet you, Loretta. I'm Talee.' She's neat. Pressed jeans and checked shirt. Dinky short hairdo and clean fingernails. Unbitten. My hand slides unwillingly into hers and she grips it for a moment then lets go. 'I'm sorry to surprise you this way, but Tony says he's been flat out all week and hasn't called. He's unbelievable. You must be so cross. I hope you'll forgive us.'

My eyes roll across to look at Tony. Everything's going slow, or else my brain is shutting down. I think I heard her insult Tony, but he's still smiling. He's shaved off his sparse ginger moustache and goatee and he seems to have spent money on his teeth. My money. My kids' money.

'Can't wait to see the kids,' Tony says.

My mouth may be open. Drool may be dribbling from my lower lip.

'Teeth,' I say.

He rubs his forefinger with a squeak across his new white front teeth and laughs.

'Cost me a packet. I clean my teeth every night now, like you used to tell me, Loretta.' He nudges Talee. 'She was always on at me to clean my damn teeth.'

'No wonder – they were a disgrace,' Talee answers smartly.

Tony laughs again and I think I'm going to faint. I close my eyes. Talee asks me if I'm all right. I hear shouts as kids come running out through the school doors.

'Well, look what washed up out of the drain.' A voice speaks behind me. 'I thought you were going to buy some hubcaps and then piss off for another few years.'

Norm's big hand lands on my shoulder.

'And you must be the new one,' he says to Talee. 'Obviously as stupid as Loretta.'

'Yes, I'm the new one. I'm Talee. I guess we all have our foibles.'

'Foibles?' Norm laughs a quick bark. 'So he's a foible now. Not the word I'd use.'

My knees bend a little. Perhaps movement will return to them before I have to go back to the car. Jake's hand slips into mine and next minute Melissa comes running and flings herself against her father.

'I knew you'd come back for us!'

'Hey, baby girl.'

Norm's hand tightens on my shoulder. Jake tugs my arm and I lean down so he can whisper in my ear.

'Is that Dad?'

I nod.

'He looks different.'

I nod again.

Melissa's clinging to Tony as if he's a life buoy. Tony reaches out a hand to Jake. 'Hey Jake, how's my boy?'

'Very well, thank you.'

Talee crouches down beside Jake. 'Aren't you a cutie. How old are you?'

'Seven,' Jake whispers. 'In four months.'

Talee looks up at me. She's got the clear skin of a twenty-year-old. No make-up except for a swipe of pink lipstick. She's the opposite of scrag.

'Could we take them to buy an ice cream? We'll bring them back in time for tea,' she says.

I'm speechless. This can't be happening. She's acting as if this is a regular visit. Norm's gasping like he's run the Stawell Gift. Tony detaches Melissa from his side and reaches for Jake, but Jake steps behind me.

'Let's go, Dad,' Melissa grasps Tony's hand and pulls him in the direction of the shops. 'Come on.'

'You've got more nerve—' Norm's wheezing now. I take hold of his arm and try to shush him.

'Listen, mate. This is none of your fucking business,' Tony says through tight lips.

'Tony!' Talee squeaks out a protest.

This is more like the Tony I know. For the first time in two years I'm desperate for a smoke. The old Loretta's taken over my body again. I want to go home and have a glass of wine and wash some dishes. I want to wash every dish in the house. I'll sit in the dark for a while, smoking Winnies. Then I'll take a few clean dishes out the back and smash them on the rusted old truck carcass that squats in my yard and reminds me every day that this bastard left me nothing but crap.

My hand's still on Norm's arm and I can feel his bicep tensing and relaxing, tensing and relaxing with each breath. With time creeping glacially through this moment I find myself drifting up and floating above the impossible happenings at the school gate. I'm dissociating, I think dreamily, the way psycho-killers do in horror movies. It feels oddly pleasant. What will I do with the money Mum's going to send me? Mmm. A list of pleasing things to do when I have a few thousand dollars. Look at Melissa's hair, I admonish myself. Flyaway tangles, and uneven lengths. That girl needs a professional haircut. And maybe I'll dye my hair. We could have a girls' day at the salon. Melissa's never been to a proper salon. Come to think of it, I haven't had a haircut from anyone except Helen for years. And cricket lessons for Jake so he can stop smashing the laundry window. My heart's slowing down at last. They're talking around me, but I can't make out the words. I might shout Helen lunch at the golf course restaurant as thanks for all those haircuts. I'll check out the BMWs in the car park. See if . . .

'Loretta!'

'Huh?'

'We've got to head off. But we'll drop around to the house later, after tea, OK?'

'Drop around to the house?'

'Just like the old Loretta,' Tony says. 'Off with the pixies.'

Damn, my heart's starting to ramp up again. I used to think I'd have a heart attack when we were together. He'd be shouting at me and my heart would be hammering so hard my teeth would start to chatter.

'Honey, maybe Loretta's busy tonight. You should ask what suits her.' Talee smiles at me.

A single mother busy on a weeknight? Who is this woman? She makes Kyleen seem intelligent. Norm wrenches his arm out of my grip and stands clenching and unclenching his fist.

'Dad, I want to go with you and the lady,' Melissa says firmly.

Tony harrumphs uncomfortably. 'No, you go with your mum. I'll see you tonight, Liss. Be a good girl.'

'OK, Daddy. What time?'

I haven't seen this kind of obedient acceptance since she was eight.

'Later, all right?'

My body feels like it's been slammed back to earth. My knees are bending fine now. They're bending so well I think I'm going to sit down right here in the dust at the school gate. Norm grabs me as I buckle. We watch Tony and Talee stroll back to the CRX. Talee slips her hand into Tony's and leans her head on his shoulder then turns and waves goodbye. Melissa waves back.

'She's pretty,' Melissa accuses me.

'What are you doing up there, mate?' Norm helps Jake down from the tree behind us.

I ask Norm to stay for tea and we eat our scrambled eggs on toast and watch TV without saying much. At nine o'clock Jake's asleep in my lap and I put him to bed. Melissa's wide-eyed and keyed up. She can't stop talking. She makes a list of things she wants to tell her dad and she writes them down in an exercise book so she won't forget. How she won first prize in English last year. Getting the best and fairest in netball the year before last. How they got a pet sheep at the school and everyone voted for the name she suggested.

'What else, Mum?' she keeps nagging me.

When the phone rings at nine thirty I hold my nose trying not to cry. Melissa picks up the receiver, but she's too anxious to say hello. She listens for a minute then hands the phone to me.

'Hello Loretta? It's Talee here, we met today? Tony's called. He's stuck out on the highway with a flat so we won't be able to make it tonight. I'm very sorry to inconvenience you. Tony says he'll call you tomorrow.'

'Fine,' I say and hang up without a goodbye. Melissa looks at me and I shake my head.

'I'm so sorry, sweetie. Maybe tomorrow.'

I follow her to her room.

'Leave me alone,' she says from the darkness.

In the lounge room Norm turns off the TV. He pats me on the back as he leaves.

I pick up Melissa's exercise book from the couch and read her long list, printed and numbered with scratchings out and arrows moving things to more important positions and asterisks with notes like *The only girl!*

Melissa's list of pleasing things.

CHAPTER 14

The next night, Norm arrives on my doorstep and tells me I'm going out.

'You're not going to mooch around here feeling sorry for yourself. I want to see the Gunna Panther in action tonight, because it's the shire meeting. No one's getting away with calling my yard unsightly.'

I sigh. 'I can't, Norm. I haven't got a babysitter.' I want to sit at home mooching around and feeling sorry for myself. Tony's postponed his visit for another night and Melissa is so furious with me, convinced it's all my fault, that she's on the internet looking up how to divorce your mother.

'It's all arranged,' Norm says. 'They set up child-care a while ago because some mothers who had a petition in front of council made a hoo-ha about equal opportunity. For the older kids they've got that computer whizz, Joey, you know, Al's kid, giving some demo in the computer room. Helen's coming. No excuses, Loretta.'

I remember being taught in school that local government is the face of democracy. If that's the case, then our democracy is an angry little ferret face pushed up against the glass of the complaints department, telling people no. Normally the monthly meeting about town issues would have two people trying to get out of paying their parking fines, someone objecting to a neighbour's building permit and the usual Hotel Association rep pushing for a bigger car park outside the pub's poker machine annexe. Tonight is different. Norm wants his Unsightly Property Notice withdrawn. Plus there's special entertainment. A witch has come to Gunapan, and she's been entered as an item on the agenda.

When we arrive, the room is packed with the biggest crowd the shire meeting has ever seen. The councillors are seated around a table at the front of the hall. They have jugs of water and bowls of mints and huge piles of paper beside them. A couple of council staff are making notes at a table behind.

Kyleen's brought two packets of chips and a can of lemonade, as if she's at the pictures, and the cadet reporter from the *Shire Herald* is snapping candid shots of the gallery. The council gallery is rows of seats divided into two blocks by an aisle. On the right of the aisle, the entire congregation of the Church of Goodwill is squashed uncomfortably next to the ten remaining aged Catholics and a few pious types who don't go to church but who you often hear boasting about God the way you would a close friend who's won a quiz show on the TV. To the left sits everyone else. The kids are in the computer room learning how to hack into NASA. Melissa's probably already found herself an internet foster family.

Two rows behind, I see Brianna. She's wearing a lot of make-up. Not enough to cover the bruise. I wander back. When I touch her arm she jumps.

'Are you OK, Brianna?' Everyone knows her boyfriend loses it after a drink or two, but we can't persuade her to leave him.

She leans into me and murmurs at my shoulder, 'I'm sorry the kids saw us arguing the other week, Loretta. It was nothing, honestly. He's a good man with a hot temper, that's all. He's getting so much better.'

I don't know what to say.

'Honestly, Loretta. It's OK.'

When I step into the aisle to go back to my seat I almost crash into a portly figure, resplendent in red and gold, sailing towards the front of the room. Our mayor, Vaughan, loves the robes. He doesn't have to wear them – after all, this is Gunapan. We think dressing up is for weddings, funerals and visits from the pension assessor. But he slips on the big scarlet cloak and the gold chain whenever he gets the chance, and he makes sure the chain jingles a little when he walks, his stomach pushed out in front and his head thrown back with the pride of leading this great community.

Tonight he walks down between the forces of good on the right and the forces of nothing-better-to-do-on-a-Thursday-night on the left without glancing either way. I heard him discussing the witch issue with Sandra, the checkout girl, at the supermarket the other day. In the background, the supermarket sound system was vibrating with the rage of a radio talkback caller from Halstead who was working his way through a long list of grievances, from the laziness of young people today to that appalling pantsuit the foreign minister was wearing at the OPEC conference and did she think orange was a suitable colour to represent hardworking Australians in front of other world leaders who wore perfectly dignified suits and never dyed their hair either except that French bloke who was a ponce anyway.

'This witch business is the biggest thing ever to hit this town,' Vaughan started saying to Sandra, like he was narrating the plot of a blockbuster movie. 'I have to be very careful, very careful indeed, to be bipartisan.'

Sandra reeled back. 'You're bipartisan?' she asked, her voice a whisper.

'I try,' the mayor said. 'It's not always easy. Sometimes one side looks a lot better than the other.'

'Does everyone know?' Sandra said, hurrying to swipe his groceries and pack them. She glanced past him at me. I pretended not to be listening and kept flipping through the magazine from the rack next to me, which happened to have George Michael on the cover.

'Oh, I think it's pretty clear that I spend plenty

of time with both sides. They all have different wants and needs. You have to satisfy everyone – I tell you, what with the shop in the daytime and my mayoral duties at night and weekends, it's exhausting. The wife's not happy. She wants me to give it up, spend more time at home.'

'I bet she does,' Sandra muttered. She thrust his change at him, holding the coins between the tips of her fingers and dropping them into his hand.

'I've been trying to get on top of this witch business. Haven't heard back from her yet, but I might get lucky before the meeting. Cheerio then, Sandra,' he said.

'Hmmph,' she said.

I pushed my carton of milk up to the register and put George Michael back on the stand.

'Did you hear that?' Sandra asked.

'Nope,' I said.

She rang up my milk and handed me the bag. On the speakers above, the radio talkback caller was winding down to a shuddering finale on refugees taking our jobs and how apples don't taste the same anymore. He seemed to have been given an excessive amount of time to talk. The DJ must have been out making a cup of tea.

'This town's changing,' she said, shaking her head. 'First the witch, then a bipartisan mayor. What next?'

The witch moved to town a month ago and began advertising on a board outside her newly rented house. The hand-painted board, strung by chains from the lacework on her veranda, offered spells, charms, curses and the lifting of curses, amulets and an invitation to a monthly new moon coven. The Witchery would open for business in July, and would start taking appointments from early June.

Helen said she was heading down the day the Witchery opened. She was going to get the town curse lifted.

'What town curse?' I asked.

'The one where men suddenly get the urge to bugger off back to the city as soon as they've fathered enough children. I used to think it was something in the water, but maybe it's a curse.'

None of us is sure who the witch is. She's been out of town during most of the month the house has been rented. No one's seen her enter or leave. A stranger was spotted around town, a tall woman with black hair who had her roots dyed at Hair Today Gone Tomorrow in the main street and bought Chinese takeaway three nights in a row. Brianna saw her driving up and down the streets looking at the houses and we wondered if she was casting some kind of spell on the town. Next, she turned up at Norm's junkyard.

'She walked straight up to the door of the shed and the dogs never barked once. I look up and there she is in the doorway with this big black hairdo and a wand in her left hand that she's pointing at me. I nearly shit myself thinking I'm about to be hexed. Turns out the wand's a bit of pipe from the yard and she's come to try to sell me KwikKerb. "Darl," I said to her, "if you can find anywhere to put a kerb in this yard, good luck to you.'"

So it wasn't her. Now we're all looking around to see the witch, but she doesn't seem to be here.

'Maybe she's made herself invisible,' Helen whispers.

The mayor calls the meeting to order. As they go through the usual agenda items, Kyleen passes around the chips while the crowd on the left side chats and laughs. Melissa creeps in and asks if she can go down to the shop with Taylah and I tell her she's not going anywhere and she pouts and I sigh and it's just like being at home.

'We have an agenda item put forward by Norm Stevens,' the mayor reads out. '"An application to lift the Unsightly Property Notice on the property of Mr Norman Stevens Snr, Lot 19 Minyip Road, Gunapan.'"

Samantha Patterson is shuffling paper on the table in front of her. She takes a sip of water without looking up.

'Would you care to speak to your application, Norm?' the mayor asks.

Norm edges past me and Helen and walks to the front of the gallery.

'I don't want to speak to my application, I want to speak to youse councillors. I don't know what you think you're doing, slapping an Unsightly Property Notice on a property that's looked like

143

this for fifteen years. How come suddenly I'm unsightly?'

'Norm, please don't take this personally. I've had a look at this and it's obviously about the resolution to beautify Gunapan. Working on our community pride. Last council meeting we voted on a resolution that said,' he lifts a piece of paper and adjusts his glasses for reading, '"Gunapan should improve its image and encourage pride in the community."' He looks up, adjusts his glasses again and pats his stomach. He often does that. He's a bit of a worrier. Probably has an ulcer.

'I've got plenty of community pride, mate. And anyway, I wasn't unsightly when you came to buy that corrugated iron for your shed last month. What's the problem this month?'

'I'll check with the staff about this.' The mayor leans across to mutter to the bloke who's sitting behind him taking notes. He leans in the other direction and mutters to a councillor, then turns back to face the gallery and Norm. The council officer tugs the Mayor's sleeve to get his attention before handing him an open ring binder.

'Norm, I'll read you the shire's definition of unsightly property. "Unsightly property is land that contains unconstrained rubbish, excessive waste and/or vegetation, disused machinery or vehicles, partially completed or partially demolished buildings, or graffiti." Now, Norm, you'll have to admit your yard fits most of those categories.'

'Yeah, like it did a month ago and a year ago and fifteen years ago. I'll ask again, what's changed? I think Councillor Samantha Patterson should answer that question.'

She looks up. She's married to the owner of a big farm out past Wilson Dam. Before she was elected unopposed to the shire council, she used to run the Ladies Auxiliary of the Halstead Lions Club. She's not only the sole woman on the council, she's the youngest councillor too. She looks the same age as me, but without the scrag factor. Her nails are polished. Her brown hair is as glossy and preened as bird feathers. I bet she paid a lot of money for that dress too. It's a soft green jersey with satin around the neckline and half-length sleeves. I hope she gives it to the op shop when she's tired of it.

'I don't know much about this aspect of shire business,' she answers calmly. 'As most people here probably know,' she looks around the room smiling and nodding at a few people, 'I was elected to council on a platform of community development.' She smiles again with the white even teeth of someone on TV. 'But as I understand it, doesn't someone have to make a complaint before an Unsightly Property Notice is issued? Perhaps Mr Stevens might like to consider that. It could well be his neighbours.'

I can see Norm is heating up. He's scratching the back of his scarlet neck. The mayor leafs hurriedly through the folder and reads out loud.

'"If a complaint is received by the shire that a property is unsightly, the first step will be for a local laws officer to inspect the property. If the officer deems that it does constitute an unsightly property, a Notice to Comply will be issued." Yep, it sounds as if that's what's happened, Norm. Not a lot we can do about it. It's a by-law.'

'And if I don't comply?' Norm's talking slowly now. You don't see Norm angry very often. He's a pretty relaxed kind of a bloke. This is twice in a week. First Tony, now the Unsightly Property Notice.

The mayor runs his finger down the page.

'Da de da de da. Here it is. "The Notice to Comply will outline the circumstances causing the land to be deemed unsightly, and will state the works required to be completed by a specific date. If the works are not completed by that date or alternative arrangements have not been made with the officer, a contractor may be enlisted to complete the work on behalf of the shire. Once the work is completed to the satisfaction of the shire an invoice will be sent for payment of these works."'

'I hope you don't think we're stupid, Vaughan,' Norm says. 'It's not about my yard, we all know that.'

'Huh? What are you talking about? I hadn't even heard about this notice until I saw the agenda. There's no conspiracy here, Norm. Keep your hat on.'

'Suit yourself. If you want a fight, I'm happy to oblige.' Norm swings around and strides back to his seat next to me, breathing through his nose.

I pat him on the arm, lean towards his ear and whisper, 'Go, Norm!' before I rear back in shock. I think he's growing spuds in that ear.

He expels a great snort of air, then half-turns to the crowd in the gallery.

'We've all been pretty bloody tolerant of the secrecy and shenanigans at this council. Well, maybe we won't be so tolerant anymore.'

Around us, a few people clap. Mario leans over and mutters to Norm, 'Vaughan is a good mayor, Norm. We don't want to put the boot into the good blokes.'

'Don't worry, Mario. If he's done nothing wrong, he's got nothing to fear, right?'

It's a side of Norm I've never seen. It is true, though, that Norm knows most of what goes on around Gunapan, thanks to the steady stream of customers who never buy anything, but stand around gasbagging for hours. If he wants to cause some damage, I'm sure he has the weapons.

'What's Samantha Patterson's connection?' I whisper to Norm. 'Has she got shares in the development?'

'She's too smart for that. But I'll find out, don't you worry.'

The next item for discussion is the water tanks to be installed by the side of the footy clubhouse. The club president says he's been waiting for four

147

months and buying water to keep the ground safe for play and the club is now broke and he'll organize a demonstration if the council doesn't pull its finger out and put in the tanks. The councillor whose brief is shire amenities tells the president that the tanks have been bought and are waiting for installation but Kev the council plumber broke his ankle and they've been waiting for him to recover, and the president says, 'Stuff that, mate, twenty-five plumbers in Halstead could do the job,' and the councillor says, 'Leave it with me and I'll see what can be done,' and the president says, 'You've done bugger all till now so why should I believe that?' and the mayor says, 'Now, now everyone,' and the president storms back to his seat and the footballers in the back row drum their feet on the wooden floor and the mayor wipes his forehead and pats his stomach again.

Finally we get to the last item, the one the crowd is here for.

'Um, yes. The final item for tonight's meeting. This is certainly the most unusual shire meeting we've had in some time,' he says with a weak laugh. 'Now Trudy Walker has put forward this item. She wants to discuss satanism in Gunapan.'

Trudy gets up and walks to the front of the room. Everyone is silent, except for Kyleen who's munching chips steadily. Once she's in front of the microphone, Trudy adjusts her hair. It's been permed into a frizzy halo and she uses both hands to pat it down.

148

'We are a Christian community,' she begins.

'I'm not a Christian,' Sammy Lee calls from the back of the left gallery. 'And I think you'll find that the Dhaliwal family aren't either.'

'He's got a point,' Norm says to me. 'I've got more faith in *Best Bets* than Jesus.'

The left gallery is muttering. 'Well, I don't go to church, but . . .', 'Sister Theresa cured me in grade four . . .'

'OK,' Trudy says, raising her hands. 'OK. But we are a God-fearing community, aren't we?'

The Church of Goodwill gallery claps. I can hear Sammy Lee in the row behind me chatting with Mrs Edwards. 'Honestly, I speak and nobody listens. I'm the invisible ethnic minority in this place. Sammy Lee, token Chinaman, non-Christian . . .'

'Mate,' Brian Mack says from the row behind Sammy. 'You think you've got problems. You should try being Aboriginal here. My family's so far out of the town's bloody consciousness we might as well be white.'

'Jeez, don't wish that on us, hon,' Brian's wife, Merle, mutters.

'You may think we are old-fashioned fuddy-duddies, but this is no joke.' Trudy sounds so serious that everyone quietens down. 'Witchcraft is not some innocent game with wands and tall hats. It's not a kids' book or a TV show. Real witchcraft is the work of the devil, and it can't be played with. You might think it's funny having a witch in the town, but you won't think it's funny when it gets out of hand. We need to stop this right now, before the devil sneaks into Gunapan while you're still laughing.'

'Yes!' the right gallery calls. 'Amen!'

'I think we ought to hear the other side of the story before we make any hasty decisions,' the mayor points out, 'except I'm not sure that the person in question is actually here. I did ask the council secretary to send a letter, though.'

We all look around like a bunch of turkeys craning their long necks.

It seems as if the show is over until a voice comes from the back of the left gallery. It's a high voice, nasal and thin, and it seems oddly familiar.

'I studied hard to get this diploma and I'm not giving up because you don't like it. Witches can work for good too,' the voice says.

She stands up and we stare with our mouths open. It's Leanne. Leanne grew up in Gunapan. She left a couple of years ago to study in Melbourne and hasn't been back as far as I know. Until now.

'Leanne?' Kyleen shouts through a mouthful of chips. 'You're the witch?'

'I'd like to be addressed as Leonora. And yes, I'm now a trained witch from the Wiccan School of Herbal and Magickal Therapy in Melbourne. And I think I deserve some respect.'

A blinding flash floods the room. My heart skips a beat as I wonder if we have been smote, then I see the cadet reporter focussing his lens on Leanne.

'Oh my Lord,' Trudy says from the front of the room. 'Leanne Bivens, what does your mother think about this?'

Leanne's mother stands up beside her. 'I'm proud of Leanne. I mean, Leonora. What she's got is as good as a diploma from the TAFE. And also, she's got rid of my shingles and I won a fifth division in Tattslotto last week and you can see her acne's completely gone.'

Everyone inclines towards the back of the room and peers at Leanne. She holds her head high, tilts it from side to side. Sure enough, that acne's cleared right up.

'This is wrong,' Trudy calls out. 'Spells. Incantations. Do you think things come for free? A price will be exacted, young lady, and it will be your soul! Don't go thinking you can seduce the women of Gunapan into a coven.'

Norm guffaws beside me then tries to cover the guffaw with a cough. I'm picturing the coven of hefty Gunapan women dancing naked in the moonlight beside the stinky Wilson Dam. I wonder whether we'd dance around the old car bodies or between them.

'I suppose you pray to demons,' Trudy goes on. 'I've read about it. You have black candles and upside-down crucifixes and goats. You're playing with forces you don't understand!'

We'll have to lock up Terror.

151

Leanne steps out from the row and walks down the centre aisle towards Trudy. She does seem a lot more confident than when she was serving behind the make-up counter at the chemist shop. When she was younger she used to babysit for us occasionally. We'd come home and find her curled up asleep on the couch like a baby herself. Now she's wearing a long purple velvet dress and heavy silver jewellery that clanks as she walks. Beside me, Helen is fingering her face.

'Do you think she can get rid of wrinkles?' Helen whispers to me.

'I've got a bit of heavy-duty Spakfilla could help with that,' Norm answers and she punches him in the arm.

As she walks towards Trudy, Leanne raises her arm and points. Trudy steps back behind the podium as if it will protect her.

'They told us in class people wouldn't understand. I want you to know that not all magick is black magick. I studied white magick. I did Herbs and Spells, Incantations and Potions, Freeing Your Inner Goddess, Small Business Bookkeeping, Marketing and Promotion. And I got the highest grade in the class for Women's Mysteries.'

The whole room goes quiet. I think we're all wondering about Women's Mysteries.

'Can you fly?' Kyleen asks.

'No, but if I do five more units and upgrade to a degree it's possible I'll be able to move from one place to another by magick.'

'Of course, in India some yogis can levitate through deep spiritual practice,' Mrs Edwards behind me comments.

'Yeah, well, that's the same thing, isn't it? See?' she adds, turning to Trudy. 'And anyway, I come from Gunapan and I went to the city, but at least I came back. Everyone says that the young people leave and never come back and that's why Gunapan is in trouble. Well, here I am! Just because I'm doing something different you shouldn't treat me this way. I'm bringing new industry to town.'

She has a point. In the last year the only new businesses to start up in town have been her and Merv Bull. Before that, a member of the Neighbourhood House Committee opened an antique shop in the main street. What she called antique was the same stuff most of us use at home – Laminex tables, Bakelite flour canisters, old bassinets. If we had a lot of through traffic it might have worked, but the highway only passes by close enough for us to have the four a.m. thunder of the road trains without a single visitor ever pulling off the highway and driving into town.

Thinking about that reminds me of the development. How did they even find Gunapan to put a resort here?

'Let us pray for guidance,' someone from the right gallery calls. The Church of Goodwillers and the Catholics get down on their knees, slowly and with much grunting and bone-cracking, to begin the Lord's Prayer.

'And one more thing,' Leanne says. 'Religious freedom. You'd never do this to a Jewish person or a Muslim person.'

From out of a pocket hidden in her flowing dress, she produces a stubby silver knife. Trudy gasps.

'Trudy, get a grip,' Leanne says, waving to her mother to come to the front of the room where Leanne begins drawing a circle on the floor with the knife.

'Actually,' the mayor says, his chain tinkling as he steps towards Leanne then back again. 'This is shire property. It's probably best not to mark the floor? Not that I want to interfere with your religious freedom.'

Leanne turns to him, still pointing the knife, and the mayor clutches at his chest as if she has pierced it.

'Oops, sorry,' Leanne says and pockets the knife. She takes her mother's hand and pulls her into the circle. Her mother is beaming proudly as if this is Leanne's wedding day. She lifts her feet as she steps over the imaginary circle line then clasps her hands together and nods at several people in the front row of the Church of Goodwill crowd.

'Hi Moira, lovely to see you,' Leanne's mother says. She seems not to have noticed that Moira believes Leanne is the spawn of Satan. I can't get the picture of Leanne behind the Revlon counter

154

out of my mind. The white smock she always wore, and the blue satin eyeshadow.

The door at the back of the room swings open with a creak. Five children are standing there, my two at the front. They've obviously heard the praying.

'I'm bored,' Jake says to no one in particular.

'Hi Leanne,' Melissa says.

'Hi Melissa. Hi Jake. It's Leonora now,' Leanne answers.

The praying fades away. Everyone's looking at my children as they wander down to stand beside me. Jake's dropped half his dinner on his T-shirt. And I hadn't noticed when we left the house that Melissa's got hold of my foundation again. She's caked it on and it ends in a dark line at her jaw. I wonder if I look like that when I wear it.

'Hey Leanne, you look great. No more pimples,' Melissa says.

'Melissa!' I say. I pull the two of them into the row beside me and wonder if anyone would notice me holding my hands over their mouths and noses. Just for a little while.

'Can we go home now?' Jake whispers.

'Have you heard from Dad?' Melissa asks, as she does every five minutes at home. No, I haven't heard from her father, even though he's staying in a hotel ten minutes from where we are now. I used to hate him. Now I despise him.

Trudy has moved to the side of the room where her congregation is still praying.

'What about love potions?' Maxine calls out. 'Can you make them Leanne, sorry, Leonora?'

'Oh yeah, no worries. And amulets and charms to attract a lover. That's easy.'

Excitement hums in a surge of current through the left gallery, made up mainly of single mothers. The Christians don't stand a chance. Before the mayor has an opportunity to make a pronounce-ment on satanic practices in the town, people are crowding around Leanne, who blushes and hands out business cards.

'I declare the meeting closed,' the mayor shouts above the hubbub.

Jake's got hold of my hand and he's trying to pull me out the door. I call goodbye over my shoulder to Norm. As I get dragged past I see the members of the right gallery look at each other.

'All we can do is pray,' one of them says, shaking her head sadly.

Jake, stronger than a runaway lawnmower, propels me through the corridor towards the car park. In the alcove near the front door stands a knot of people. Perhaps they came late. Helen has spotted them too. It is as though all the unmar-ried men of Helen's dreams have come together to taunt her. The grade-three teacher is talking earnestly with Merv Bull. Beside them, the widowed farmer from beyond Riddley's Creek stands with his thumbs hooked through his belt loops, staring into space.

I smile at the group as we pass. Helen tries to

nod at the men, but she's carrying her neighbour's two-year-old on her shoulders and the sudden shift in balance makes her stagger past like a drunk.

'At the end of the day,' the grade-three teacher says to Merv Bull, 'it's all about civil liberties, isn't it.'

Merv nods. 'And a little bit of magic in your life never hurts either,' he says.

I glance back when I hear him say that. He's looking straight at me and I feel a heat in my face. He nods. My face starts to burn. Jake tugs at my hand and before I know it I'm out on the street.

CHAPTER 15

The shire meeting last night was a distraction, but the moment I put the kids to bed and tried to get some sleep myself, the night demons arrived to torment me. Perhaps Melissa is right: it *is* my fault that Tony hasn't visited the kids. I am horrible. I am an ogre. He is right to have left me. And so on and so on until I sobbed myself to sleep. This morning I drifted through my chores in a dreary haze. In the afternoon I arrive at the school to pick up the kids. Helen is at the gate too. Today my life is small and pinched and the sky seems vast and filled with a relentless glare.

'What's wrong with you?' she asks, prodding my forearm with a finger. 'Have you heard anything I've said?'

'No,' I answer.

'I said we've only a two-year extension for keeping the school.'

'I know.'

'So are you going to do something about it?'

'Not right now.'

Helen stares at me. I stare back. My eyes are so

tired that staring makes them water and I rub them with my fists.

'Don't do that – it'll make your wrinkles worse,' Helen says.

We peel ourselves away from the side of Helen's car where we have been leaning as we wait for the kids to get out of school. She's picking up her cousin's eight-year-old twins. Helen had her boy, Alex, when she was eighteen and now he's doing an apprenticeship in Melbourne, so she's one of the people we call on to help out with our kids. She says she'll get it all back when Alex comes home with his own children, which will be fairly soon if family history is any indication.

'It's Tony. He left a message on the machine last night about how he's going to have them visit him in Mildura. He hasn't even left Gunapan! He hasn't even visited the house! Why is he taunting them with these stupid promises?'

I've left a sweat print of my body on the faded red paintwork of the car that could be mistaken for the crime scene outline of a corpse. I pluck my T-shirt away from my sweaty back.

'What did he say anyway? You didn't tell me. How did he explain three years without a word?'

'He didn't. He acted as if nothing was special. And the girlfriend's behaving like we're all going to be great mates . . .' I trail off, suddenly realizing.

'What?'

'He hasn't told her.'

'What?'

159

'That's so typical.'

'Loretta!'

'She doesn't know he ran off. That explains the other day here at the school, why she was acting as though it was a regular visit.'

Tony's method of dealing with difficult situations was always to wait and see if he could get away with it. He never did. Only smart people can do that. Rather than get into trouble by telling the truth, he'd hedge or lie outright, even when he was bound to be caught out. If I asked him whether he'd been at the pub, he'd say no, he was working. That was after he'd parked the car on the flowerbed, vomited at the foot of the steps and tripped on the torn lino in the kitchen before landing on his face and shouting abuse at the floor.

'She's still a dimwit,' I mutter. 'Got a flat on the highway. Sure.'

As kids come belting out of the school I look up and down the road. No sign of Tony and Miss Happy.

'I'll call you tonight,' Helen says. The twins zoom up and immediately start asking what's for tea. Helen takes one in each hand and heads off. 'Come on, we've got baked beans. The best money can buy.'

'We don't like baked beans,' they whine simultaneously. I'm sure their mother was in a childbirth fog when she named them Timothy and Tamsyn. Everyone else calls them the Tim Tams.

Jake climbs straight into the car and starts kicking the back of the passenger seat. Melissa shades her eyes and gazes up and down the road.

'They're not here, sweetie.'

No response.

'Let's go home. They might call.'

'No, wait. I want to wait a bit.'

'Ten minutes, then we're leaving.' I open the four doors of the car to let the air circulate and drape a towel across the windscreen.

'Your back's all sweaty,' Melissa says with distaste.

Jake roots around in his school bag and comes up with a piece of pre-chewed bubble gum he's stored for emergencies such as this. I wave at Brenda and Kyleen and Maxine and Brianna and the grade-three teacher and the headmaster and Liz and the grade-six teacher and some woman I don't know but who waves at me. Small towns. Soon only two kids and us are left waiting at the gate.

'Melissa, we're going home.'

In ten minutes of full sun her face has burned. I find some cream in my bag and try to dab it on her face, but she pushes my hand away and gets into the back seat of the car. We slam the four doors and I roar away from the kerb, putting my foot down even harder than usual. Just like when we were married, Tony makes me angry when he's around, and even angrier when he's not.

As we're passing Norm's junkyard I toot the horn. Norm's skinny brown arm reaches out of the door of the shed, gives a thumbs up and disappears back inside.

'Why do you always do that? And why's he always coming around? And why do we go there all the time? That junkyard's stupid. You never buy anything.'

'Because he's our friend, Liss. He cares about us.'

'He's old and ugly. And he smells of petrol.'

At home she pulls out the phone book, looks up the number of the pub where Tony's staying and calls. I leave the room. When she comes into the kitchen I ask if she got hold of him.

'It was her,' she says. 'She doesn't know anything.'

I'm glad we feel the same way about that. After tea, with Melissa crying in her room, I ring the pub again. They put me through to the room and the idiot child bride gets Tony on the phone.

'Listen and only say yes or no.' I speak quietly so the kids won't hear. 'You've made up some crap about seeing us regularly and sending us money and your girlfriend believes it, right?'

He makes nothing but a mumumum sound in reply.

'I'm way past taking any bullshit from you, Tony. Am I right?'

'Yes.'

'And she wanted to come here and meet the

kids, but you can't let her near them because she'll find out you deserted us.'

No reply.

'Then leave her at the pub and get in your precious car and get down here. Your daughter's almost slashing her wrists in the bedroom, you bastard.'

Silence.

'I'm not going to dob on you unless you make things worse by not seeing Liss. Get down here and pretend to be a father. If you don't turn up tonight I'll tell your girlfriend everything.' I slam down the phone and then pick it up and inspect it to make sure I haven't broken it. I definitely cannot afford a new phone.

I've finished chewing my fingernails and moved on to the skin around them by the time he arrives. He stomps past me at the doorway. It reminds me of when we were together. Because he stomped everywhere I could never tell from his footsteps whether he was in a good mood or a bad one. I had to wait and cop it.

He's smiling. Those expensive white teeth put me in even more of a fury. He's carrying a bulky white plastic bag stamped with the logo of a department store in Halstead.

'Loretta.' He grins even wider and bends down to kiss me on the cheek. 'You're a bloody champ. I swear I'll make it up to you. Talee's a great girl. She's making me a better man, you'll see.'

My breath is steaming in and out of my nostrils like cigarette smoke. I try to steady my respiration, in through the nose, out through the mouth, yoga style. Helen did a yoga class once. She used to come over after the class and demonstrate the positions to me in the lounge room.

'The positions massage different inner organs. Apparently this pelvic floor one makes your sex life dynamite. If you have a sex life, that is.'

One of the positions she tried to demonstrate, before she got the cramp, was called The Camel. She was on her knees, face scarlet from the exertion, rump thrust in the air. The problem happened when she realized she was bent over in the wrong direction and attempted a backflip. After she had finished screaming, she explained to me what she'd done wrong from the get-go.

'It's the breathing. The key is how you breathe. Once you're doing the good yoga breaths, everything flows from there. Good breathing will change your life, that's what the teacher said.' We practised our yoga breaths between sips of wine cooler.

I warn Tony to stay twenty minutes only, and to come and see me before he leaves, then I call Melissa and Jake out to the lounge room. Melissa runs mewing like a kitten to her father and wraps her arms around him as he drops the bag of expensive presents by the wall.

A better man, ha. While I'm waiting for him to come out I perfect my yoga breathing in the dark

164

on the veranda – breathe in through the nose, gnash the teeth, breathe out through the mouth. I should visit Leanne and find out what she's got in her bag of spells.

CHAPTER 16

'What the hell am I supposed to do?' Norm says straight away when I answer the phone.

'Pardon me, Norm?' I use my poshest voice, trying to indicate that elegant ladies like myself prefer a conversation to be opened with a courteous greeting and an enquiry after our health.

'Justin's out on parole. He's coming to stay.'

'Who?'

'My son.'

The shock is too much. I sit down. Norm's son? Somewhere deep down I knew Norm and Marg had a son. Somewhere deep down I knew their son had gone to prison for armed robbery. Somewhere deep down I had decided to forget that information.

'Oh.' My heart is beating a little too fast. I can hear my own breath. 'Norm, can I ask you something?'

'No.'

'OK then,' I say in a sprightly voice.

'He was a stupid kid when he did it.'

'Norm, if you're Norm Senior, isn't your son called Norm Junior?'

'He never liked it. Justin's his second name. Made us start calling him Justin when he was in high school.'

'Ah.'

'It was his bloody high-school mates who got him into it. No one got hurt in that stunt they pulled. But he wouldn't dob on his mates so they gave him fifteen years. Then while he was inside he got caught up in some fight and they gave him another five.'

'Twenty years. Hmm.' I don't know what I'm supposed to say.

'He's out in fourteen, though. Good behaviour.'

'Well, that's got to be a good thing.' Five years on top of your sentence? Doesn't sound like good behaviour to me.

'He never wanted me to visit. I went when he was first in, but he wouldn't come out to the visitors' room. Ten times I turned up at visiting time. I sat on my own for an hour every time, hoping he'd at least come and say hello.'

I've never heard Norm string this many sentences together. It's as if we're having a conversation in reverse. Usually I'm the one banging on and Norm's going 'Hmm' and 'Yep' and 'Is that right?' while he tinkers with a piece of scrap.

'Is that right?' I say.

'Marg neither. He never let her see him. She goes every year at Christmas and waits, but he's never shown his face.'

'Is it that he . . .'

'I thought he hated us. We both thought he hated us.'

Jake's tugging on my sleeve and making faces. He's been told so many times not to talk at me while I'm on the phone that now he mimes messages at me. He wrinkles up his face into a bad smell kind of expression, then makes a big face of surprise with an O mouth and points at the sky. It could mean anything. OK, I mouth back at him, pushing him away. He's not screaming, so it can't be that bad.

'So, Norm, your son is—'

'Loretta, you don't get it. He sent a letter. He wants to come here. He wants to stay with me.'

'And that's . . . I mean, is he . . . Gee.'

'Marg's pretty upset. But what does it mean? What am I going to do? After all this time he's a stranger.'

'Gosh, Norm.'

'Jeez, Loretta, let me get a word in here. I don't know what to do, all right? What am I supposed to say to him?'

'Hello?'

'Hello, are you there, Loretta?'

'No, I mean, say "Hello". Start with hello. Let him do the talking.'

He heaves a big sigh at the other end of the line.

'When's he coming, Norm? You'll have to get stuff in. Set up a room for him. Buy some food. You can't expect him to eat takeaway hamburgers every meal the way you do.'

'Three o'clock.'

After I put down the phone I understand what Jake was trying to tell me. The tomato soup I was heating for lunch has thickened up, burned on to the bottom of the saucepan – that would have been the bad smell face – then sent small semi-liquid missiles flying around the kitchen, which have stained the walls and floor in a gory red spatter pattern like a TV massacre scene. And – here's the surprise O – one dark brown gob of it is stuck to the ceiling in the shape of a map of Tasmania. At least Jake managed to turn off the gas before the saucepan burst into flames.

Cleaning the kitchen can wait. I bundle Melissa and Jake into the car and we run around the super-market loading up with the basics that people keep in their houses – bread, butter, milk, eggs, cheese, fruit, a few vegetables, lollies, chocolates, more lollies.

'Take them back to the shelves,' I tell Jake. 'And bring me a jar of peanut butter. And Liss, you go to the deli section and get some bacon.'

'What if he's vegetarian?' Melissa says.

'He can eat the eggs. Hurry up, Lissie. It's twelve o'clock and we've got to get to the yard and make up a bed and clean the house and be out by two.'

'Why can't we meet him?'

'We will, later.'

Norm's house is quite difficult to distinguish from the surrounding junk in the yard. He shifted here when Marg threw him out eight years ago, worn down by his irredeemable passion for scrap. He couldn't stop bringing stuff home. After Marg woke up one day to find half a boat in the dining room, she sold their brick veneer house and moved to Warrnambool. Norm lived in the junkyard shed for a while, then the house began to assemble itself around the shed. He had to knock up another shed as an office. 'What's the point in having a scrap yard if I can't make use of it?' he always says.

The *Closed* sign is hanging on the gate. This is the first time I've seen the yard closed in the daytime when Norm's here. Norm is sitting at the kitchen table with his head in his hands. Jake climbs on to his lap the way he used to when he was a toddler.

'Hey mate,' Norm says.

Jake leans his head against Norm's chest. I don't know how he knows something is wrong. Norm gives him a hug.

'My dad came to visit,' Jake tells Norm.

'I heard. Did you enjoy that?'

'He brought me a car and a machine gun and a truck and a T-shirt.'

'Oh, bloody hell. I didn't buy Justin a present! I should have bought him a present.'

'Don't be silly, Norm. He's a grown man. You and Jake put the groceries away and start cleaning the kitchen,' I say. 'Liss and I'll get started on the rest of the house.'

Melissa steps into the bathroom and steps right back out again quick smart.

'I'm not going in there,' she says.

It's years since I've been into this bathroom. Norm gave me a tour when he first built it. I remember nodding politely and admiring the claw-foot bath with bricks instead of claw feet, and the real-estate agent's sign as flooring. I did wonder about the lack of windows and fans, but Norm said he liked his bathroom steamy. He said Marg had always complained about his steaming up the house, and now he could do it to his heart's content.

Today Melissa has glimpsed the terrifying results of that steaming process. I send her off to make up the bed in the lean-to room off the lounge where Norm's mates sometimes stay if they've had a few and don't want to drive, while I arm myself with gloves, cleaners, scrapers, brushes, disinfectants and a headscarf before venturing in to do battle with the green velvet wallpaper.

By two o'clock, I can't lift my arms above my head anymore. Crippled by mould. I don't know how I'll explain that to Beamer Man when he has to help me into a cardigan after our armless lovemaking session. Melissa runs gratefully to the car, dragging Jake behind her, and we leave Norm standing in his doorway, his tall stooped frame bent over a little more than usual. He's given me a letter to drop into the postbox on our way home. I'm very curious. It's addressed to the editor of the *Shire Herald*, the local rag.

'What's Norm scared of?' Melissa asks as we

pull away from the yard and Norm gives us a half-hearted wave. It's a good question.

'That's a good question. What do you think he's scared of?'

Melissa tips her head back and stares at the roof of the car.

'Intimacy,' she finally pronounces.

'When's your birthday?'

'You're my mother! You're supposed to know that.'

'If you were really Melissa Boskovic, you'd be turning twelve in August, but I seem to have a forty-year-old sitting next to me in the car. Intimacy indeed. And what kind of intimacy do you think Norm might be afraid of?'

'He's afraid of having to connect with the son he hasn't seen for a long time and he's worried they won't have anything to say to each other.'

Hmm, that's exactly what I was thinking. But I'm not letting an eleven-year-old out-psychologize me. Isn't this the child who still believes her father's promise that he's coming back to Gunapan to visit again any day now?

'Actually, I think Norm's got a number of issues.' I sound like Dr Phil, but that's OK because Melissa's at school when his show's on TV.

'You sound like Dr Phil,' Melissa says.

'What's an "issue"?' Jake asks.

'Have you done your homework?'

They both groan. 'That's what you always say when you don't want to answer questions,' Melissa complains.

172

We're pulling into the driveway when Melissa asks the question I've been dreading. 'Where has he been? How come Norm never talked about him?'

I try not to lie to the kids. I know that one day they'll find out stuff anyway. But this is a hard one.

'It was somewhere bad, wasn't it?' Melissa tilts her head as she asks.

'Why do you say that?'

'Der. No one talking about him?'

'Sometimes people do things without thinking,' I start.

'Was he in jail?' She seems calm about it. I glance in the rear-view mirror. Jake's eyes are wide.

'Yes, he was. But he's not a bad person. He made a stupid mistake when he was a boy, and he got locked up.'

Melissa looks out of the window. Jake's edged forwards on the seat.

'Is he a murderer?' Jake whispers.

Melissa laughs. She leans over and tickles Jake under the arms. 'And he's coming to get yoooooo,' she says in a spooky voice. Jake squeals and wriggles away from her tickling fingers.

'Of course he's not,' she says to him. 'He's Norm's son.'

Once we're home I send them off to do their Saturday chores, and I turn on the computer. Information about Justin is impossible to find. I'd imagined that I would type in his name and find out everything from his favourite colour to a blow-by-blow description of the crime he committed. But all that comes up is a world of worthless information. Norman Justin Stevens is the name of a young gynaecologist in Maine, a jazz musician, an athlete and some maniac who set his hair on fire and filmed it for the internet. I watch that video a few times before I wheel the computer back into Melissa's room. I'm starting to think the internet is completely useless.

I want to ring and find out how Norm's going, but that would probably make Justin anxious. He might think people are ringing to check up on whether he's gone mad with the sudden freedom and chopped up his dad. Instead, a more productive task would be to begin organizing, one more time, the Gunapan Save Our School Committee.

When the minister visited Gunapan and gave a speech about the value of education and his government's commitment to our rural communities, what he meant was he'd give funding to the school for two more years under a one-off assistance program for disadvantaged country towns. And that was probably only to stop me writing more letters.

At first, hearing that the school would stay open, the headmaster and teachers and parents thought I was some kind of hero. Not as good as Joshua Porter, the local footy player who was selected for the Australian Football League and now tells people he comes from Halstead instead of

Gunapan. More like Hector from the abattoir, who did go on to win the Australia-wide championship and had *Speed Butcher* stencilled in silver Gothic lettering on the side of his black Falcon. For weeks afterwards, blokes around town would raise their fists in a victory salute when the Speed Butcher drove by, similar to the way parents I'd never met would nod at me when I picked up the kids after school.

Now our fame has faded. The Speed Butcher's 'S' has been scraped off his car, probably by Bowden who doesn't like anyone else's car getting attention. At school, when I pull up in a cloud of Holden exhaust, the other mothers have gone back to coughing and spluttering in the exaggerated way they used to before I was a hero.

As I pull the file of the last Save Our School campaign out of the dresser drawer, I wonder again whether the Gunapan school is worth fighting for. The town's not growing. We've only got a population of a thousand, including the outlying farms. We have some local industry: the abattoir, a couple of organic farms, the alpacas.

The alpaca people set up five years ago on an old property out past the Wilson Dam. Last year I took Melissa and Jake out to see the animals. We left the car on the road and started walking down the driveway, hoping to see some cute fluffy alpacas. When we finally reached the end of the long farm road, we found a woman standing with her hands on her hips watching two alpacas in a pen near the house.

'I hope you don't mind,' I said, introducing myself and the kids. 'We wanted to see the alpacas. My daughter loves animals.'

'No worries,' the woman said. 'Just don't leave any gates open, OK?'

In the pen, the male was sitting on top of the female and groaning. Melissa blushed and Jake asked what they were doing.

'They're making babies,' Melissa muttered.

Jake stepped up close to the fence and peered at the alpacas. The female, crushed under the male, was chewing cud, staring off into the distance. The male rolled its eyes and groaned again.

'He's been at it for an hour already,' the owner remarked.

Another drawn-out groan.

'That's enough,' the woman shouted. 'You've finished, you moron. Get off it. G'awn, get off.'

She stepped inside the pen and flicked a whippy tree branch at the male, who rolled his eyes at her and moaned again. The female angled her long neck around, yawned, stared for a moment, then went back to chewing. They clearly don't bother faking it in the alpaca world. One more flick of the branch and the male fell off, scrambled to his feet and strutted through the gate and into the paddock. The female tucked her legs further under her and nodded off. Their behaviour seemed familiar, but I decided not to think too hard about it.

176

On the way back down the driveway we were followed along the fence by five alpacas that stared at us without blinking.

I heard the alpaca family turned a profit for the first time last year. What a good reason to keep the town alive – developing industry! And the meatworks is going great guns, as the minister saw. We produce a lot of children. Everyone says we need more children in this country. Yes, Gunapan certainly needs a school and a new, improved committee. Maybe I'll spice it up by making it the Save Our School and Stop Our Development Committee. We can help Norm out with his Unsightly Property Notice.

Luckily I kept my list of anyone who had ever turned up to a Save Our School meeting, offered to turn up to a meeting, asked about the meetings, mentioned the word meeting or had not definitely said they would never attend a meeting. But I'm not quite ready for the whole telephone thing, so I settle down to write a letter of irresistible charm that will have everyone wanting to join the Save Our School and Stop Our Development Committee Mark II.

Dear local parents and concerned citizens,
  The school term is now well underway and—

No. I sound like the principal.

Dear local parents and concerned citizens,
  You may remember the visit to Gunapan of

*our Minister for Education, Elderly Care and
Gaming—*

Oops, another problem. Not only has the
minister who came to Gunapan lost his minister-
ship, it's no longer the Ministry of Education,
Elderly Care and Gaming. The new minister, a
woman, is the Minister for Education, Social
Inclusion and the Service Economy. If we have to
give her a tour I don't know what we'll show her.
The school, the pub and the meals on wheels? I'll
leave that problem for later. Now I need to write
this letter.

*Dear comrades, local parents and concerned
citizens,
    Our community is faced with a crisis of—*

Although, is something that will happen in two
years' time a crisis? Or is a crisis something that
is about to happen right now?

'Mum, I've finished dusting the lounge room.
Can we go to a movie?'

'Call it a film, Jake. Movie makes you sound like
an American.'

'But I want to be American. Americans have
cookies and cream.'

'Ice cream, that's what we should have bought
for Justin.' I can't imagine what Norm's doing
right now. How do you talk to a son who's been
in prison for fourteen years?

178

'Mum, can I have some ice cream?'

'OK,' I tell Jake.

He stands still beside me, astounded that I've given in without a fight.

'Go on,' I tell him. 'It's in the freezer.'

Jake narrows his eyes at me as if he thinks it's a trick.

'I can't reach the freezer,' he says. He's testing me back.

'Why don't you get the chair I saw you using last week and climb on that?'

He sits down beside me to think about the implications of this and I turn back to my letter. I've lost my enthusiasm. Norm and Justin are playing on my mind. I can't compare them with Tony and Melissa who have only been apart for a few years, but even in that relationship the cracks are starting to show. When Tony left us, Melissa was a little girl who doted on her daddy. She thought she still doted on her daddy until her daddy turned up in the flesh as his old unreliable untrustworthy self. He only stayed in Gunapan another two days after his visit to us. He told Melissa a few tall tales about the magnificent house where he lives and how he's going to have her and Jake over to stay and buy them whatever they want and he'll come back here and visit regularly. He went to the toy shop in Halstead and bought Melissa and Jake another armful of toys. Then he shot through again with Miss Happy Talee and sent a postcard. *Will call soon. Love, Dad.*

It's been two weeks of silence already, and I can see Melissa hardening. It's too much for an eleven-year-old. Too much disappointment. At least she's got Terror. Terror gallops over to Melissa when she goes out in the yard and nearly knocks her over in her joy. Sometimes Melissa sits on the back steps for half an hour combing the tangles out of Terror's coat while Terror makes little moaning noises of ecstasy. There isn't a single shrub standing in the yard.

'OK, I'll use the chair,' Jake says, watching me intently to see my reaction.

'Clever boy.' Tomorrow I'm going to buy a freezer lock.

If I start up the letter-writing and meetings again I might lose the few friends I have left in Gunapan. That's something worth thinking about. Will Helen ever answer my phone calls if she thinks I'm going to ask her to do the door-to-door petition thing again? Will Kyleen almost decapitate the headmaster a second time, carrying a sign? And Norm seems so tired lately, I'm not sure he'd even have the energy to turn up to meetings. He's got his Unsightly Property Notice and Justin to deal with as well.

Plus, I am aware of one particular difficulty with starting up again. Melissa. She's going to be turning twelve soon. That means her mother-mortification-meter will be calibrated to a degree only matched by Swiss watch-style precision engineering. And the way she blushes means that everyone knows when Melissa's embarrassed.

It's all too hard.

'Jake, Melissa,' I call. 'We're going to the pictures. Tidy yourselves up and we'll head off.'

It seems that no time has passed before Jake is standing in front of me all dressed up in his best T-shirt.

'Get that off and put on a clean one.'

CHAPTER 17

As we head off to Halstead along the road where Norm's junkyard is the spectacular landmark, mounds of glowing red rust, the metal Uluru of the south, I try to slow down the Holden enough to see properly, but not so much that anyone can tell I'm trying to stickybeak.

'Mum, you're making me carsick. Can you please drive at one speed?' Melissa pleads.

'Tell me if you can see anything at Norm's. I have to keep my eyes on the road.'

'See what?'

'Anything.'

'Well, I can see Norm and I suppose that's his son with him.'

I resist the urge to veer across the road and stare. 'What are they doing?'

'They're staring at some piece of machinery.'

'That's good. Very good.' Norm's back to behaving like Norm again.

It's a forty-minute drive to Halstead and the cinema. By the time we get there, Melissa and Jake have had three fights in the back of the car. Jake's snivelling and Melissa is humming a pop song that is driving me mad. She's told me five times already that her father's friend Talee was once an extra in a movie about a Melbourne rock and roll band. I wonder if I can sneak away during the film and leave these horrible children to be raised by vagrants in Halstead. Or perhaps I could have them put in jail and fast forward to when they're adults. I'll bake a cake for their release.

Inside the cinema is cool, verging on Arctic. Across the aisle, in the garish flickering light of the previews, I can see a family of four children and one woman. Something about them makes me think it might be the Gunapan family I saw at the waterhole. On the other side of me, Jake and Melissa are in the trance state that overcomes them whenever they're put in front of a screen. They each have a box of popcorn and a fizzy drink.

This excursion has cost me a fortune. The kids have no idea, of course. Tony turned up with a bagful of expensive presents and from now on they'll sneer at anything I buy them. 'Why can't I have a console for the computer?' Jake asked yesterday.

'Because the computer's so old it's got arthritis and Alzheimer's. It would be like buying Nanna a skateboard.'

'I don't mind if she gets a skateboard.' He's always been a generous boy.

I wonder how the woman with four children can

possibly afford to bring them out to the pictures. I lean forwards. The kids aren't holding popcorn boxes, but they are eating something. Probably mixed sandwiches filled with sprouts and carrot or health bars she whips up in her free time and sells as a sideline in Halstead's trendy cafés. Other mothers seem to be able to do these things. I reach across and take a handful of Jake's popcorn. He whines something unintelligible, never taking his eyes off the screen.

At the end of the film, while the credits are rolling, Melissa yawns and asks if we can look in the Halstead mall clothes shops. Jake hands me his empty popcorn box as if it's a gift. The lights come on in the cinema and everyone starts talking and stretching. When the Gunapan family stands up I turn to ask Melissa who they are, but she's gone. She's already halfway up the aisle, pulling Jake behind her and leaving me to gather up the bags and empty drink containers before I stumble up the aisle after them like their baggage-handling lackey.

'Young lady, do you mind?' I shout after her.

When I get outside she's already halfway up the main street heading towards the mall. Jake has dropped back and he's looking past me with an expression I can't quite identify. Horror, perhaps? I don't want to look. If Jake's expression is any indication, I don't want to see what's coming. Anyway, I'm puffed out. Melissa has disappeared around the corner and I refuse to chase an eleven-year-old as if she's a toddler. We'll see how she enjoys walking home from Halstead.

I can see myself in the shop window. Jake's backpack is slung over my left shoulder and my handbag hangs from my right. I have two popcorn boxes and two soft-drink containers in my left hand. My right hand is clenched around the waist of my Target jeans, which slide down my hips like a pole dancer whenever I walk too fast. My hair has turned into a strange beehive shape from slumping in the cinema seat and, since that same action gave me a bit of a crick in my neck, my head is tilting sideways. We could call this the Gunapan shuffle.

I dump the containers in a rubbish bin, and take a seat beside it. I'm not moving. One of my children has run away and the other is staring at something behind me which could possibly be the monster from under the bed. On a more positive note, unlike in my dream of two nights ago, I am fully clothed.

'Let's go, Mum.' Jake's looking at the ground now. 'Let's go, come on.'

'No.' I wiggle myself backwards on the bench outside the shop and drop Jake's backpack on the ground. I know I've hidden a packet of Caramellos deep inside my handbag. I keep them to bribe the children, but since one of them has run away and the other won't even look at me, those Caramellos have my name on them. At last I find the roll at

185

the bottom of the bag, peel away the paper and pop two into my mouth at once. My worries disappear in a haze of chocolate and caramel. My eyes flutter shut.

It seems like a pleasant quarter of an hour, but when I open my eyes, only seconds have passed. Jake is now behind the bench and the family I saw in the cinema is coming towards us. The mother grasps the shoulders of the smallest child, who looks about five, and pulls her close. All four children are staring at Jake sniffling behind me. I'm starting to wonder – have these kids been bullying Melissa and Jake? Are they the ones calling Jake a bush pig? They don't look like bullies, but I suppose people usually don't. The mother isn't staring at Jake. She's keeping her eye on me as if I'm holding a machete and about to lunge. She gathers her children in a huddle around her as they pass us.

'What's going on, Jake?' I ask once they've rounded the corner. 'Is one of those kids being mean to you?'

'No.' He's still sniffling.

'You can tell me.'

'I want to find Melissa.'

'We'll find her in a minute,' I say, perfectly aware that she's lurking around the corner inside the mall waiting for us. I can see her reflection in the window opposite. She's standing in a small crowd watching Brian Mack and his friend Al who are busking at their usual spot.

As Jake swings around and heads for the mall I heave myself off the bench, pick up his backpack, sling my handbag over my shoulder and hitch up my pants. I feel about a hundred years old. When I round the corner Brian's finished his song and Al's blowing the last mournful note on the didgeridoo. The onlookers toss a few coins into the guitar case and wander off.

'Hey Loretta, doing some shopping?' I can tell Brian's politely trying not to look at my baggy pants and worn-down heels.

'I wish. I've just spent a fortune on a family trip to the pictures. Making much today?'

'Nah, stingy bastards can barely even give us a clap.'

'Probably wouldn't even give us *the* clap if we asked for it,' Al says, wiping the mouth of his didg with a cloth.

'Already did that when they first got here,' Brian says.

'Mum.' Jake pats my thigh. I can tell he's about to ask what they mean so I grip his hand and give Melissa a touch on the back to urge her forwards. She moves on to the next shop and gazes at the tops in the window.

'Got to head off. Hope you do better.'

'It won't pick up as long as that friggin' statue is down there. Makes a packet from standing still. Where's the talent in that?' Brian's glaring down towards the other end of the mall, where a small woman dressed in a ballgown and covered in grey paint stands on a rock-shaped pedestal in front of the chocolate shop.

She sees us watching and raises her hand in a slow-motion wave that takes a full five seconds to reach the top of its arc.

'Hmph,' Brian says. He begins twisting the pegs on the arm of his guitar and tuning the strings. 'What that statue needs is a good chisel.'

For some reason, the thought of taking a chisel to the statue person makes me feel cheerful. 'Hey Brian, speaking of building, what do you know about the development down the Bolton Road?'

'Don't get me started, Loretta. That place is bad news.'

'So what is it? What's going on? Is it true they've got a licence to take water out of the ground?'

'They've got a licence to do whatever they bloody want.'

'Is that land a sacred site for you?'

'No, not for our mob. Our country's further out west. It's a beautiful piece of bush though. Or it was until the council stopped maintaining it. Let it turn into a rubbish dump. I heard they sold it for a song.'

'Mum, let's go.' Jake is tugging at my sleeve.

'Can I call you about it, Brian? I'm trying to find out what's going on.'

'No point calling me, love. I don't know anything.'

CHAPTER 18

The Bolton Road seems particularly long today. My foot lifts off the accelerator as I pass the gash in the bush and peer down the dirt road towards the development site. I think about stopping and walking in, but only because I'm feeling a little wobbly about today's plan, which is to visit Merv Bull and get my windscreen wiper blades replaced. But before I can make up my mind to take a stroll into the development, the Holden, which needs at least a kilometre's warning before it can stop, has coasted into Merv Bull's yard and is throbbing uncertainly outside his shed. I turn the key and the engine dies with a shudder.

The blue heeler is at the door of the shed, basking in the sun. It lifts its head and looks at me for a moment, then flops on to its side and thumps its tail in a stretch before snoozing off. Last time I came the yard held an aqua Monaro, a Combi van and an old Escort but now it's jammed with cars of all shapes and sizes. I have to edge my way between two sleek new cars to reach the door. Lined up along the new cyclone wire fence are three earth-moving machines.

'Mr Bull?' I call from the doorway. The heeler opens its eyes and watches me without moving.

Shadows inside the shed sway and dip, and then he's in front of me, wiping his hands on a rag.

'Yes?' he asks. He tucks a corner of the rag into the back pocket of his overalls, and lifts his hand to shade his eyes. 'What can I do for you?'

'I brought my car in when you first came to Gunapan, I'm not sure if you remember.' I point to the Holden.

'Of course. Windscreen. Second-hand,' Merv says, nodding. 'Is there a problem?'

'Boss,' a voice comes from inside the shed, 'can we have smoko now?'

'All right,' Merv shouts back then turns to me again. 'Slackers, the lot of them.'

Three boys file out of a small door further along the wall of the shed and sit on plastic chairs in the sun. They pass around a packet of biscuits.

'So . . .' Merv says.

'It's only the wiper blades. The windscreen is great, but it rained the other day for the first time in ages and I couldn't see a thing.'

'No worries. It's an '85 Holden, right?' Merv says. He disappears inside the shed for a moment and comes back with plastic-wrapped wiper blades.

We weave our way back to the car and while he fits the rubber blades, I try to make conversation. I remark on the heat. I remark on the fading paintwork of my car. I remark on the colour of the wilted scarlet geranium by the fence. I can hear my voice starting to quaver. When I told Helen I was coming to Merv Bull's garage, she raced around to the house and made me wear a pair of her high heels and put on make-up. I tried to protest that I only wanted new wiper blades, but she insisted. 'He's an attractive man, you can't deny it,' she said. 'So why knock yourself out of the race by turning up in your trackie-daks?' I was cross about that. I never wear my tracksuit pants out of the house unless I'm one hundred per cent sure I won't have to leave the car. Then once I'd got dressed up, it seemed as if I was on a date, or a mission, and I started to feel sick. All this for a pair of wiper blades.

'Nice shoes,' Merv says after he's dropped the plastic wrapping and bent to pick it up.

'Thanks,' I say in a cheery voice. A twitch above my left eye flickers like a broken neon and I thrust my hips forwards in an attempt to balance on Helen's high heels. I'm pretty sure I could pass for Quasimodo. I remark on the earth-moving machines. 'I suppose they're for the development. When's it going to open? I heard—'

'Um,' he interrupts. 'Geez, I'm sorry, but I can't remember your name.'

'Loretta Boskovic.'

'Of course, sorry. So, Loretta, they brought the machinery up the other day and I signed an

191

agreement. Part of the deal, you know. Commercial-in-confidence stuff, they said. So I'm not supposed to talk about it.'

'Sorry! I didn't want to know anything secret,' I say hurriedly. The sun is quite hot, even though it's only ten in the morning. I think my face is melting.

'Like I said, I've signed that thing.'

'Sure.' I try to think fast and stand steady on high heels at the same time. Make conversation, make conversation. 'No problem. I was just excited. About having the development here. It's going to be great for the community, isn't it!'

'Yeah,' Merv says. 'Hey, hang on, aren't you the lady who organized the Save Our School thing? With the chocolate drive?'

'Mmm,' I answer. I'm not sure I want to be known as the chocolate-drive lady.

Merv glances to the side and I realize the three apprentices are staring at us. One nudges the other and they slump back in their chairs and pretend to talk casually.

'I'd better be off. How much do I owe you?'

'Don't worry about it. Complimentary service,' Merv says, and I hear a low whistle from one of the boys.

As I totter around to the driver's side with Merv following, I apologize for having disturbed him, for parking in the driveway, for not having brought my car in for a full oil and grease change. He has to catch my elbow when I stumble in my heels on a rut in the driveway. His hand is warm and firm on my arm. He doesn't let go, but guides me to the door.

'I must get the car tuned soon,' I say stupidly. The yard is so packed with cars he must need five more apprentices.

'Anytime,' Merv says. 'We can always find a spot.'

The car door squeals as I pull it open, ease myself in, then slam it shut.

'Can't have that,' Merv says. He tells me to hang on while he gets something from the shed. In a minute he's back, spraying the hinges of the door. 'There we go,' he says, swinging the door sound-lessly open and shut. 'The smell won't last long, don't worry.'

'Thanks.' I hesitate. He didn't have to do that. 'Thanks a lot.'

'Boss! Phone!' a shout comes from the shed.

Merv looks around. One of the boys is holding the phone handset up at the door of the shed.

'It's the Fiat guy!'

Merv leans down to my window.

'Whenever you want that tune,' he says.

I nod. He nods. My heart starts to thump a little. The boy shouts again, and Merv shouts back that he's coming.

Once I start the engine of the Holden I can't hear a thing. Merv says something, who knows what, as I give a wave while I back out of the driveway and into the road, completely forgetting to look behind me. The screaming horn of the car that follows me down the Bolton Road is quite melodic to my ears.

CHAPTER 19

It's uncanny seeing Norm and Justin together when I drive into the yard on the Monday. They're sitting in the shed, side by side, as if they've been here forever. Norm's got his radio up full volume, listening to the races at Moonee Valley, while Justin is bent over the table screwing a plate on to a bicycle frame. They both look up when I knock on the corrugated iron wall. Even their movements are in synch, like an old couple who've lived together for years.

'Made too much pasta last night, Norm.' I plonk the pot on the table. 'Thought you might be able to use the leftovers.'

'Thanks, Loretta. Have you met Justin, my son?'

Yes, I should answer, I snuck in and met him while you were listening to race three. Instead I put out my hand and we shake.

'Loretta Boskovic. Loretta can't sing, but her pasta's all right,' Norm tells Justin.

Justin nods and smiles. So this is how Norm looked thirty years ago. I only met Justin's mum, Marg, a couple of times, but I can't see anything of her in Justin. Only Norm's long face, wide

195

mouth, sticking-out ears. The son's a lot cleaner, though.

Justin brushes dust and wood shavings off a chair and uses a hand gesture to offer me a seat. He hasn't spoken a word yet. I was nervous coming here this morning. I'd never met an armed robber before. I expected Justin to have a mean snarl and tatts up to his ears, but he seems to be an even gentler version of Norm.

'How are you enjoying Gunapan?' I ask him.

He presses his lips together in a half-smile and looks at the ceiling and nods a few times.

'He hasn't seen much of it yet,' Norm says. 'We might head out for a counter tea tonight, right, Justin?'

Justin nods again. I'm starting to wonder if he has a tongue.

'They've put Thai curry on the menu at the Criterion.' I'm trying to keep up the conversation.

Justin raises his eyebrows as if to say, 'Really?'

'What do you think of curry, Justin?' Norm asks.

Justin shrugs and shakes his head. I think this means he's never tried it. I suppose if he lived in Gunapan until he was twenty, then moved to Geelong and promptly got fourteen years for armed robbery, he's probably never eaten anything more exotic than a banana fritter. Sammy Lee's father used to run the Chinese café here fourteen years ago, but his Chinese food had more to do with Rosella tomato sauce than Chinese herbs and spices. Now the Chinese café is run by an Indian family.

196

'Well, that's settled,' Norm says. 'An early counter tea then home to watch the footy on telly, eh?'

Justin smiles gratefully at his dad. He looks tired. So does Norm. Justin goes back to screwing the plate on the bike frame.

'Justin's thinking of working at Morelli's Meats,' Norm says.

I guess we're going to chat about Justin as if he's not here so that he can go on being shy without having to pretend to enjoy talking, so I join in the spirit of the conversation.

'Has he ever worked in an abattoir?' I ask Norm.

'No, but he's been living in one, by the sounds of it,' Norm says, perfectly straight-faced.

A soft laugh comes from Justin's bent head. He has a crew cut and under the bristly dark hair I can see a scar on the back of his skull, running from the crown right down to his neck. As I'm sneaking a look at him he rolls his shoulders and flexes his fingers. He's long and muscular, like a racing greyhound.

'I suppose if the work's there.' If I'd just been released from prison, I don't think I'd want to work in an abattoir. But what would I know?

'I hear they're short-staffed because Heck's competing again. Justin can probably get casual work to fill in for a couple of weeks.'

I can't see Justin's face, but his scar shifts a little, as though his face is moving. I wonder if he truly wants to work at the abattoir.

'I offered him a job in the yard, but he said no.' Norm looks away at the wall of the shed, which he has plastered with colourful centrefolds of Massey-Ferguson tractors.

An awful silence drags on. Justin doesn't raise his head. He's finished attaching the plate to the frame and now he's sanding rust off the wheel forks. He's a natural for the yard. I can't imagine how Norm would pay him, though. People come into the yard, spend two hours talking at Norm, and leave with a five-dollar purchase. He doesn't sell a lot, but he knows everything about everyone. He could set up a good sideline in blackmail. Norm Stevens Snr: spare parts, scrap and confidential information to order.

'Anyway, Norm, are you coming to the next Save Our School Committee meeting?'

'Sure. I can help make up the numbers.'

'Great. I want to talk about the development as well. And I'll make orange cake.' I have to create an incentive or no one will come. 'Feel free to come along, Justin.'

'Thanks, yep. Ta,' Justin mutters without raising his head.

Having succeeded in getting Justin to speak, I feel as if I've already done a good morning's work. 'Well, I guess I'll be off. Have to clock on at the Neighbourhood House soon.'

Actually, I don't want to go. This morning was chilly with the crispness of new autumn, and now the fog has disappeared and Norm's rusty shed is

198

bathed in morning sunlight. I wouldn't mind sitting in companionable silence in the sun with the two Stevens men. I could pick up a piece of machinery and try to take it apart.

'Meant to say, Loretta.' Norm turns down the volume of the racing, which has been droning on in the background. Outside the kookaburras are going crazy laughing in the stand of messmate trees across from Norm's yard. 'Meant to say, Loretta,' Norm says again. 'Have you met the people in the old MacInerny house?'

'Nope. Why?'

'The lady with the four kids?'

'I think I know who you mean. What about them?'

Norm reaches up and touches his forehead, the place where he had the cancer cut away. I haven't seen him do that for ages. When he goes outdoors these days he always wears a hat, a battered straw boater he found in a cupboard of a caravan someone dumped on the side of the road near Magabar.

'She's a nice lady. From that place in Europe, Bosnia Herzagobbler, where they had the war. A bit shy. Maybe she could join your committee, meet some people.'

'You don't want to tell me anything else?'

He shakes his head. I hate it when Norm does this. He's got more agendas than a school committee but he'd never admit to it. At least now I know they're not bullies. That's not something

Norm would keep to himself. He's more protective of my kids than a Rottweiler.

'OK, I'll drop a letter at the house. The old MacInerny house on Ross Road?'

Norm nods. I step out of the shed and wave at the darkness inside. Two moving shadows show me that Norm and Justin are waving back. As I turn to head for the car, the fine colour of rust shimmers in the thin sunshine. It has a strange beauty I will always associate with Norm.

Next day I finish work at eleven, so I drive to Ross Road on the outskirts of town. The MacInerny family left their house a long time ago but everyone kept calling it the MacInerny house because no one else had moved in. I thought it was derelict.

The house has dingy lace curtains in the window and a tan-coloured dog the size of a horse lying on the veranda. When I pull the car into the driveway the beast raises its head and woofs one deep bark, then drops its head back on the veranda with a thump that shakes the neighbourhood.

I've been driving inside a twister thanks to the bits of paper flying around the car. I unfold one of the pieces wrapped around the gearstick. It's a committee begging letter dated months ago. I scratch out the date with a biro that doesn't work anymore and fold the letter so the crease covers where I deleted it.

The moment the Holden door slams behind

me, the house comes alive. Curtains tweak open in the left-hand window, the dog tries to haul its massive frame off the veranda floor, the door opens and the woman I recognize from the Halstead mall steps outside and puts her hands on her hips. I guess they don't get many visitors out here.

I'm starting to get a bit of a hillbilly feeling, what with the car on blocks beside the house and the oil drum in the middle of the front yard stuffed with pieces of an old paling fence. I hesitate beside the car, waiting for the banjos to start, until it occurs to me that my yard has an unhappy similarity to this one, thanks to having my own rusting truck on blocks and a goat tethered to the washing line.

'Hello,' I call out. Damn, Norm forgot to tell me her name.

She steps back inside the shadow of the door. Norm wasn't kidding about 'a bit shy'. She looks like she's going to be absorbed into the wall.

'Hi. I wanted to drop in this invitation.' I'm shouting, but only to make sure she hears me from wherever she's disappeared to.

Inside the house someone speaks curtly in a foreign language. It has the commanding tone of an order. The curtain in the left window falls back into place.

'Hello?' Maybe it's not a hillbilly movie I'm stumbling around in but a horror. They probably have bodies stacked five deep in the shed.

'What you want?' an accented voice calls from the darkness.

Hmm. I want to invite you to join a committee. Even thinking those words puts me in a coma of boredom. Surely I can find a better way to describe it. I will be talking to the air and an empty doorway, but I suppose she'll be listening from inside.

'I'm worried about our kids' future,' I call out, realizing as the words leave my mouth that I am using the same line as a maths software salesman.

She darts out of the doorway and into the light like a spider that feels a tug on its web, her finger pointing at me.

'Your kids, no!'

The monster dog starts to growl. I was right. It is a horror movie.

I hold out the folded letter. I'm beside the car, next to the front gate. I'm not moving while the monster dog is alive and making noise.

'No good!' She's still pointing as if a laser is beaming from her fingertip, and my hand reaches up involuntarily to touch my chest.

The curtain tweaks open again. I'm close enough to see an old creased face peering out. I smile. The face frowns and the ancient one makes a shaky fist at me.

I never knew I could make such a strong impression. I creep along the fence, tuck the letter into the rusted old letter box beside the gate and hurry back to the car. I'll be thanking Norm later for this experience.

Driving back from the MacInerny house, I see her kids get off the school bus. The little boy is holding the hand of a smaller girl, and the two others, an older boy and girl, are walking behind them. The young boy seems to be crying.

I gun the Holden down the road. Maybe someone's sick, I think. Maybe the young boy has leukaemia and they're exhausted from looking after him. Or the mother's suffering from post-traumatic stress after the war and she locks them in the house and won't let them out except for school. Or maybe that old crone in the window is . . . is something. I don't know. A witch, maybe, but a real one, not a glorified aromatherapist like Leanne. I feel a little shaky after that reception. I hope the new Mrs MacInerny doesn't join the committee.

At the school gate Melissa's standing with her hands on her hips, lips pursed, squinting into the sun. If she keeps maturing at this rate she'll soon be a fully fledged Gunapan woman. She'll have married, had kids and been deserted by the time she's fifteen. She and Jake climb into the back seat and I head off in my usual role of chauffeur.

'How come you always sit in the back, Liss?' I ask. 'It's not as if you need a booster seat anymore. You could sit up with me and chat while I drive.' If she's going to be a Gunapan woman, she'll need to learn the art of the car nod. A half-nod for acquaintances, a nod for friends and a knowing head toss for best friends. This can only be done from the front seat. And while driving at speed. Preferably with an arm hanging casually out the window.

'Because you drive like a psycho,' my daughter says casually. 'And I don't want to die.'

The minute that girl gets her licence I'm never letting her in my car again.

'Are any of the kids from that new family in your class?'

'What new family?'

I check the rear-view mirror. Melissa's sitting with a back as straight as a ballerina and staring at her hands. She's lying.

'The one from Bosnia Hergesobbler. The foreigners.'

Another glance at the reflection. Jake's looking out the window.

'Well?'

'Yeah, a girl.'

'What's her name?'

'I don't know.'

'You must know. There are only sixteen kids in your class.'

'Something. I can't pronounce it.'

'Well, what do you call her when you want to speak to her?' I'm starting to channel Constable Plod.

'Nothing.'

A modern mother never resorts to violence. That's why I don't screech to a halt, lean over the back of the seat and give my daughter a good thwack over the head. Instead, because I am a reasonable modern woman and a caring mother, I screech to a halt, lean over the back of the seat and warn Melissa that serious consequences will occur if she doesn't smarten up and stop avoiding my questions.

'What serious consequences?' she asks.

The serious consequence is that my head may explode, but that's not going to sway Melissa.

'No TV for a week.' I try not to think about the fact that Melissa is only eleven. If she's this way now, what will happen when she turns into a teenager? I might have to leave home. Get a flat in the city. Join an exercise class and discover the body that's been waiting underneath my flab for all these years. I'll be tired of Beamer Man and Harley Man by then. I'll be ready for Merc Man. Merc Man has divorced his ungrateful wife and is looking for someone to pamper. 'Loretta,' he says to me after we've made love on the king-sized bed in his penthouse with views of the Sydney Harbour Bridge, 'you are one delectable hunk of woman. You know, looking at this taut body, I can't believe you have children.' 'Actually, I don't,' I'll tell him. 'I sold them.'

Melissa's been checking the letter box every day since Tony left town, and this afternoon I see her pull a few bits of mail out of the box, flip through them, then slip one into her pocket as she looks furtively around at the house. I am not hiding. It is a fluke that I am standing behind the curtain, from where I can see her but she can't see me. Exactly where I have been while she checked the letter box every day since her father's visit.

'Bills, Mum,' she says with pretend innocence, dropping a few envelopes on the dresser and heading off to her room.

'Thanks, Liss,' I answer with a winning smile, like a character in an Enid Blyton book. Sometimes I am amazed at how we learn to play these roles, as if we are in a movie.

Tony is too lazy and selfish to try to take the kids away from me, but whenever I think of the possibility, my stomach rolls over and I can feel my insides being rearranged. What if Talee wants them? I wonder. What if Tony and Talee have Melissa over for a visit and Melissa doesn't want to come home? Or Jake? They'd only have to buy Jake a Lego set and he'd go anywhere with them. Later in the night, when Melissa's asleep, I sneak into her room and slide the card from under her pillow.

Hi Liss and Jake,
   Hope school's good and everything is great. Can't wait to see you again. Say hello to your mum.
   Love Dad and Talee

Which would be fine, except it's not his handwriting. Miss Happy must have written it. They won't be coming to take my children. Tony has probably, once again, forgotten he even has children.

Next morning I ring Helen and tell her about my experience with the new family at the MacInerny house. She's never met the woman.

'I mean, I kind of know her. I've seen her and the kids plenty of times. We nod hello. I just never had a chance to talk to her. She's a refugee, poor thing. Try the Church of Goodwill. They have that outreach program.'

After work, on the way to the church I drop in at the shire office. Norm's asked me to get the official documents for the development to use in his next try at getting the Unsightly Property Notice lifted. He's convinced they're connected.

'Give me everything you've got on the development on the Bolton Road,' I say to the receptionist in my best private detective voice.

She yawns and turns to her computer. 'You mean the resort?' she asks.

'That's it. I'll have whatever you've got. Plans, permits, letters, objections.' That's odd, I think. 'Did anyone object? I don't remember seeing any notices about this. Aren't you supposed to be able to object to new buildings?'

'Don't know. You'd have to ask in Planning about

that.' She taps and clicks with her keyboard and mouse, stifling yawns. 'Nothing here, sorry.'

'It's a huge development. Isn't there anything?'

'Yeah, but I can't find anything for the public. All the stuff's in files I can't access and the manager's not in today. You'll probably have to put in a written request.'

Next I head for the church.

The Church of Goodwill shopfront is on the main road between the betting shop and the fish and chippery. Hand-drawn pictures of rainbows and doves are sticky-taped to the window and Christian rock and roll music blares in distorted waves from a tinny speaker above the front door. Inside, Trudy sits at the desk staring at a computer screen.

'I hate these things,' she says to me when I walk in. 'I preferred it when we wrote letters to each other by hand, and added up the week's offerings in a hardbound book with two columns. I'm not entirely convinced that computers aren't the work of the devil.'

'Is that right?' I try to look as if I talk about the devil every day.

'I'm joking, Loretta. What can I do for you?'

'Have you ever met the Bosnia Herzabobble people down the old MacInerny place?'

'Mersiha and her family? Yes, of course. They're part of the Gunapan Revitalization and Welcoming Committee Community Project.'

I might be imagining it, but Trudy seems to be

avoiding looking me in the eye. I've been getting that feeling a lot lately. As if people are afraid to tell me the revived Save Our School Committee is a waste of time. I don't know why they'd hold back. They didn't last time. I distinctly remember Trudy telling me, 'That Save Our School Committee is a waste of time, Loretta. Why don't you do some real work in the community and help clean up Wilson Dam next Saturday?' I wanted to answer that I didn't feel like contracting tetanus, but I didn't because Trudy's a Christian and a good worker in the community and one day I might need her help for Save Our School.

'She's already on a committee. Oh, that's OK then. Norm thought she might be good for Save Our School. But if she's busy . . .'

'She's not on the committee, Loretta. She's a refugee, struggling to get herself and her family settled here. Her sponsor is Maxine. Anyway, you must have seen her at the school and the fair and around the place. Mersiha's lovely. She's making a real effort to join in. People are starting to welcome her very warmly.'

'Oh. Well, maybe I could ask Maxine to contact—'

'Actually, Loretta,' Trudy looks at the ceiling as if she's getting instructions from above, 'Maxine and I have been meaning to talk to you. So here you are, and I think I'd better say it.'

'About Save Our School?'

'No.' She takes a deep breath. 'About the bullying. Something has to be done.'

'I knew it. I knew it was bullying.' My face is tight with rage. 'I'll do something all right.' I feel the breath blazing out of my nose, hotter and angrier than the snorts of a bull at a matador fight. 'They'll find out no one messes with my kids. I'll call their father to come and sort it out if I have to. I'm going around to that woman's place right now.' I want to paw at the ground. The whole room is red.

Trudy stands up and squeezes out from behind the desk. She edges her way between me and the front door.

'Step away from the door, Loretta.'

I take a long deep breath, swell to twice my size like an angry puffer fish. 'I'm going now, Trudy. Get out of my way.'

Trudy presses her back against the door. 'I can't let you.'

'This is not about you, Trudy. It's about my children. Get out of the way or I'll throw you through that door.'

'Loretta, listen to yourself. Think about where your children have learned their bad behaviour. I had no idea you were this kind of person.'

'My children's bad behaviour? What about that woman's children? Oh, it's a lovely welcome for them, even though they're making my children's life hell. I know, they're traumatized by war and everything, but that's no excuse for bringing their problems here and bullying my kids. I won't take it, Trudy. Out of the way, please.'

'Oh, dear,' Trudy says. She has slumped against the glass of the door. She reaches out and takes my hand. 'Oh, Loretta. We'd better have a cup of tea.'

CHAPTER 20

When I arrive, bawling, at Norm's yard, Justin is by himself.

'Dad's gone out,' he says. He's sitting at the table in the shed, listening to the races and using an artist's paintbrush to paint fire-engine red enamel on an old toy car the size of a shoebox. 'Thought your Jake might like this.'

I hiccup in reply. Justin gestures to the seat on the other side of the table, but I shake my head. It's two o'clock. I have one and a half hours till the kids get out of school and I need to do something, but I don't know what.

'Cup of tea?'

I shake my head, then nod, then sob, then sniff a long wet snotty sniff.

'When's Norm back?' I manage to ask.

'Not till later tonight. He's gone down to the city.'

I wonder what Norm would be doing in the city, but I can't allow myself to get off track. I have an urgent problem and I have to find a way to fix it.

'My daughter's a bully,' I blurt out to Justin. 'My son's a follower. They've been tormenting the new kids in town.'

Justin nods slowly. I'm still standing in the doorway of the shed, the sun burning the back of my neck in stinging fingers.

'I don't know what to do.'

Justin nods again. 'Seen a few bullies in my time.'

'I'm going home.' I start to sob and hiccup again. 'Can you tell Norm I came by?'

'I might follow to see you get home all right. You probably can't see too well right now. Drive slowly, OK?'

He's right. My eyes are stinging and smarting, my whole face is swollen. I must look like I'm the one who's being bullied.

I only bump the veranda lightly when I steer the Holden into the driveway. Justin pulls up in the truck and waves to me, but I don't want to go into my empty house and cry, so I call him in. He sits patiently at the kitchen table as I start the kettle, lay out the cups and a plate of biscuits, work my way through five tissues then finally stop crying. I pour the tea and slump into a kitchen chair.

'I'm a terrible mother,' I tell him before I bite into a Chocolate Royal and suck the marshmallow. I've lined up the ten Chocolate Royals from the packet in two rows on the plate. Number one is still on its way down my throat when I pick up number two and start to peel the chocolate covering away from the marshmallow with my teeth. It's not easy to speak with my mouth full of chocolate, marshmallow and biscuit base, but I do have experience.

213

'Melissa has been calling the Bosnian kids "bush pigs". She passes the little girl notes during class with curly pigs' tails drawn on them. She whispers to them that they should go home to the stinky country they came from. She—' My voice cracks here. I can't believe this is my daughter. 'She tells them they smell bad and that they're dirty foreigners.'

Justin blows on his cup of tea to cool it down before he takes a sip. 'Does she hit them?'

'I don't think so. You'd better have one of these.' There are only four Chocolate Royals left on the plate. I'm starting to feel nauseous as I suck the marshmallow off the biscuit base of number six.

'That's got to be a good thing. She doesn't hit them.'

'Jake follows the younger ones around the schoolyard at recess making squealing noises. They escaped from a war, only to come out here and be bullied by my children! Is it because they're growing up without a father?'

'Dad said your kids have missed their dad.'

I want to blame Tony. When he was here he was a bad father and now he's gone he's still being a bad father. I wonder if I should try to contact him. He neglected to leave his new address. I suppose I could ring around the country towns near Mildura and ask about a man with unnaturally white front teeth and a child bride.

'He never taught them how to behave. He was always stomping around in a permanent rage.'

Justin nods, looks at his tea.

'How can I teach a little boy to be a good person? That's a man's job. Sure, it was fine to leave me, but did he have to abandon his kids?'

Justin keeps nodding, a quiet, calm motion.

'I thought everything got better after he left. We were happier. I thought I could bring them up on my own . . . I always joke about giving away the kids, but they're my life.'

For a moment we sit in silence as I come around to the truth.

'I've done a bad job. I'm the worst kind of mother. I've raised monsters.'

'So what do you reckon you'll do about it?' Justin asks.

'Here, you take this one,' I say, pushing the last Chocolate Royal towards Justin. He shakes his head. As I swallow the last gluey crumbs, I wonder whether I still have that old block of rum-and-raisin chocolate from Christmas in the back of the freezer.

'I think. I think, I think . . . I think I'll wait till Norm gets back. Yes, that's what I'll do.'

'Good idea.'

'They probably hate me. That's why they're doing this. They hate me and they want to punish me. Unconsciously. You hated your parents, didn't you? Norm said that.'

Justin sits back in his chair and stares at me. 'Of course I didn't hate them. Did he mean because I wouldn't see them while I was inside?' He presses his lips tightly together for a moment, breathes in through his nose. 'I was ashamed. I was a shitty ungrateful kid who got caught and then when they sent me to jail I realized what a fucking idiot I'd been. Sorry about the language.'

I shake my head. That kind of language slides off me after ten years with Tony, who thought 'fucking' was the most descriptive word in the English language. For Tony, 'fucking' meant good and it meant bad. It meant funny and it meant someone who needed a good kicking. It meant hello or goodbye. Thank you or I never want to see you again. Delicious, or red, or belonging to the human race, or not.

'I told Mum,' Justin mutters. 'When I went up to Warrnambool. I explained why I couldn't come out when she visited.'

'Because you were ashamed?'

He shrugs and picks up his mug, peers into it then holds it up high so he can look at the base. 'Cracked,' he says. 'I'll get a new one for you.'

'Don't worry, it's been like that for years.'

Watching him at the table, I can't get over the resemblance. Justin hasn't seen his dad for fourteen years and yet even the way he holds a cup is identical to Norm. His hands are the same plate shape. He looks off to the side when he's asking a question and he snorts softly when he doesn't believe something. And the ears. If he and Norm could learn to move those ears at will they could form a circus act – the Flying Stevens.

216

'My friend, Helen, was going to come around tonight to watch a film after the kids have gone to bed. Maybe Norm and you could come too? To have a talk about this . . .'

He does his look over and out through the window thing while I gather the cups and switch the kettle on for another cup. He is so quiet and still that I feel like a punchy drunk, flailing around and rattling the whole kitchen with every move. I'm not helped by the wonky floor that bounces up and down every time I take a step and sets the kitchen dresser juddering and the plates chattering across the shelves.

So far poor quiet Justin has seen me blubbering, self-flagellating, moaning, complaining and eating an entire packet of Chocolate Royals in eleven minutes. Prison and its standards of etiquette are probably looking pretty fancy right now.

'I'm not sure Dad'll be up for it tonight, but I'll ask him.'

The kettle boils and I pour water on to two more teabags and settle back at the kitchen table.

'I shouldn't keep you,' Justin says into his teacup.

The trouble with gentle, calm, quiet people I don't know well is that I find myself babbling to fill the spaces between bits of conversation. Useless information wells up out of me and dribbles all over the silence.

'I'm starting up the Save Our School Committee Mark II. I want to make it about the development too, because of what they've done to Norm.'

217

'Dad said.'

'No one will join now. I'm the mother with the bully children. Everyone else is probably hoping the school will close so they can get their kids away from mine.'

Justin laughs. 'Where I was, real bullies made a career out of it. Some other people did stupid bullying things because they were afraid. They thought it made them look strong. Once they found their place in the hierarchy, they settled down.'

I suppose I'm in shock. I think about Melissa passing nasty notes to the girl in her class and Melissa seems to have become someone new, not my smart-arse daughter who's full of bravado but loves to cuddle up on the couch with me and hug me from behind when I'm at the sink. How could she be doing this?

Half an hour later, as I wait in the car outside the school, Melissa walks out of the school gate with Jake in tow. She has her father's narrow pointy features, I can see now. She looks behind her. The children she's been bullying are coming down the steps of the school in a tight group, not looking sideways or forwards, only staring at their feet. Melissa pulls Jake aside and they stand hidden outside the gate.

Melissa could see me in the car if she turned around, but she doesn't. She's concentrating too hard on what's happening at the gate. Her arm, stretched behind her, holds Jake protectively against the fence as if she's afraid someone is going to snatch him away. The other children step out through the gate in one movement, then hurry off down the street in the opposite direction to where Melissa is standing. I see her call something after them. The oldest one turns around and for a moment she and Melissa stare at each other like animals, each waiting for the other to make the first move. The girl, hissing something so loudly I can hear the hiss but not the words, turns, gathers her siblings around her and starts off for home. Melissa's body goes limp and her head nods towards her chest as if she is exhausted. Jake steps around her and takes her hand. She might be crying.

I have no idea what's going on, but I want to take her in my arms and hug her. They say she's a bully. All I see is my little girl, frightened and alone.

CHAPTER 21

Norm turns up at nine in the evening with a couple of stubbies of beer and a packet of beer nuts. He's got a Band-Aid on the inside of his arm.

'What happened?' I nod at the Band-Aid.

'Oh.' He seems startled. Puts down the beer and nuts and rolls down his sleeve to cover the Band-Aid. 'Scratch. Piece of metal.'

'Make sure you get a tetanus shot,' I warn him. Norm snickers.

Helen greets Norm when he comes into the kitchen. The kids are in bed, but I've left the TV blaring in the lounge room so they can't hear what we're saying if they wake up.

'Come to help sort out the children of the corn?' Helen says to Norm.

'Bloody menaces to society.' He thumps into the same kitchen chair that Justin sat in this afternoon.

'Norm, tell Justin thanks for me, will you? I cried at him for a while then forced him to drink about ten cups of tea and wouldn't let him have a single Chocolate Royal out of the whole packet.'

'So what's new?'

'It's not funny, Norm. My children are bullies. I raised two bullies!'

'Sometimes these things fade away,' Helen remarks. 'Aren't the kids going to your sister's place next week? Maybe it'll blow over while they're gone.'

'It might blow over, but I don't think I'll ever get over it.'

'So they're calling kids names. So what? You didn't raise real bullies. Brenda Giles' boys, now they're real bullies,' Helen says.

'Yeah, settle down, Loretta,' Norm adds. 'It's not like you're drunk every night or your kids are hacking babies into little pieces.'

'Norm, you've got to stop reading the news-papers.'

They may not have been hacking up babies, but last summer the Giles boys, Glenn and Gary, spent nights terrorizing anyone who dared to venture out on the streets. Brenda was having a bit of a bad patch with the stress of having all those children to feed, and she was passed out on the couch by nine every night. The younger kids stayed home eating rubbish and watching TV shopping shows till dawn, but the two older boys started to roam.

Any kid walking around after ten o'clock was in trouble if Glenn and Gary caught them. They were the angriest boys anyone had seen in this town for a long time. Bill, the local policeman, drove around the streets in his patrol car trying to keep an eye out, but they were fast and on foot and they always got away over fences and down lanes and through the paddocks on the outskirts of town.

The local lads who'd thought they were tough until Glenn and Gary were let loose came home with black eyes and bruises and a sudden desire to spend more time with their families. Bill once joked to me that the Giles boys had done a better job of cleaning up the streets than he ever could. But they got more and more violent. The black eyes turned into cuts. The bruises became broken bones. They started carrying chains and bats.

One night, after most of the local kids had learned their lesson about staying indoors after dark, a couple of boys visiting their cousins down the end of Ables Court ran into the Giles boys out in the scrub behind the abattoir. The visitors were from a tough part of Melbourne where proper gangs identified themselves with tattoos and pledges and special haircuts. No one knows exactly what happened, but the Giles boys disappeared for two days. Then, on the third day, they turned up at the emergency ward in Halstead Hospital. Glenn slipped into a coma and only woke up after five days. That's what got Brenda out of her bad patch. She had to farm out the other kids for a week and stay in the hospital while Glenn was in danger of not pulling through. When she got home the kids made her swear she'd never drink again. They told her that the people they'd stayed with had made them do their homework and no way were they going back to that.

I wonder if I've been neglecting my children. Is that why they've turned into monsters? A stinging tear forms in the corner of my left eye. Perhaps I should give up the campaigning.

'Have I been neglecting them?' I say out loud. 'All the Save Our School stuff and the rest, don't they realize I'm doing it for them? So they have a good place to live? No one else is going to do it. No one cares about us in the small towns. We have to fight or we'll go under. But maybe they're asking why me? Why have I decided to do it? Maybe that's what's happened. I should be doing more things with them. Nature walks. Art projects. I'll start sewing lessons, learn to make them clothes. I'll—'

'For God's sake, Loretta, snap out of it. Where's your sense of humour gone? It's not the end of the world.' Norm sounds impatient.

I sniff. Pull another tissue from my pocket. Helen's tapping her foot and leafing through the TV guide.

'Sorry, love,' Norm says. 'I didn't mean to jump down your throat. I'm a bit tired. But will you leave it for a few days? Let the kids go to your sister's place and we can talk about it when they get back.'

'You don't have to deal with it, Norm. I have to deal with it. Let me ask you something important.

Should I try to get in contact with Tony? Is it because they haven't got a father?'

After they've finished laughing so much that Helen has a coughing fit and Norm spills his beer, Norm leans back in his chair and sighs.

'Norm's right. Give it a rest, Loretta,' Helen says. 'Let things settle. There's such a thing as being too proactive.'

Too proactive? Helen's been reading the back of my breakfast cereal box. The other morning I was gazing dreamily at the box and the word caught my eye. Proactive. Or was it a margarine container? Whichever. I read it and realized I'd been in a non-proactive slump. That's what decided me to start up the SOS Committee Mark II. But how did Helen know? How does she know these things about me? It's unnerving. It makes me cross.

'I have no idea what you mean by proactive, Helen. You must be picking up jargon from that therapist of yours.'

Helen blinks slowly. 'Actually, Loretta, therapy helps people with anger issues. You should try it. You and your bullying children.'

So this is how a friend behaves when you're in trouble. Puts the boot in.

'Yes, Helen, you're right. My bullying children might need to see a therapist. At least they have a real problem. They're not middle-aged women so desperate for attention they'll pay for it.'

Norm pushes his chair back from the table. 'Right. I'm out of here.'

From the bedroom comes one of Jake's shrieks. I ignore it like I usually do, knowing it's not a desperate shriek, only one of his night shrieks.

'Aren't you going to see what that's about?' Helen asks.

'It's nothing,' I answer impatiently. 'They both scream at night.'

Helen raises one eyebrow. I've sat with her and laughed when she used that look on someone else. Now I know how it feels to be the victim of the single superior arched eyebrow.

'Not real screaming. Night cries.'

'Everyday screaming, then,' Helen says. If anything, the arched eyebrow goes even higher. She'll lose it in her hair if she's not careful.

Norm heaves himself up off the wooden kitchen chair and picks up his old straw hat.

'I'll drop by Sunday, once the kids are gone. Leave it a bit, OK, Loretta?'

They obviously don't care. I can't leave it. I'll have to do something before the kids go to Patsy's.

Helen, still looking miffed, is stuffing her phone into her handbag and rummaging around for her keys. Norm ducks on his way out the back door, but I notice he's shorter, or stooping lower, or something, because the top of his head is nowhere near touching the architrave anymore. He must be getting old. I hear him talking to Terror as he heads down the back stairs and the thudding of her hooves following him down. She likes to escort visitors to the gate.

'Do you want a coffee tomorrow?' I ask Helen as we walk down the hallway to the front door. I talk softly so I don't wake the kids.

'I'll be busy attention-seeking tomorrow,' she says, looking at me in the dim light of the moon that comes through the glass panel in the front door.

'Oh, Helen, don't. I didn't mean it. I'm sorry.'

'You never mean it, Loretta.'

She steps out through the front door and pulls it shut quietly behind her. I stand in the half-light, shocked, suddenly shivering.

CHAPTER 22

The next day is the last day of term and the parents are at the school gate early. Helen's here to pick up the Tim Tams. She's making a big show of chatting and laughing with everyone but me. I stay sitting in the driver's seat of the Holden, my left bum cheek almost impaled on the broken spring that poked its way through the vinyl last week.

Melissa and Jake are so excited about their visit to Patsy's house that when they get into the car their shrill voices sound like squeaking bats. Melissa is talking about the shops she's going to visit in Melbourne and Jake keeps interrupting with descriptions of the food George cooked both times she came to visit us. He seems to expect she'll spend his whole visit in the kitchen, whipping up culinary masterpieces to thrill a six-year-old – chocolate crackles, hot dogs, toffee, pancakes.

'Auntie George is a chef!' he screams at no one from the back seat.

I can't understand how I made these children.

It takes them a while to realize we're not going home.

'I have to pack!' Melissa shrieks. 'Mum, we have to go home now!'

Who knows what she thinks she's going to pack. It's as if the promise of a trip to Melbourne has addled her mind and she thinks she has more than four outfits.

'Sit tight,' I tell them. 'We're going on a little trip.'

In the rear-view mirror I see Melissa fall back against the seat. How on earth will she have time to choose between her three good shirts if we waste our time driving around the countryside?

I take a full tour of Gunapan, starting at the CWA Hall, following the route of the annual Rhododendron Parade, which passes the eleven Gunapan houses with rhododendron bushes and ends at the local park, then I ease the car off north to the footy ground and travel the dirt road out to Wilson Dam and then further north. Melissa and Jake quieten down and sit staring out through the windows.

This is all a ploy to buy time while I plan what to say to them. I considered leaving 'the talk' till they got back from their holiday, as Norm suggested, but I know I'll fret the whole time anyway so I might as well have a crack at this problem now.

When we reach the lookout on Bald Hill, I climb out of the car. Melissa and Jake stay sitting in the back. They won't look at me.

The wind is barely blowing down in town, but up here it's brisk and biting. We're the only people here. The view looks over Gunapan, the abattoir, the farms. The first autumn rain came last week, but the land is still dry and the grass and trees are like children's models made of straw and sticks. I can see our little house over to the south with the neatly paddocked hobby farm opposite. It's incredible to think I've been in Gunapan for thirteen years. Shouldn't I get some kind of award?

A long way away, to my left, the Bolton Road winds through the forest. The gash of the development is even bigger than I'd realized. In the centre of the cleared land is a deep rectangular hole with large yellow machinery parked around it. Maxine told me she drove past last week on the way to Merv Bull's garage and they've put *Do Not Enter* signs all along the road. That used to be public land. I'm mad about this. Right now I'm mad about everything.

When I'm completely chilled through and the kids still haven't got out of the car, I go back and get into the driver's seat. At first I turn around to look at them, but twisting my neck is painful, so I turn to face the front and adjust the rear-view mirror to see their reactions. They're both looking down as if something very important is curled up in their laps.

'You're bullying those new children.'

They don't reply. I thought Melissa would jump in to defend herself. I thought Jake might cry. Nothing. They sit still and stare at their hands.

'I'm ashamed.' It's me who starts to cry. I press

my lips tightly together and hold my breath, but tears gather at the corner of my eyes and run down my face. My nose fills with snot and I have to breathe through my mouth. I'm afraid to say anything else because my voice will give away that I'm crying, and I don't think they can see that I am because I'm facing the windscreen. I want them to know I'm angry, not think I'm a pathetic crying mother.

The wind is buffeting the car, whistling through the perished rubber seals around the windows. A single splat of autumn rain hits the windscreen. Inside, we're saying nothing. The tears stop dribbling. I pull a hankie from my pocket and dab away the wetness, then blow my nose as quietly as I can, but the wet snot sound is a dead giveaway that I've been crying.

'Why? Are you unhappy?' I decided on the drive here not to mention Tony. If it's about Tony, I'm sure Melissa will let me know.

Bald Hill isn't bald anymore. The Gunapan Beautification Committee built a park up here, with benches and a lookout tower and shrubs and trees and a toilet block. The vegetation is stunted from the hot wind in summer and the sudden frosts of winter. When we first moved to Gunapan, Tony and I came up here for a picnic. I dropped the sandwiches in the dirt, Tony drank too much beer and got a headache in the hot sun, his car battery went flat for no obvious reason and we had to wait two hours for a tow truck. 'Welcome to Gunapan,' I said to Tony, laughing, as we sat waiting on the picnic bench and watching nothing move in the town below. He didn't laugh. That would be lesson number twenty-three no one taught me: don't marry a man who has no sense of humour.

'We're not leaving till I get some answers.'

The only time they're this quiet is when they're asleep. I can outwait them. I know Jake simply cannot say silent for much longer. I'm fairly certain that Melissa is building a case in her mind and will soon present the argument for the defence. I reach for my bag and my trusty Caramellos. Chocolate and caramel can soothe any situation, if administered early enough. Naturally, my evil bullying children will have to do without. They watch me cram three into my mouth. I consider a fourth, but decide that only a death in the family is a four-Caramello crisis.

I like to close my eyes when I'm sucking on a Caramello. It makes the taste stronger and the bad things of the outside world disappear for a few minutes. However, having my eyes closed doesn't mean that I lose my other faculties. I hear the click and creak as Melissa opens her door.

'Montchu dare nget outf dis kaa,' I say, mouth glued up with Caramello.

The door groans and clunks as Melissa pulls it shut. In the rear-view mirror I see her look at Jake. Jake looks back at her. I can't read their expressions. The silence continues, punctuated by the

231

whistling of the wind. The Caramellos melt to nothing but a sweet aftertaste. As I'm wondering what to do next, a thick foul miasma creeps over the seat and encloses me.

'Jake!' Melissa screams. She flings open her door and falls out of the car. So do I. It's incredible that a six-year-old can produce so much stink. Jake sits with his legs clenched together.

'I need to do poo,' he says firmly. 'I need to do poo very soon.'

The grey concrete public toilet block squats on the very peak of Bald Hill. I point Jake in that direction and stuff a wad of tissues in his hand.

'No more than five minutes!' I shout after him as he hurries off in a tight waddle. He's inherited his father's habit of spending fifteen to twenty minutes on the toilet, pondering whatever they ponder.

Over at the picnic area Melissa perches on a table with her feet resting on the bench below. She's having a growth spurt and her school dress is too short. I can see the faint outline of her budding breasts pressing against the cotton of the dress. I have to take a deep breath and remember how hard it is to be a girl going through puberty. Of course, my puberty only arrived when I was fourteen. A late developer in so many ways.

'What happened?' I ask when I'm sitting on the bench next to her feet.

'Nothing.'

'What did you do to them?'

'Nothing.'

'If you didn't do anything, how come I'm being told you're a bully?'

'I'm not a bully! They started it.'

I reach up and hug myself against the cold. 'Did you call them bush pigs?'

'No! Well, not before she called Jake a bush pig after our lesson about feral animals. He got upset so I joked about it to make him feel better.'

'And what did you do to that girl to make her call Jake a bush pig?'

'She can't even speak English properly! She said the essay I read out in class was a lie and her sister said I was big and fat. She smells and she's always got those brothers tagging along.'

I'm having trouble finding anything to hang on to here. 'I think we'll have to cancel your trip to Melbourne. If you won't be honest, I can't trust you to be in charge of Jake. Maybe when you've grown up a bit.'

Oh, hell. I believe I heard my mother speak through my mouth. I accused my child of being immature and threatened to punish her unless she grows up. My hands reach up and tug at my turkey neck. I look down and see, with despair in my heart, that I am wearing squarish sensible shoes.

'Melissa?' I heave myself up backwards to sit beside her on the table. It's time to be straight-forward. 'Don't do it anymore. I don't understand what's going on and I don't care. Don't be mean. That's all. Don't be mean. If someone's mean to you, come and tell me. Don't be mean back. Don't call people names, don't tease them, don't try to scare them.'

'Mmm.'

'No nasty notes. Don't encourage Jake.'

She stares down at her shoes.

'I mean it, Melissa Boskovic. I am so ashamed that my child is a bully. Those kids have come from a war zone! You should be helping them.'

Tony told me once that his great grandfather migrated to Australia during the gold rush. It's only dawning on me now that the name Boskovic might actually come from the region of that war zone. My kids could carry the same kind of blood as the children they are tormenting. When Helen and I were watching TV reports of the war and the ethnic cleansing, we talked about how we might behave if we were in a war. Would we be cowards? Would we be able to kill someone? War must make you do things you never imagined. Now that thought only makes me feel worse about my children, brought up in a safe quiet country town and still behaving like bullies. What is their excuse? What is mine for raising them to be like this?

Melissa's voice has risen an octave. 'They started it! It's not fair. I get the blame and she's the one that said I'm a liar and everyone believed her and not me!'

'What did you say that she would call you a liar?'

Melissa flushes. 'Nothing.'

'I'm warning you, young lady. I want the truth, or no trip to Melbourne.'

'I said my dad was a spy who was undercover.'

Tony an undercover spy? In the middle of these terrible negotiations, that nearly makes me laugh. 'I see,' I say in my most serious voice. 'And is that because he's not around?'

'Yes,' Melissa mumbles miserably.

'But most of the children in the school don't have a father around.'

'Yeah, but they're losers.'

'So are we losers too?'

'No!' she shouts indignantly. 'That's the point!'

'Don't you realize that bullies are losers? They're the real losers because everyone's scared of them. No one respects them and absolutely no one likes them.'

She turns her head and looks off into the distance.

'I won't have it, Liss. You stop this rubbish, or I'll come to the school myself and make you apologize to those children.' I can see the tremor of horror that goes through her at the idea of me turning up in her classroom. 'Will you promise to stop? To stay away from that girl and those children and not say nasty things to them?'

'What if they say something to me? Or Jake? What am I supposed to do then?'

Biff them, is what I want to say, because I hate the idea of anyone being nasty to my children. But that is exactly what a bully might do. And I am supposed to be the adult here. 'You ignore them, and you walk away. And if it goes on you tell me or your teacher. Clear?'

Melissa nods, still looking off to the horizon.

Maybe it's one of those situations you get into where you can't see a way out until someone tells you to stop. Two weeks of holiday are coming up. Even that might be enough. Kids move on, forget their enemies and turn them into best friends.

'And sweetie, you do know you're not fat, don't you?' The girl's comment is obviously why Melissa wouldn't change into her bathers and swim at the waterhole that day, and why she's been wearing winter clothes in the hot weather. I'd thought it was some weird fashion thing. It had crossed my mind that she might be anorexic, but her continuing enthusiastic appreciation of food of any kind eased my mind on that issue. 'That girl only said you were fat to make you feel bad. She was retaliating, that's all. You're not fat at all.'

'Really?' she says, hesitantly.

'Your grandmother told me she thought you were a skinny thing, and she never lets tact or flattery get in the way of her opinion.' I put my arm around Melissa and pull her close. 'Remember when she told us that we looked like escapees from Outer Woop Woop?'

She nods.

'And the time she thought Jake might be retarded because he couldn't tie his shoelaces? He was only three.'

She nods again, and giggles. 'And when she said you looked like an English sheepdog after you spent all that money on a haircut in Melbourne.'

That smarts. I'd forgotten that particular remark. I'd thought my new cut was rather stylish, and I'd been practising a sultry look from beneath my feathery fringe until we went to visit Mum.

'OK then. Now come with me while I get Jake out of that damn toilet.'

She jumps off the table, no doubt relieved that our little chat is over.

When we reach the toilet block, Melissa calls from outside.

'Jake, let's go! We're ready to go home.'

'Am I in trouble?' His high voice echoes around the concrete walls.

'Only if you don't come out immediately,' I answer. A boy-toilet stink of ammonia clings to the block. I hope he doesn't smell like that when he gets into the car.

'Liss, I want Jake to understand what I've told you. You have to be an example to him. All right?'

Melissa nods. Her sandy hair is whipping against her cheeks. Her eyes are red.

I remember how hard school is, especially when you are growing breasts and having hormone storms. In Patsy's class one girl tried to bleach her moustache because the other girls were laughing at her and she ended up in hospital with a blistered lip. Every day for a month in grade seven someone put a note in my desk with a description of another of my horrible features. 'Your nose is so bent they named a hairpin after it.' 'Your hands are so ugly they won't serve you in shops.' I kept up a brave face at school and went home and sobbed every night.

CHAPTER 23

Yesterday I drove down to Melbourne, dropped the kids at Patsy's house, visited Tammy and did a wee in her toilet that blows air up your bottom to dry it, then drove back in the dark. This morning I set to cleaning the house thoroughly, giving it a scrub like it hasn't seen in years. Twenty minutes later, I am exhausted. I need to ring Helen. I've been a cow and I have to make it up to her.

'Please forgive me. I was worried about the kids and I was being a bitch. No wonder they're bullies.' I take a breath. 'Let's go to Halstead tonight and have dinner and a bottle of wine. My shout.'

'I don't know. I'd have to check with my therapist first.'

'Helen, please. I'm so sorry.'

Silence. I wait. The house pulsates with the germs I've failed to destroy, the dust lurking in every crevice, the piles of dirty washing.

'Don't ever say that kind of thing to me again, Loretta.'

'I won't. I won't, Helen, because it's not true and I didn't even mean it. I'm really sorry.'

If she could see me now, flooded with shame, she wouldn't need to tell me not to do it again. After Tony left, it was my friends who pulled me and the kids through. Friends like Helen and Norm. And without them, I'd have to play bingo or join the CWA to pass the time. I'll do anything to keep them onside.

After a rattling bus ride from Gunapan through the slums of outer Halstead, Helen and I end up at the Taste of India. We order lamb korma and butter chicken, which are suspiciously alike except in colour, leaving us with the impression that there is only one taste in India, before walking to the pizza and pasta place in the mall for dessert. Helen pops the second champagne cork and we toast each other again, finding each other's lame jokes hilarious and laughing like we've had too much to drink. We toast again.

'Good evening, ladies. Your menus.'

The last time I saw Bowden he was chatting up girls at the Gunapan waterhole, wearing jeans that were way too big for him and a grubby singlet that showed off his skinny white arms. His nose was scarlet with sunburn and when he stopped squinting to glance around at me he had white lines around his eyes where the sun hadn't reached.

'Hi Loretta,' he'd said as I walked by on my way to deliver a tube of suncream to Helen.

'Mrs Boskovic to you, Bowden,' I replied.

'Bowie to you, Mrs Boskovic,' he muttered.

I was tempted to give him a clip over the head until I noticed his family a little way up the hill.

'Hi,' I called up, smiling and waving. Not that I thought Bowden's father would ever hurt me, but even an accidental bump from someone with shoulders that wide could break your collarbone.

'Thank God you're here,' Helen said, grabbing the cream from my outstretched hand. 'I've completely destroyed the effect of the facial I had yesterday and gained ten more years.'

'I don't think smearing your face with yoghurt and laying slices of potato over the top can be called a facial.'

'It's the poor woman's facial, Loretta. And I had no cucumber.'

That was last summer. Now here is a brand-new Bowden, standing beside our table in ironed black pants and a white shirt, with a snowy napkin draped over his forearm and a pencil moustache so narrow and perfectly shaped that I think he might have drawn it on.

'Could we have the dessert menu please, Bowden.'

'Ladies, please call me Bowie.' He's using a voice much deeper than the one he uses to order a hot pie and sauce at the milk bar. He saunters away and pushes through the swing door to the kitchen.

'So. Have you heard about the mechanic?' Helen leans in conspiratorially.

'Merv Bull?'

'Yes, Merv Bull,' she answers impatiently. 'He had a date with Maxine.'

'Maxine?' I keep smiling, trying to hide the glum face underneath. When I went to see Merv Bull for my wiper blades I thought I felt something. A flutter. A hint in the way he looked at me, the way he said I was welcome to a tune anytime. I read all kinds of innuendo into that line. So I was going to get tuned, I mean get the car tuned, except that Terror learned to open the gate latch and ruined everything. She somehow found her way to the alpaca farm and started cosying up to the alpaca herd. I thought it must be some kind of identity problem. And who would blame her, living with us? But apparently goats need constant company. Norm never mentioned that when he delivered our lawnmower. I ended up taking in another goat, Terror's sister, who Melissa immediately named Panic. So the money I had set aside for some well-earned tuning went on extra feed costs. Now it looks like I've lost my chance at a thorough tune-up.

In the Merv Bull stakes, Helen had positioned herself at tight odds, thanks to a split radiator hose, a dud alternator, and a full service including cleaning the fuel injectors and adjusting the computer.

'It's cost me a fortune, but I think he's about to ask me on a date,' she told me a couple of weeks ago. 'Kyleen was the odds-on favourite because she's so pretty, until she accidentally ran over his dog when she was backing her car out of the yard.'

'Oh!'

'Don't worry, the dog's OK. Those heelers are built of steel. The car bounced off the dog, only gave it a fright. Merv had been shouting and waving at Kyleen to stop and she'd thought he was waving goodbye so she took her hands off the wheel to wave back. That's when they heard the yelp. Kyleen said Merv wasn't so friendly after that. So I think I'm closing in. Probably four to one now.'

Things have obviously changed since then.

'Maxine. Who'd have thought.' I can't deny I'm disappointed. A whisper of hope was thrilling me for a moment back there.

Bowden appears and produces the dessert menus with a flourish, before backing away to stand against the wall with his hands demurely locked in front of him as if he's the maître d' in a five-star restaurant.

'Is he making fun of us?' Helen whispers.

'I believe so. No tip for him.'

'He'll really miss that two dollars.'

We call him over and order the tiramisu to share and, when Bowden is gone, Helen pours us a sobering glass of water. The only other people in the restaurant are an older couple sitting near the wood-fired oven that's shaped like a clay igloo. The man is red and sweating. Outside the windows of the restaurant, the Halstead mall is lit by thin

243

light. Neon brand names flicker feebly in shop windows, and every now and then kids in groups push each other past the window.

'So do you think Melissa will stop what she's been doing to the foreign kids? What about the girl? She might want to complain.'

I tell Helen about getting the cruel notes when I was at school. 'I didn't want revenge. I wanted to pretend no one had ever called me ugly.'

It must be the champagne. My throat is tightening at the memory of the notes. I would sit at my desk wondering all day who had written them and why they hated me so much.

'Are you going all soppy on me, Loretta?'

I shake my head. Take another sip of champagne with a water chaser. The tiramisu arrives and we both scoop our spoons into the soft creamy centre. That school episode never had a proper end. One day there was no note. After that I never had another one. Once I realized it was over I cried with relief.

'This tiramisu is almost as good as Caramellos.'

'Hey, look.' Helen points with her spoon.

Vaughan, the mayor, is walking arm in arm with his wife past the window of the restaurant.

'Back in a sec.' I drop my spoon on the table and fling my napkin on the chair as I get up. Even as I stand I can see the mayor glimpse the movement from the corner of his eye. His eyes widen when I wave at him, and he waves back quickly then grips his wife's arm and starts walking fast, away from the restaurant. He can't beat me though. I've been chasing goats around the back-yard and I have legs like pistons.

'Vaughan!' My voice echoes against the shop windows in the empty mall.

'Hi Loretta. Great job on the school, we must have a meeting about what to do next,' he calls back over his shoulder, still scurrying along at a surprisingly speedy pace and dragging his wife behind him.

'I need a signature from you for the next letter to the minister,' I shout, even though I've nearly caught up. They stop, panting, and I lean over to catch my breath.

'How dare you,' the mayor's wife, whose name I have forgotten, says to me. In the neon light of the mall, the fine spray from her mouth looks like a tiny rainbow-sheened fountain. She is dressed in black trousers and an orange silky top as if she's been out to a fancy dinner. Rings glint on her fingers. She has a gravelly voice like a transves-tite, but I'm fairly sure she's not.

'Pardon?'

'Why are you making trouble like this? You should be looking after your children, not running around like a nutcase. Everyone knows you're only trying to get attention. You're probably trying to get on to council yourself, is that it? You're going to stand for election?'

'What?' I'm gobsmacked.

'Leave us alone. Don't you think you've done enough this week?'

'Vaughan? What's this about?'

The mayor looks at his feet. Or, if he could see his feet he would be looking at them. 'Loretta, I think you went a bit far with the newspaper.'

'What?' My vocabulary has shrunk to one word thanks to all the champagne.

When the wife leans in close to me I stumble backwards. I don't want to be standing in the shower when she speaks.

She points at my chest. Her finger isn't exactly poking me, but I can almost feel the pressure on my breastbone. 'Who do you think you are?'

'Darling, don't get upset.' Vaughan takes his wife's arm, the one not pointing at me, and tugs her away. 'We don't know for sure it was Loretta.'

'What?' I say one more time.

'Of course it was her. She's the one who keeps sending out those endless letters about the school. She's the one who's always putting up signs and calling meetings. And she hangs around with that old junk man. I told you, Vaughan, she did it for him, to get that Unsightly Property Notice lifted.'

'Stop calling me HER!' I shout.

'What?' Vaughan and his wife say together.

'I don't know what you're talking about. Why can't we discuss this like . . .' My words peter out as I wonder what I'm trying to say. 'What *are* you talking about?'

'Don't get me started.' The wife's lips are all tight and wrinkly. 'Vaughan, let's go.' She swings around, her shiny silk top rippling in shades of orange and ochre in the mall light.

'I'll call you, Loretta,' he mutters as he turns to follow her, but she finishes the conversation for him. 'You certainly will not. Goodbye.'

'Whoa.' I flop back in my seat at the table. 'Have you read the newspaper lately?'

'The *Shire Herald*? Of course not. That's five minutes of my day I don't want to waste.'

'I'll have to go to the library.'

Helen pours more champers into my glass while I spoon up another velvety mouthful of the tiramisu.

'I've got news. I had a date too,' Helen says.

I stare, open-mouthed, which must be disgusting considering what I'm eating.

'Last week. At the Thai restaurant down the road. I had green curry. We drank two bottles of wine. Then we had another date on Saturday. And spent a day together.'

'Don't make me ask.'

'Peter Rudnik.' She grins at me.

I think that, in my thirteen years here, I have met every living person within twenty minutes' drive of Gunapan. Who is Peter Rudnik? It's obvious Helen expects me to know. 'And . . . it was good?'

'It was fun. He relaxes when he's out of that environment. He's got a good sense of humour. And we're exactly the same height.'

I'm starting to suspect. 'So he's not gay, then?'

'Definitely not. And he's some kisser. Found that out at the end of the night on the first date.'

'At the end of the day, you mean.'

'Oh, ha ha. Everyone has things they say all the time. It's a habit.'

'You sly dog. You kissed the grade-three teacher!'

'Oh yeah.'

'I'm jealous.'

'I know,' she says triumphantly.

'Actually, I have a prospect of my own.'

'A biker?'

'No, this one drives an Audi. He's widowed, a tragic light plane crash that only he survived. His grown-up children put in together to console him with a beach house at Sorrento and an annual trip to Tuscany.'

Helen is still grinning.

'Are you going out again?'

'Wednesday on a picnic. It's school holidays, so he's free for two weeks.'

'I'm very, very jealous.'

'I know.' If she was grinning any wider her face would split.

'If you get together with him, seriously, he has to join the Save Our School Committee Mark II.'

'I'll keep that in mind.'

'In fact, he has to be an office-bearer.'

'I like him.' She shakes her head at me and I laugh before plunging my spoon deep into the tiramisu.

'Eat up,' I tell her. 'You're going to need your strength.'

'For what?'

'For when you start the horizontal foxtrotting.'

Helen belts out a laugh and has to catch bits of tiramisu in her napkin. 'Too late. We've already practised the foxtrot, the waltz and the barn dance.'

CHAPTER 24

'Looking a bit the worse for wear,' Norm says when I lean in the doorway of the shed.

'Tired,' I mutter. Last night with Helen was fun, but I got home and cried about the kids and their bullying and how the mayor's wife told me I should be looking after them better and woke up ten times during the night and thought I heard a murderer coming in the back door and lay rigid for five minutes with my heart hammering until I realized it was Terror and Panic burping and butting each other on the outside stairs. Now that I'm up and about, the sparkly morning light has penetrated my exhausted hungover head and is making my brain wrinkle.

Norm stands up and pulls a seat from underneath a pile of newspapers, which cascade gracefully down to form a new pile on the ground. He empties the dregs of a cold cup of tea outside the shed door, wipes the rim of the cup on his shirt hem and switches on the kettle.

'Hey, are any of those newspapers current?' I

ask, remembering what the mayor's wife said last night.

'You saw it, then?' Norm's smiling.

'What?' I'm starting to hate myself for this word.

He points to a sheet of newspaper tacked to the cupboard door at the back of the shed. I get up and walk closer so I can read it. It's the front page of Saturday's edition of the *Shire Herald*. A perfect specimen of Norm's thumbprint in oil adorns the margin.

'"Councillors Need Probe",' I read aloud and laugh. 'They shouldn't let that cadet write the headlines. Last night the mayor's wife nearly punched me out, I guess because of this.'

'Apparently,' Norm says with a feigned look of horror, 'not all our councillors are as honest as they should be.'

It's hard to be shocked. Everyone knows local councils are about people making sure their friends' building projects are approved and travelling overseas on 'research' missions and getting their names in the paper.

'But Vaughan? I can't believe Vaughan is corrupt.'

'It's not Vaughan. He's all right. But he's been letting the others get away with things. We all have. I'm not putting up with it anymore, Loretta. They've gone too far.'

'There's oil all over the newsprint on this, Norm. I'll read the article at the library. Where's Justin?'

'He's at work. Got two weeks at the abattoir. Hates it.' Norm glances at the dashboard clock attached to a car battery on the bench. 'His shift will be over soon.'

An odd smell is permeating the shed. Usually it smells of metal and oil with a hint of old hamburger. I sniff and try to figure it out, but my senses are out of whack today. It seems to be a clean smell. In this shed where every surface is marked with the liquid tools of Norm's trade – oil, petrol, grease, beer and tea – it is a very odd smell indeed.

'Has he been cleaning up in here?'

'Justin? Not in here. He knows better than to mess with my filing system. Mind you, he keeps that room of his tidy. Must be all those years in a cell.'

Norm turns off the whistling kettle and pours hot water into my cup, then drops a teabag into it. He offers me milk, but I always think it's wise to stay away from dairy goods that have been sitting opened in Norm's shed for any length of time.

'It's quiet at my place, Norm. Terror's missing Melissa. She stands at the back door burping, then she chases Panic around the yard.'

'She's a goat. Goats burp and play. And the kids have only been away two days.'

We sit in the warm shed blowing on our tea and sipping it slowly. I move my feet closer to Norm's two-bar radiator under the table.

'Have you—'

Norm raises his hand for me to stop speaking. He nods towards the transistor, where the race caller is screaming like an assault victim. We wait until the caller has reached his highest pitch and sobbed out the result. Norm sighs.

'Bloody old nag. Knew it wouldn't win.'

'So why did you bet on it?'

'Justin did. He's done his tenner. I told him he should put five each way on that old crock, but he likes to put his money on the nose. So, Loretta, heard you had a word with the kids.'

How is it, I ask myself, that everyone knows these things about me? I talked to my children on Bald Hill out of sight and hearing of everyone except the fat black crow hopping around the rubbish bin, and somehow Norm has heard about it.

'I see,' I answer huffily. 'And what did I tell them?'

'They'll be all right now. Things get out of hand, that's all. Kids don't know how to stop. Yep, I think it's going to be fine.'

He reaches under the table and pulls out an old tin.

'You deserve a biscuit.' It takes him a while to prise the lid off the tin, but when he does, a delicious aroma of orange-cream biscuits drifts out.

'How old are these?' I turn my biscuit over and examine it for signs of mould. It's worth asking, because I'm fairly sure that lid was rusted on.

'Those use-by dates are a con so we'll throw things out. Don't take any notice of them, Loretta.'

While Norm talks I can feel something happening in my head. Like a depth charge. A thought begins deep in my tired and fuzzy brain-stem, working its way through the left and right hemispheres and out to the surface. I become convinced that the smell I caught before was antiseptic. Antiseptic is a smell I have never experienced in Norm's vicinity. And it smells like my mother. The connection sparks. Or it would do if I had any spark left in my brain. What happens is more like an underwater explosion. The smell is what I smelled back when we visited Mum in hospital.

'Heard you went into town last week,' I say casually before slurping some hot tea. It tastes good and bitter. I take another sip. The caffeine is definitely helping to wake me up.

'I think that's Justin now.' Norm inclines his head.

All I can hear is a faint whine somewhere down the road. Out in the yard the dogs start barking as if they know Justin's coming too. He's length-ened their chains and started feeding them more regularly. Norm told me he even walks them some-times.

'By the way, has that dog near the gate changed colour?'

'He washed them. He's turning them into bloody lapdogs.'

'Right. He's probably booked them in for a spa and massage too.'

The whine is becoming a throb. A rhythmic pulsing throb powering down the road towards us.

'What is that noise?' The throb sounds a little like what was happening in my head all night as I lay awake fretting.

'The boy bought himself a Honda 500cc on the never-never.'

Justin pulls up outside the shed with a spurt of gravel, swings his leg over the bike and eases off his helmet. Norm's already poured him a cup of tea by the time he gets inside the shed. Justin nods at me as he pulls out a chair from behind a cupboard. Norm's shed is like a magician's trunk. Whenever you want something you reach under the table or behind a cupboard, and presto, there it is.

'Have you told her?' he says to Norm.

Norm shrugs and turns up the radio. Justin reaches over and turns it back down again.

'Tell her.'

'What am I, a child?' Norm's using his long-suffering voice, the one he puts on whenever he complains about the poor return on scrap metal.

I'll sit quietly and mind my own business while they bicker. I wonder how Norm's enjoying being a parent again. At least he's past the stage of cleaning up vomit. And he doesn't have to drive Justin to school and back every day. If we moved closer to the school Melissa and Jake could walk. I'd save a good forty minutes each day, which I could then use sewing chic evening wear and looking after my skin. My scrag-woman image would slowly fade. I'd learn to walk with my head up and my shoulders back, instead of hurrying around like the hunchback of Gunapan. But we could never afford a proper yard that close to the school. What would we do with Terror and Panic? I've grown rather fond of the goats. They're excellent listeners. Of course, they're not the perfect pets. They do burp a lot. Sometimes it's alarmingly loud. And they do shed a little. Not to mention the poo problem. But they seem so smart. I wonder if they can be house-trained?

'Loretta?'

I pick up my cup of cold tea and smile at Justin. 'Sorry, off in a dream.'

Justin looks down at the table. Norm clears his throat.

'I'm going to lose my hair,' Norm mutters.

'It's a bit late to be realizing that.' I look at his fast-receding hairline.

'From the chemo,' Justin adds.

The whole shed seems to slide sideways. I feel the cup wobble in my hand and I reach up with my other hand to grip it and lower it carefully to the table.

'Chemo?' I repeat.

'The big C. In the liver.' Norm sounds tired.

'Liver?' My voice sounds like an old record.

256

Justin lays his hand on mine. He closes the palm and fingers tightly over the top of my hand and nods at me. One of the dogs in the yard barks and the rest follow, growing louder and crazier until one starts howling.

'Customer.' Norm pushes himself up off the seat.

'I'll get it, Dad.' Justin waves Norm down.

My hand is instantly cold when Justin takes his away. He swings the door open and a gust of chilly air swirls around my ankles.

'Liver cancer? But you're not a drinker.' I should have noticed how thin Norm's got.

'There's only a sixty per cent chance the chemo'll work. I don't want to do it, Loretta. Remember when Jim from the railways had the stomach cancer and they gave him chemo? And he looked like shit and he said he felt like shit and all his hair fell out and he couldn't eat and then he bloody died anyway. What's the point?'

'Sixty per cent, that's the point!' I answer hysterically. 'Norm, what are you talking about? Of course you'll have it. Don't be stupid.'

'If it wasn't for Justin making me swear, I don't think I would.'

'Not for me? Not for Melissa and Jake?'

'Exactly. I don't want your kids to see me looking half-dead. I'd rather they remember me like I am now.'

'Stupid, you mean? You want them to remember you as the stupid man who wouldn't get treatment?'

'Settle down, Loretta. I said I was getting it, didn't I? Justin's made me promise.'

Even in my state of fury, I can see how odd it is that my best friend, the man who is like a grandfather to my children, has told me he's very ill and my reaction is to want to cut his throat. We both look out through the window at Justin, who's listening, head bowed, to a bloke talking as he pulls bits off some kind of engine. We can't hear their conversation from inside because the dogs are still going at full throttle and someone else is driving a pounding ute right up to the door of the shed. Norm heaves himself up off the chair and opens the door.

I don't know what's wrong with me. I look at Norm standing at the door and gesturing the driver to come into the shed, and I want to punch him. I want to slap him. I want to stamp my feet in front of him and scream like a two-year-old having a tantrum. I am furious. I feel as if my heart is about to explode. How dare he be sick? How dare he have cancer?

He comes back into the shed followed by Merv Bull.

'Merv, you remember Loretta, don't you?'

'Of course.' He lowers his voice and turns away from Norm to speak. 'Actually, I was hoping to have a quick word with you if you've got a moment.'

'Sorry, have to rush,' I say. Right now, I need to go home and scream. 'Nice to see you, Merv.'

I set off smiling and waving goodbye and get into the car and rev the engine so hard it almost has a prolapse. Then I scream backwards on to the road before powering off, leaving two smoking streaks of rubber on the tarmac.

CHAPTER 25

Norm's news has given me the strength of seven Lorettas. In six days I've stormed the post office with letters asking for old and potential new SOS committee members to come to the first meeting. I've coaxed sponsorship from the abattoir, the supermarket, the CWA and the winery outside Halstead for a fundraising dinner. I'm organizing an auction on the night of donated goods. So far Leanne's put up a voucher for a spell or hex of the winner's choice, Morelli's Meats has offered a side of beef, Norm's repairing a vintage stationary engine that should be ready for the night, the Church of Goodwill is donating a month's housecleaning and the local pub is giving a dinner for two.

My children's absence has also helped to inspire my burst of activity. Terror and Panic have put on so much weight they look like they're about to have kids of their own. Yesterday I found myself thinking how attractive Terror would look with a ribbon in her beard.

I had dreamed that while Melissa and Jake were away I'd be out at romantic dinners, tossing my newly styled and tipped hair as I laughed and made witty repartee with Merc Man or some other suitably loaded and charming suitor. But I couldn't even get an appointment at the hairdressers until next Tuesday, and once that part of the plan collapsed, it seemed like I'd have to go on with my old life. I'm not allowed to tell Norm's news to anyone, even Helen, but I can't stop thinking about what might happen to him and I can't stop trying not to think about it and I can't sleep. That adds five more hours in the day to fill.

And on top of all that, I can't find out anything about the development. I've failed Norm completely. I've heard plenty of rumours, but no facts.

'Are you sure there's going to be a pool and spa and sauna?' I asked Kyleen.

'Of course,' she scoffed. 'How could you have a top-quality luxury resort without them?'

The whole population of Gunapan, one of the region's most disadvantaged small towns, has become an authority on what makes a top-quality luxury resort.

'I hope they don't get Sleeplover linen,' Brianna remarked. 'It doesn't last. They'll have to go better quality than that. And I can't wait to see what kind of TVs they have.'

'What are you talking about? They won't let us within cooee of the place. Why is everyone being so nice about it?'

'More to the question, Loretta, why are you so mad about it?'

'Because they're taking our water! Because Norm's been landed with an Unsightly Property Notice!'

'It's not our water. Our water comes from the Goonah Reservoir.'

'Which is at fourteen per cent capacity. And we go selling off water that bubbles up out of the ground!' I can hear my voice rising in frustration. Soon I'll be reaching the high notes of opera, only with a kind of whining sound. A lot of complaining goes on around here. We could set up the Gunapan opera company. Performing live every weeknight, the Gunapan Whingers. You pick a topic, we'll complain about it.

Brianna shrugged. 'Anyway, I'm going to get my Responsible Service of Alcohol certificate. Maybe get a job in the bar. I bet those guests will leave good tips.'

'Sure, why don't you help them suck the water out of our town? Well, I'm not going to put up with it. If I'm going to keep campaigning about the school, I might as well campaign about the development too.'

My friends have been as encouraging as usual.

'Give it up, Loretta,' Helen said this morning. She looked down at the latest letter to the Education Minister.

'I can't. It's turned into an addiction. I can't stop writing letters to ministers.'

'Like heroin.' She nodded sympathetically.

'Or beer, but not as pleasant. Actually, it's more like an addiction to ground glass, or whipping yourself with wet rope every morning at dawn.'

'Great. My best friend has turned into a pain junkie.'

'Helen, do you remember what I said when I first started the Save Our School business?'

She shook her head.

'I said that you should tell me if the whole town started to hate me. It's happened, hasn't it?'

'What makes you say that?' Helen inclined her head doll fashion, smiling a fake smile showing no teeth, only tight lips with upturned corners.

'I saw Maxine in the grocery store yesterday. She didn't have time to say hello. You know why? Because she was running. Yes, people are running away from me now.'

'Maybe she was busy?'

'She hadn't bought anything. She dropped a tin of tomatoes as she ran out the front door.'

'I think you're exaggerating, Loretta.'

'I didn't ask her to pay for the biscuits in the meetings.'

Helen rolled her eyes. 'Don't blame me when this obsessive compulsive thing puts you in a strait jacket,' she said on her way out the door.

Underneath every conversation, like having an electric current buzzing through my brain, is the fretting about Norm. Each day I ring or drop in and try not to ask him about his health.

'Don't start asking about my health all the time,' he warned me on Monday. 'I know what a terrier you are. I'll tell you if there's anything you need to know.'

So I don't. I've been pestering Justin instead. Yesterday Justin asked me if I wanted to know about Norm's bowel movements.

'Well,' I said dubiously, 'I suppose. If it's important.'

Justin looked away, smiling.

'Oh, you were joking.' I thought I should probably go home. Norm's illness seemed to have stripped me of my sense of humour.

'He's doing OK. Really.' Justin was still smiling. Thought he was a pretty funny bloke.

'Hey, forgot to mention, you're signed up for the Save Our School and Stop Our Development Committee. Norm said you're good at maths, so you're the treasurer.'

No more smiling for Mr Funny Man. I pulled a meeting flyer from my handbag and dropped it on the table. He's not really the treasurer, but neither is anyone else, and since he didn't say an immediate no, I think I might have done something smart for a change.

'See you tomorrow night!' I called back gaily over my shoulder on my way out of the shed.

This afternoon I remembered to drop into the library and read the article in the *Shire Herald* about the council needing a probe. I had to race a fifteen-year-old for the only comfortable chair in the place, and when I beat him he stood against the opposite wall sulking. Talk about needing a probe. Brenda should teach that boy some manners.

Council Needs Probe
It has been leaked to the Shire Herald *that last year certain shire councillors and council staff took trips, sometimes with spouses and children, which our source claims were paid for by a corporation involved in land acquisition in the shire. Three of these trips were to Western Australia, ostensibly to investigate small-scale agriculture, and included winery tours and boat cruises. The cost of the trips is estimated by the* Herald *at approximately forty thousand dollars.*

And I was worried about the amount of petrol it took to drive the kids to Melbourne.

It has been suggested by the source close to the council that there are inappropriate links between council and local builders, as well as larger development companies based out of the shire. The source suggested that there may have been intervention in planning processes for building applications that violate the local building codes.
The Shire Herald *is also investigating allegations that a major development company*

made large campaign donations before the election, but that these donations were not declared.

Hot stuff! No wonder Mrs Mayor almost went at me with her handbag the other night. Even if Vaughan isn't one of the people the article is talking about, he looks like an idiot for letting this go on.

I made twenty copies of the article to bring to the meeting tonight. I had already changed the night of the meeting so we wouldn't be competing with the Church of Goodwill so this time we're in the big room. Brianna has offered to mind the kids again – she really has no fear.

When I arrive, Helen's sitting alone in a circle of orange plastic chairs at the front of the room, reading. Behind her is the stage where every year the Halstead Players do a performance of a musical, which has been *The Sound of Music* five years out of eight. We Gunapanians feel obliged to pay good money to hear them yowling and yodelling, then tell them over a cup of tea afterwards how much we loved it.

Helen looks up as I head for the board to write up the agenda. 'Peter sent his apologies. He's had to stay back for a school staff meeting tonight.'

'OK. Good book?'

She turns it over and reads the blurb aloud. '"Heather thinks this holiday in her hometown of Darwin will be just the thing to cheer her up after the breakdown of her marriage. But when she meets a mysterious man claiming to be her long-lost uncle, family secrets emerge that will rock her world and set her on a surprising course to new love." How come thrilling secrets never emerge from my family?'

'I've discovered some dark secrets in mine.'

'Yeah, right.'

'It's true,' I tell her. 'A mysterious man. Five Chihuahuas. A sudden trip to a tropical destination.'

'Your mother marrying a geriatric and retiring to the Gold Coast is not thrilling or mysterious.'

'Here's a real secret. I got the cheque from Mum from the sale of her flat. Five thousand dollars!'

Helen whoops as Justin walks in the door. He's alone.

'Norm not coming?'

Justin shakes his head. 'Next meeting, he says. He's sent me to represent the Stevens.'

'And don't forget you're the treasurer.'

For the next ten minutes I sit on the edge of my vinyl chair biting my nails while Helen reads and Justin wanders around the room, hands clasped behind his back, looking at *Vaccination Works!* and *Literacy Week* posters. The hall is the original building that the community centre has been constructed around. It's panelled in oak and the ceiling is painted the original toilet-block green. On one wall is a portrait of Queen Elizabeth, who never made it to Gunapan on her coronation tour but sent a framed picture instead.

The back wall has the names of all the mayors listed in gold lettering.

I can't wait any longer so I pass them copies of the *Shire Herald* article. 'Did you read this?'

'Typical.' Helen goes back to reading her book.

'I saw a copy on Dad's door,' Justin says. 'And I don't think he's finished with them yet.'

Now Helen looks up. 'Norm's the source? He is full of surprises, that man.'

At seven fifteen, Leanne appears at the door. She looks around the empty room.

'Is this . . .?'

'The Save Our School and Sod Off Development Committee.' I gesture around the empty room. 'Maybe someone's meeting in the room next door, but I haven't heard anything.'

'That's right, I'm here to save the school.' Leanne sweeps into the room. Ever since she re-appeared as Leonora, she's been wearing clothes that sweep and swish and pretty much walk around with a life of their own, while little Leanne gets carried inside. And she loves the heavy jewellery. Tonight she's wearing a necklace and bracelet of ruby-red glass baubles the size of knucklebones.

'Did your mum send you?' I ask.

'I'm not your babysitter anymore, Mrs Boskovic. I'm a grown woman and a practising Wiccan.'

'Sorry, Lea— Leonora. And you'd better call me Loretta.'

'So why are you here?' Helen asks Leanne. 'No offence.'

Justin meanders back to the chair circle and sits beside Leanne.

'That's OK. I want to have kids one day. And I want a proper town for them to grow up in. Everyone thinks I'm weird coming back here, but I like Gunapan.'

Justin and Helen and I nod as we ponder this.

'Why?' I ask finally.

'That's what everyone says! I dunno. It's home.'

'The vision splendid,' Justin murmurs.

'Pardon me?'

'I mean, is it the countryside? Fresh air, all that. You "see the vision splendid of the sunlit plains extended and at night the wond'rous glory of the everlasting stars".'

'I'm guessing you didn't make that up,' Helen says. At least she's showing enough interest now to drop her book into her bag.

'Can you do the whole thing?' Even as the words come out of my mouth I wonder if I've gone too far by asking shy Justin to recite a poem to three women. But he leans back and closes his eyes and starts to intone.

'"I had written him a letter which I had, for want of better knowledge, sent to where I met him down the Lachlan years ago.

He was shearing when I knew him so I sent the letter to him just on spec, addressed as follows, Clancy of the Overflow."'

He continues with the poem. I'm stunned at his memory. I'm lucky if I can remember the three things I went to the supermarket to buy. Quite often I arrive home with seven completely different items, none of which we need. That is why we have a whole cupboard for toilet paper storage. If there is ever a major oil spill in Gunapan, my household will have enough absorbent paper to effect a full clean-up.

'"But I doubt he'd suit the office, Clancy, of the Overflow,"' Justin finishes, and opens his eyes. Which are blue, washed-denim blue.

Leanne and Helen clap wildly.

I can take a joke. 'I see, Justin. You're telling us that Gunapan is "the vision splendid". Obviously it would be from the west with the glowing mountain of Norm's junkyard on the horizon. Or at night, the wondrous glory of the abattoir's all-night shift lighting up the sky. And that must be why you came back, Leanne – sorry, Leonora.'

'Don't worry, everyone still calls me Leanne. I'm not sure about a vision splendid, but it is nice here. And I can rent a house for a quarter of what I'd pay in the city.'

'Yes, Norm's yard.' I'm on a roll. 'The vision splendid. You can see it from the moon – all those bits and pieces of broken machinery glinting in the sunshine. Well, the parts of them that aren't half-rusted away. And it is smack bang in the middle of the, what did you call it, "sunny plains extended"?'

'Settle down, Loretta,' Helen says. 'Norm's yard is so far from splendid it needs a new word. It's

270

a blight on the landscape. So, Justin, do you know any other poems?'

'A few. Had a bit of time for reading. I read a book of poems and they kind of went in without me even trying. I can recite them all.'

'What were you doing?' Leanne leans forwards in her chair.

'Time.'

Leanne opens her mouth to ask the next question, but I jump in. 'Do another one.'

'What kind?' He doesn't look very enthusiastic.

'Anything, honestly, anything. Love poem, hate poem. Whatever.' I'm stalling. If we sit through the time it takes Justin to recite another poem, fifty excited Gunapan citizens might storm the room, pitchforks raised, ready to make kebabs out of the Minister for Education, Social Inclusion and the Service Economy if she won't save our school. Because if someone doesn't arrive soon, I'll break into the wailing country music song of self-pity my mother always hoped would issue in glorious twang from at least one of her daughters. Except without any kind of tune because we've all inherited her tone deafness.

'Another day, maybe.' Justin keeps his head lowered.

We sit in silence for a few more moments.

'All right then, we might as well go home. The Save Our School and Stupid Obnoxious Development Committee is obviously finished.'

No one charges in to protest. At least if Kyleen

was here she'd be telling me not to let the carburettors grind me down, but she's in Halstead working her new job at the cinema's candy bar.

I turn to Leanne. 'I'm sorry you came along for nothing.'

'No, it was good.' She's still staring at Justin.

I think she's in love. A strange bubble forms in my gut. 'I'm sorry everyone. You go, I'll pack up the chairs.'

Against their protests and offers to help tidy up, I herd the three of them out the door and shut it behind them. After I've dragged the chairs back to their spots lining the walls and rubbed the agenda off the whiteboard, I lock the door and head for the car, thinking about the Freedom of Information application I put into the council yesterday to find out about the development. It took me two hours to fill in the forms and, what's worse, it cost twenty-six dollars. I wonder if I can get that money back.

CHAPTER 26

It's dark in the Community Centre car park. We've asked the shire a million times to put some lighting in here. It would serve them right if I got raped and murdered right here on the concrete. Then they'd be sorry. Or I could trip on this poorly maintained surface and crack my head open. I find tears springing to my eyes at the satisfying image of how right I'd be and how sorry they'd feel when they visited me in hospital and found me hovering at the edge of death, pale and delicate, the trauma surgeon – who has fallen in love with my quiet courage – at my bedside wringing his hands and praying for steady nerves to perform the surgery that could save my life.

A rap on the driver's side window makes me jump so high I nearly do end up with head trauma. My heart is still battering the wall of my chest as I wind down the window.

'Didn't mean to startle you. Are you OK?' Justin leans in close.

'Apart from this heart attack?'

'Wondered if you were all right. You sounded a bit wobbly before.'

'Thanks, but I'm fine.' I wait until he's ambled off and the rumble of his motorcycle engine has faded into the distance before I slump into the seat.

This is the freedom I used to dream about. The kids off at their auntie's house and me with a tank full of petrol and an empty evening ahead. I only wish I could think of something to do. Now that mine is the only car left, the gloom in the car park seems to be even darker. In fact, over near the community hall, a patch of darkness is moving as though it's caught on a breeze. Must be the shadow of a tree, I think, until it emerges from the bushes and starts moving towards me.

I know I'm screaming because my ears are hurting, but I don't have any control over it. The darkness slips closer to me as I suck in another lungful of breath and scream again so loudly that the steering wheel thrums. My keys, which were in my lap, have jiggled loose and I know they're on the floor, but I can't lean down in case the black spectre flows into the car and smothers me while I've got my head between my knees. The darkness is pressing in on me and I can't help turning my head and seeing . . . a smiling woman in dark clothes standing outside the car door. I wind down the driver's side window. That's two terrifying moments I've had tonight. I don't think my heart can take it. I must stop reading those books from the Neighbourhood House donations shelf.

'I come to meeting,' says the mother of the

children my kids were bullying. 'Your friend, Mr Stevens, he tell me to come.'

I explain to her that the meeting is over without mentioning that it's because no one came. The night is chilling down. She is shivering and holding her arms close around her.

'Hop in, please.'

'Thank you. Mr Stevens say you bring me home.'

Trust Norm to have worked it out so that we end up together in a confined space. Heroic war widow and mother of four, beautifully dressed on a shoestring budget, well-mannered, helpful and toast of the town, clutching the dashboard and sliding around on the vinyl seat of the Holden beside me, the old scrag, deserted mother of two Gunapan-bred bush pig bullying children. I'm certain Norm only does these things to humiliate me. On the drive back to her house, I find out her name and the correct name of her country and repeat the names to myself twenty times so I won't get them wrong. Mersiha, Bosnia Herzegovina. Mersiha, Bosnia Herzegovina. Mersiha, Bosnia Herzebogova. Mersiha, Bosnia Herzeboggler ... In between gear changes and mental exertions, I attempt chit chat about the weather, about the school, about the annual Kmart underwear sale in Halstead next week.

'It's a highlight of the Gunapan calendar. I'm heading over with Helen and Kyleen first thing Monday. Feel free to come along if you need undies.' The moment I've spoken, it dawns on me

275

that I don't often have the opportunity to converse with people outside my normal circle. Perhaps underwear isn't the most appropriate conversation topic for a first meeting. It will have to do though, because I'm desperate to avoid the other topic, the real topic – my bullying children.

'I find that the elastic only lasts ten to eleven months, which makes these last few weeks before the sale pretty dicey. I try not to run or make too many vigorous movements and that usually—'

'I'm sorry,' Mersiha interrupts.

'Pardon?'

'My children. They say rude things to your children. I am very sorry. They had a hard time. Their father, the war, the camp. I speak to them. I tell them to be kind, to be good—'

I burst in and apologize to her for *my* horrible children. They should have known better. It's my fault, I say. I'm a delinquent mother. I tell her that I'm sending them to the revenge camp for bullies and their bullied where they'll find out what it's like, and she gasps and I have to stop the car and explain that it was only a joke. How stupid am I to make a joke about revenge camp to a woman who has come from a war? Stopping the car also allows her a moment to unclamp her fingers from the edge of the dashboard. Perhaps Melissa is on to something about that refresher driving course.

While we're stopped on the side of the road near the turn-off to the old MacInerny place, the headlights of the car catching flitting night bugs and a few seedy grass heads in their beams, I make Mersiha promise she will tell me if my children ever bully her children again.

'My children too, please tell me if they say the bad things again. What is the word they say to your children? Bogan? I think it means bad thing.'

That's depressing. My children are being called bogans. I admit, I have occasionally called myself a bogan in jest, mainly when I was wearing sheep-skin slippers or enjoying an AC/DC song on the radio. But I'm not a bogan. Bogans are proud wearers of checked flannelette shirts and trackie-daks as their costume of choice. Women bogans colour their hair auburn and swear loudly, all the time, while swigging beer from long-necked bottles. Or there are the new bogans, the over-the-hill footballers who end up living in ridiculous houses and appearing on TV shows being rude to their fans, or the multi-millionaire children of successful businessmen who swan about the world in tasteless expensive fashion and cockatoo hair-styles trying to be photographed. No, neither of those types are me, I'm certain. If my children are bogans, they must have got it from their father.

'Mrs Loretta?' Mersiha presses her warm hand on my arm. 'Are you all right?'

I nod glumly and put the car into gear. The tyres spin on the gravel on the side of the road as we take off, sounding suitably boganish. As we turn into her road I start on the polite questions she

277

must have heard a hundred times. How long she's been in Australia. Where she lived before. Her family.

'My husband was killed in war.' She shakes her head in the dark car beside me, as if she wants to shake out what she has just said.

'I'm sorry. It must be so hard for you.'

'No!' she says so loudly I almost slam my foot on the brake before I realize she's not angry. 'No, please do not be sorry for me. For us. Everyone always staring at us, always sorry.' She thumps her hand against the dashboard. The radio turns on, but she doesn't seem to notice. 'I do not want sorry.'

'I see.' I hesitate. Should I stop asking her questions?

'No one ask me about my husband because they are so sorry. When they introduce me, they say this is Mersiha, the refugee.'

'Right.' I'm treading carefully because this is exactly the kind of moment where I'm likely to say the wrong thing.

'I am more than refugee. I am normal person. My kids, they are normal kids. We want to be normal, not always everyone so sorry, so sorry.'

'Got it.'

Driving down the road to her house, I think about what she said. One day I will ask about her husband. When we reach the house, the veranda light is on and the monster dog is lying in its usual spot.

'That is an enormous dog.' I remark.

'You know this dog?' Her eyes are wide. 'You know who belong to this dog? Please take this dog!'

'You mean it's not yours? Who feeds it?' I wonder if she used to have more children.

'I do not know. In the morning it goes away. In the afternoon it comes back and stays all the time until the next morning.'

While we sit in the car talking, the ancient evil woman I saw the day I came here twitches open the curtain to the left of the front door and spears me with a death ray.

'My grandmother,' Mersiha says. 'She is very old.'

No kidding. I think she might be a first cousin of Methuselah. 'I'll get Norm to take the dog to the pound. And thanks for coming to the meeting. The committee is finished, though. No more Save Our School.' I have to admit it. I've failed.

Mersiha shrugs. 'That is too bad.'

'But if you'd like to join a committee, the Neighbourhood House Management Committee has a vacancy coming up.' At last, we might have a committee member who doesn't own a four-wheel drive and property. They won't be happy about that. I feel an uncharitable glee. We could stack the committee with migrants, refugees and bogans. Of course, we'd never get another grant. We're supposed to help the disadvantaged, not be the disadvantaged.

'Please, come inside. A cup of tea.'

I tell her I'd better head off. It's only eight o'clock, so I'll drop by and ask Norm to take care of the monster dog. Another excellent excuse to see how he's doing.

The screech of my car tyres must have alerted Justin. He's standing in the doorway of Norm's place, framed by light, when I walk up the drive.

'Loretta?'

'That's me,' I reply, still chuffed at the thought of our new Neighbourhood House committee member.

'How did you know?'

The thumping of my heart begins as a slow erratic stutter and quickly rises to a fast drum roll.

'Know what?'

'He's gone in the ambulance to Halstead. I'm about to follow.'

CHAPTER 27

'Stop it,' I tell Norm.

He breathes quietly. His chest lifts the bed sheet in a small, quick billow, like a puff of air under a silk dress. He is sunburned dark brown against the whiteness of this hospital ward, with the scar on his forehead a lighter colour, as though he has missed with the fake tan.

'Stop this rubbish and wake up, Norm.'

I take his hand and rub it briskly in mine. Justin sits on the other side of the bed watching as I fuss around. Norm's hand feels strange. The skin slides over the flesh and bones like a soft glove when I rub, as if his body has separated into different parts.

The doctor told us earlier that Norm might not wake up.

'Don't be stupid. Of course he'll wake up,' I replied.

The doctor nodded sympathetically at me as if I was the sick one.

'He's repairing a stationary engine for my

auction,' I explained. 'It's one of the big-ticket items.'

He nodded again and patted me on the arm before moving to a bed further down the unit.

I'm tucking the bed sheet more neatly under the bed when I think Norm has stopped breathing. With my heart banging so loudly I can't hear anything anyway, I lean down and place my ear against his chest. The sparse grey hairs tickle my ear. His chest rises to meet my ear and Norm's warmth presses against my cheek. I stand up and take a deep shuddering breath. No matter how much air I suck in, I can't get enough into my lungs, as if I'm leaking from a thousand tiny pinpricks.

'Loretta, sit down,' Justin says.

'Did he knock back treatment? I'll kill him if he refused the chemo.'

I move Norm's hand gently along the heavy cotton sheet. His other hand is wired up. So is his nose and there's another line snaking up under the bedclothes from a machine on a wheelie stand beside the bed.

'What's wrong with him?' I hear my voice becoming increasingly shrill. 'He said he'd be fine. He said even if he didn't have treatment he'd be alive for years.'

'He has been having treatment. It's an infection. The doctor just told us that, Loretta.'

Justin stands up. He pats his own cheeks as if he's trying to wake himself up.

'You go home. I'll call you if there's a change,' he says.

'No, I'm here till he wakes up.'

'Mum's coming soon. We're only allowed two visitors at a time.'

So that's it. I'm being thrown out. My life with Norm tossed aside by a son who hasn't seen him for fourteen years and a wife who dumped him. I never did understand the story of the prodigal son. The one who has been good and faithful and devoted all those years is taken for granted while the one who abandoned his family gets a party and a pig on a spit. What's right about that?

My feeling of airlessness grows even stronger in this stuffy hospital room. I'd better get home and clean up for the kids. They'll be home the day after tomorrow. I have to make a good home for them so they don't go out and rob a bank and go to jail and abandon me, then waltz back in after fourteen years and turf out the poor sods who've been my good friends while they were gone.

I can't even squeeze out a goodbye. I swing around and charge out through the open door of the ward, wheel past the nurses' station and thunder down the hallway, tears blurring my vision and a trail of runny snot winding its way around my top lip.

★　★　★

At home, Terror edges her way hesitantly into the kitchen and begins nosing around the kitchen table.

'Help yourself,' I tell her as I take the kettle to the sink to fill it.

Panic clatters into the room and butts her way past Terror to join in.

A bar of soap sits on the kitchen window sill for Norm to wash his hands when he comes to tea. He is everywhere in this house. Lemons from the tree in his yard fill the fruit bowl. Terror, his lawnmowing gift to us, stands in front of me with her spooky green eyes. I pull her close and she burrows her head into my armpit. Her coat smells of hay and eucalyptus. She's wearing a bell that Norm welded together from a Toyota cylinder housing and the key to an old tractor.

At eight in the evening I drive back to the hospital. The nurse making notes at the nurses' station tells me that Norm has two relatives with him, so I'll have to wait in the visitors' room at the end of the floor. A man and a child are waiting in there too. The little girl sits astride her father's knee playing an electronic game while he stares, with the same hollowed expression as mine, at the gaudy figures on the television screen flickering silently on its bracket above us. As the minutes tick on, I wish my children were here for me to hold, to hug tight, even though I know it is better that they don't have to experience this descent, this excavation of hope. The longer I wait, the more I sense the dreadful impending absence of my closest friend.

At nine twenty, Justin and Marg walk slowly past the visitors' room towards the lifts. Marg is weeping. Neither of them sees me.

At nine twenty-four I stand beside Norm's bed. An orderly waits at the entrance to the intensive care unit. Around us the hospital is alive with the sounds of coughs and televisions and muttering and squeaky trolley-wheels and the hum of machinery. The activity makes the silence and stillness at this bed seem like a hollow core.

Norm's face is stubbled with grey as usual. His head is turned to the side, as if he was looking off to the horizon before he closed his eyes. I lean my face down to his, dripping tears on to his creased skin. No breath comes from his mouth. No smart-alec comments, no bad jokes, no deadpan asides. He isn't telling me off anymore, or shaking his head in disbelief.

'Take your time,' the orderly says before he draws the curtain around me and Norm.

I sit down on the bed beside his long skinny body. I take his cool hand in mine, examine the fingernails, their black rinds of grease from broken machines and rusty spare parts. I press his cobbled fingertips against my cheek. I imagine I can feel his body turning into something other than Norm, powering down to a cold hard object like a machine that has been turned off.

He has no last words for me. I turned my back and he slipped away.

'Damn you. Damn you, Norm Stevens.'

CHAPTER 28

When I wake up the next day, the house is roaring with emptiness. I lie in bed most of the day waiting. Waiting, like the house, for Norm to appear, his narrow frame leaning against the doorjamb. Waiting for the phone to ring so he can ask me to drop by and help him get the lid off a jam jar. He could fix any machine, could build anything given enough time, but he could never get the lids off jam jars. Or maybe that was an excuse to ask me to come around. The house creaks with faint echoes of his voice. It is so unbelievable that he is gone that I doze and wake up with a shout of shock. He's not coming around. How will I tell the kids? My breath is all caught up in my chest like a wound-up scarf. How will I tell the kids?

When I wake up the next morning I know I have to drive. I stop at the hole in the wall in Halstead and take out money for petrol. I fill the tank of the Holden, and I head out to the highway. An emptiness seems to follow me, so I put down my foot and speed along the bitumen past the Myrnabool junction until I reach a road I've never heard of, and I turn off. Thoughts about how to tell the kids, whether to call them at Patsy's or wait, drift into my mind but I push them out. I don't want to think, only cover distance, feel the tarmac grumbling against my tyres, the engine throbbing and choking and roaring as I swing around curves, accelerate through level crossings, fly up and down the hills of the countryside. Always the emptiness looming up behind me like a darkness in the rear-view mirror.

I drive past houses with neat trim gardens and colourful flowerbeds, past broken-down shacks whose roofs are rusted and patched with tin. Past farms of fluorescent green canola and past dry dusty paddocks where sheep scratch around for a few stalks of yellowed grass. Through single-road towns with one general store and one pub, a park bench outside for the smokers, an antique shop and someone selling free-range eggs from a self-service stand on the side of the road. Through bigger towns with a bakery sending out the stink of confectionery sugar and a fish and chip shop with a Friday family special painted on the window. I gun the Holden up hills to local look-outs from where the vast flat plains of the country stretch out and a tired old sign declares this to be a place where Burke and Wills stopped on their ill-fated trip.

On a road outside a grain town I see a small half-starved brindle dog trotting along the verge of the road and I cry. The reptile tourist park near the Goonah Reservoir has a hand-painted tin sign attached to the gate saying *Closed for Business*. I cry. A magpie swoops across the road so close to the car I am afraid I've killed it, and even when I see it soar into the air behind me, I cry.

After two hours, the car's temperature is heading towards the red zone, so I pull over into a truck rest stop and turn off the engine.

I don't know how I can live in Gunapan without Norm.

CHAPTER 29

I remember Norm saying to me once that he wished he was Irish because they knew how to send people off.

'A slab of beer, a barbie and a good laugh,' he said. 'That's how I like to say goodbye to a mate.'

But no one laughed at Norm's send-off. It was too sudden. We weren't prepared.

In the days after he died, the *Shire Herald* was full of notices from people everywhere. Melissa and Jake and I cut them out of the newspaper and pasted them into a book. We put in photos of Norm that I'd taken over the years, and some of the notes from him – often written on the backs of betting slips – that I'd stuck to the fridge because of their Normness.

The service passed by in a flash with women crying and sobbing and blokes consoling each other with handshakes, arm jabs and nods. Marg said a few words and so did Justin. I hardly heard a thing because I was blowing my nose most of the time, or trying to cuddle Melissa, who wanted a cuddle, but was trying to pretend she didn't, or grabbing hold of Jake every time he started inching towards the door of the church where men had gathered in the back pews to slap each other's backs and nod and grunt meaningfully before they headed off to the pub for a few beers. I heard there was some unrestrained male sobbing in the pub car park later that night.

Now that a week has passed, the number of people dropping off casseroles and cakes and frozen meals has slowed down. I'd been delivering most of them on to Justin anyway. I'm sure they would have taken stuff directly to him, but barely anyone in town has officially met him yet, although a few blokes have started turning up to the yard again, probably missing their long consultations. When I delivered the last batch of food, I found Justin standing in the middle of the yard, staring at the horizon. He looked so lonely I wanted to hug him.

'Are you OK?' I asked after I had dropped off the three frozen soups at the door of the shed. We turned towards the warming sun and both crossed our arms as we squinted out over the yard.

Justin nodded. 'Thanks, Loretta,' he said.

'Marg's gone home?'

He nodded again.

I hesitated before I said, 'You know, Justin, I'd never seen Norm as happy as when you came to live here.' I wasn't sure whether that would please Justin or make him even sadder, but it was worth saying.

At home, we are in shock, unable to believe

Norm isn't going to appear at the back door with a bag of lemons and all the news of the town. It's as if no one has any news to tell anyway. Gunapan has gone quiet. We're all in mourning.

It seems important to go back to routines. For a week Melissa and Jake, distraught as they were, got away with doing no chores, eating whatever they wanted whenever they wanted and watching endless hours of television. Today we stop that. Today we go back to life and try to find a way back in without Norm.

'I don't want to go to school,' Jake says in the car. 'The holidays were good. Let's put more pictures of Norm in the book.'

When I pull up at the gate, Melissa and Jake stay sitting in the car.

'What's up?' I ask.

'What if they ask us about Norm?' Melissa puts her hand up to her mouth and begins to nibble at a nail. Another bad habit she's got from me.

'Sweetie, everyone knows Norm died. Don't worry, they'll try to make you comfortable.'

They climb reluctantly out of the car and shuffle towards the school steps. Around them, kids stare silently. I was wrong. No one knows how to behave when someone close to you has died. My poor kids will probably sit alone all day while the other children gawk at them as if they're zoo animals.

At the Neighbourhood House, the reaction is quite different.

'Welcome back,' Gabrielle says at the front door.

She holds the wire screen open while I unlock the front door, then follows me into the office.

'How come you're here today? The committee meeting's not for another two weeks.'

'Oh, darling, I wanted to see that you were OK. I heard your friend, Mr Stevens, died. That's so awful. I am sorry, Loretta.'

'Thanks, Gabrielle.' I am more than surprised. I was certain she didn't know my name.

Gabrielle sits in the office armchair with the foam spilling out of the holes in the fabric and leafs through some old committee minutes while I walk around turning off the alarm, unlocking the rooms of the House, switching on lights. The House seems even shabbier than usual today. We can't get money to paint the rooms, so the walls are scuffed and the paint on the woodwork is chipped. The colours they chose originally were jolly lemons and greens, supposed to cheer people up. Now they look like prison colours. The furniture is all mismatched. The polished floorboards have lost their polish where everyone walks and dirt is being ground into the boards. I trudge back to the office, making a note to apply for funding to repair the floors.

'So how are you coping, darling?' Gabrielle asks once I've dropped into the office chair.

My email opens as she speaks. I have three hundred and forty-four unread messages after two weeks of being away. I don't want to talk about how I'm coping. For the first time in my life I want to work slowly through a huge number of outstanding emails and think about nothing else.

'We're OK. Thanks for asking, Gabrielle,' I answer in a crisp, businesslike voice. I move a pile of papers from the left side of the desk to the right. 'Look at all this. I'd better get on with it.'

Gabrielle doesn't look as if she's about to move, so I open my emails one by one. The first twenty or so are course and childcare enquiries. Why these people can write an email but not look at a web page is beyond me. I reply with a link to the web page. At least thirty emails are from the funding bodies who think the main purpose of the Neighbourhood House is to fill in forms about funding. If you fill in enough forms and are lucky enough to get some funding, you'll spend the rest of the year filling in forms about how you intend to spend the funding, how you are spending the funding, and then how you did spend the funding. And then they'll want a report on the success of the funded project. Which you haven't had time to do because you've been flat out filling out forms about funding and they only gave you a quarter of what you needed to do the project anyway.

Helen's sent me a joke. I'm scared to open it because it might have sound, and Gabrielle is still sitting beside me in the House's most uncomfortable chair, the one we put in the office to discourage people from sitting and complaining for hours. The last joke I opened from Helen was a jaunty song about penises that rang out across the office of the Neighbourhood House for what seemed like an hour while I withered at the desk, apologizing, because I didn't know how to turn it off. Helen doesn't realize that I'm a professional woman doing a professional job and I have an image to uphold. Plus we have a large sign over the office window saying *Offensive language will not be tolerated in this House,* which Maria put up after her son Damien heard one of the visitors shouting abuse at someone on the phone. I was the first to be graced with his new vocabulary when I arrived on the Tuesday morning and said, 'Hi Damien,' only to be answered with, 'Hi you fucking slag.' Maria was mortified.

'What's going to happen to Mr Stevens' yard?' Gabrielle asks out of the blue.

'I don't know.' I keep clicking through my emails as we speak, hoping she'll get the hint.

'It is an eyesore. I don't think many people will be sorry to see it go.'

'An eyesore?' I repeat. I remember Norm's description of it – an abstract interpretation of the changing face of Gunapan – and smile. 'I find it rather attractive. An unusual work of art.'

'But most people won't think that way, will they, darling. Most people will be glad when it's gone.'

'I'm not sure why we're talking about this, Gabrielle. The yard is none of my business. And I don't feel up to talking about Norm, I'm sorry.' I turn reluctantly away from the computer to face Gabrielle and find to my astonishment that she has tears on her cheeks. 'What is it? What's wrong?'

'I didn't know he was ill,' she says, breathing in with a stutter between words.

'Nobody knew. It's OK.'

'It's just that we were at supper and talking about the yard and how ugly it made that road and how it wouldn't look good for people driving to the resort, and I don't know, suddenly I was the one who was going to make the complaint. I didn't want to. And if I'd known he wasn't well . . .'

'You mean to the council?'

'I only said to them that they should ask him to put up a fence! And then they sent him that notice and everything blew up.' She takes in a long shaky breath. 'And then he died.' She pulls a tissue from her bag and honks into it.

'Who was at supper?'

'No one special. Just our book group.' She does another honk and brings out her make-up mirror. 'Oh, look at me. I'm a mess.'

'Who's in the book group?'

'It's no one you'd know, darling. A couple of ladies from Halstead, a councillor, members of the Lions Ladies Auxiliary. We have a glass of wine and a nibble once a month and sometimes we even talk about the book.' Gabrielle's perking up now. She smiles as she mentions the glass of wine.

'Samantha Patterson?'

'Yes, Samantha. And Ann-Maree, who makes the most delicious tiny party pies. Or maybe she buys them from that Halstead patisserie. I try to put on a lovely supper too, but some of those Lions ladies can cook like chefs. It's rather intimidating, I have to say. I've been tempted to cater, but that wouldn't be in the spirit of things, would it.'

'Samantha Patterson,' I mutter again. 'Samantha Patterson suggested you complain.'

'No. No, it wasn't Samantha. I can't remember who it was. It was everyone. We were all talking about it. It just came up.'

'He was a sick man.'

Gabrielle's eyes fill with tears again. 'I didn't know.'

'It *was* Samantha Patterson, wasn't it?'

'I can't remember. We were chatting. It was only a harmless little message to get him to clean up.'

'But it wasn't harmless, was it? He was ill. It caused him terrible stress.' I feel a little ill myself, hearing these words coming out of my mouth. But I'm furious. Norm knew Samantha Patterson had something to do with it. How dare they do this to Norm, my Norm.

Gabrielle dabs at her eyes with a new tissue. 'I'm sorry. I'm so sorry.'

'I have to get to work now, Gabrielle.' I feel unkind, but not as unkind as I'm going to feel when I get hold of Samantha Patterson.

The day flies past as I answer emails and fend off sympathetic calls and when I knock off I only have two hours until I have to pick up the kids.

297

Luckily, I know exactly where Samantha Patterson will be. She'll be where all the wealthy women of this area appear on the first Monday of the month. The mobile day spa.

CHAPTER 30

The women who go to the day spa would never have a haircut at Hair Today Gone Tomorrow in the main street of Gunapan. They have their hair done in Melbourne. But once a month a van arrives in Gunapan and spills young Asian women carrying manicure and pedicure kits and boxes of creams and lotions into Hair Today. The blinds go down in the windows. The pub delivers bottles of champagne. Four-wheel drives pull up and park along the street like some beauty-hunting club and the women disappear into Hair Today, which is closed to normal business for four hours in the afternoon. Helen tried to book in last year, but they told her it was full up. 'Full up, my arse,' she said to me.

When I push open the door of the salon, the first person I see is Gabrielle in a bathrobe. She's sitting with her hands spread flat on a table. The girl on the other side of the table is shaking a bottle of nail polish. Further inside are two women, lounging in reclining chairs with their feet in footbaths, chatting and laughing. Several more towards the back of the room are lying on massage tables, their faces covered in goop. Jazz music and a delicious smell of orange and cardamom fill the room. Candles are burning. A young woman comes towards me carrying a tray of hors d'oeuvres. Am I still in Gunapan?

'Do you have a booking?' the young woman asks, surprised, looking me up and down.

'No, I'm here to see someone.'

At the sound of my voice Gabrielle looks up. When I shake my head at her she looks away again, her face pink. I don't want to cause Gabrielle any harm. I have never wanted to cause anyone harm – until today.

'Sorry,' the young woman says quietly, 'this is a private club.' She puts the tray on the shop counter and moves behind me to open the door and usher me out, but I'm headed for the back of the salon.

The elegant figure lying with its eyes closed and cream all over its face on the table near the basins is unmistakeably Samantha Patterson. Her sleek hair is fanned across the pillow. Like the other women she's wearing a fluffy white robe and pink towelling scuffs. Her fine-boned hands, which have obviously never encountered a scourer, are crossed daintily over her flat stomach.

At this moment, the full extent of my scragness is very clear to me. My rage deserts me. I have a terrible feeling I'm going to open my mouth and a screech will come out.

Samantha opens her eyes, frowns at me for a moment, and closes them again.

'Tran, somebody's here,' she says, her eyes still closed. 'Can you look after them, please.'

So much for my rage deserting me. It was only on a brief holiday. 'I'm here to speak to you, Samantha.' I can hear a shade of screech in my voice, but there's nothing I can do about that.

She opens her eyes again and gives me the once-over. 'I'm sorry. I don't think I know you.'

'I'm a friend of Norm Stevens. You know Norm, the one with the unsightly property. I'm also interested in the development on the Bolton Road. I think you might be the person to talk to about that.'

Samantha doesn't even blink. She lies on the massage table like Cleopatra waiting for her slaves and turns her face away from me before she says, 'I am in the middle of a facial. Do you mind?'

'Yes, I do mind. I want to know what's going on.'

'I'm sorry, I don't know what you're talking about.' She sits up and swings her legs over the side of the table so she's facing me. 'I can't believe you've been so rude as to barge in here and interrupt our afternoon. If you've got some issue with the development, take it up with council.'

'No.' That screeching voice coming out of me is getting louder. 'I want to take it up with you. Norm told me you were behind this. I'm going to finish what he started.'

Everyone's listening now. The girl doing the pedicures has her scalpel poised in the air and is staring at us.

301

'I hardly think the ravings of some filthy old junk man are anything to rely on.' She looks around at her friends who half-nod and half-smile, not knowing what else to do. 'And coming in here like this is completely inappropriate. Please take your concerns up with council.' She waves an indolent hand at the girl near the counter. 'Tran, can you show this person to the door.'

'No, Tran. Don't bother. I'm not leaving.'

The salon, usually full of chatter and the rush of water and the hum of hairdryers, is so still I can almost hear the guttering of the candles. Tran holds on to the counter.

Samantha looks around at her friends, but they're staring at the floor or the wall. I recognize one of them from the creative-writing class at the Neighbourhood House. She seemed like a kind person. Her list of pleasing things included hugging her granddaughter and smelling the flowery scent of her flyaway hair. Why would she be friends with this nasty woman?

'My friend, Norm, died. He was a good man.'

'I'm sure he was.' Samantha relaxes her shoulders, rolling the left then the right, and brings her hands to rest in her lap. 'I'm very sorry. I am really very sorry.'

As soon as she says this everyone in the room starts to breathe again. Relief ripples through the salon. I start to see the funny side of this. Samantha's face is covered in cream. It's like talking to a pavlova.

'Should I call the council and make an appointment for you? Tran, could you please bring my handbag here?'

'No.' I will not be put off. Norm is dead and I owe him.

Tran hurries past me with her head down and passes Samantha a red leather bag.

'You're obviously grieving. I'm very sorry about your friend. Go home and rest and we can organize an appointment with the council for you.' She pulls a gold notebook and matching pencil from her handbag. 'Now, what's your name and phone number? I'll get my assistant on to it first thing tomorrow.'

I can hear murmurs of approval from the front of the salon. So her friends think she is doing the right thing. Perhaps I *am* blowing things out of proportion. Samantha has her pencil poised over the open notebook.

But no. Grief, stubbornness, anger, whatever it is, she's not getting rid of me this easily. 'I want you to tell me about the development and your connection with it.'

From her small pink mouth I hear a tiny *tsk*. She turns to the woman at the next table and rolls her eyes. 'For heaven's sake,' she mutters.

I am not sure exactly why this sets me off the way it does. It's not only about Norm, or the development, or the council. It's everything about who Samantha Patterson is and who I am and who Norm was. It's Samantha Patterson rolling her eyes as if I'm some annoying bug that got inside her big air-conditioned house. It's the way she said, 'For heaven's sake,' as if my life and Norm's life and the lives of most of the people I know in this town are a waste of time. It's enough to make me take a step forwards and do something I've never done in my life.

I slap her face.

Even as my hand connects, I realize what a stupid thing I'm doing. Not because it won't give me satisfaction – it will – but because her face is covered in cream. What should have been a resounding smack that leaves her with a stinging cheek and a good dose of humiliation becomes a slithering swipe that unbalances me and leaves my hand greasy and Samantha with the look of a half-eaten cream bun. A giggle rises in me.

'Tran, lock the door,' the cream bun says through gritted teeth. 'Call the police. I've been assaulted.'

'Geez, Loretta, what do you think you're playing at?' Bill asks when I'm sitting in the passenger seat of the police car heading for the station.

I shrug.

'Samantha Patterson is not a person to get offside.'

I shrug again. I don't care.

It's only a ten-minute drive from the salon to the police station, a small brick office at the front of Bill's house. We should drive past the CWA Hall and the school on the way, but Bill swings the car around the corner at the supermarket and heads along Grevillea Street. He says he doesn't want my children to look out of the window of their schoolroom and see me in a police car. I tell him I would probably go up ten points in Jake's estimation if he did see me in a police car. We drop by the doctor's surgery, where I run inside to ask Helen to pick up the kids after school and take them to her house. When she asks why and I explain I'm under arrest for assaulting Samantha Patterson, I think I go up ten points in her estimation too. An old lady I know from the Neighbourhood House hauls herself out of her chair in the waiting room and asks to shake my hand. Unfortunately my hand is still greasy from Samantha's face cream.

At the station, Bill sits across the desk and gazes at me with the sorrowful expression of a disappointed father. He shakes his head as he reaches into the drawer and pulls out a form with several coloured copies attached.

'Full name?'

'Loretta Judith Boskovic.'

'Address?'

'You know that perfectly well, Bill.'

'Answer please, Loretta. This is serious. Mrs Patterson has insisted I charge you with assault.'

'Fine. I'm glad I slapped her. Do you have a tissue?'

'You know you could lose your job if you get a conviction?'

That shuts me up.

'You'll be charged on summons. You'll come up in front of a magistrate. You'll be a criminal if you're convicted, Loretta. It's not a joke.'

CHAPTER 31

The kids sit quietly in the back on the way home from Helen's place. It's likely they can see the steam pouring from my head and they're worried it's about them. I keep thinking about Samantha Patterson calling Norm a filthy old junk man, and each time that phrase goes through my head another surge of steam builds up. Sure, Norm was the local junk man, and I do admit that on occasion he was filthy, but that's not for her to say. And now I might lose my job.

'If you're looking down – or up – from somewhere, Norm Stevens, I'll show you what a battler I am. Nothing is going to stop me bringing that woman down.'

'Mum!' Melissa says crossly. 'You're talking to yourself again. And you missed our street.'

'All right, all right, no need to blow your top.'

'Not like some people,' she says, pursing her lips in that special Gunapan way.

I swing the car into the next street then do a blockie, heading for our road. With the silence broken, Jake can't help himself.

'Our class got a mouse today and the teacher said if anyone screamed she'd send them home and Jamie wet his pants and he had to wear the spare ones and they were blue and I got—'

He's stopped midstream for the same reason I'm applying the brakes. Sitting outside our house on a trailer behind an old Bedford truck is a massive yellow machine with a bucket at the front. It has caterpillar treads and a square cabin on the top with a seat in the shape of an upturned hand perched above the engine and levers sticking up from the floor. From this angle it looks like it could scoop up the whole house.

I'm expecting Justin to jump out of the truck, but when we pull up in the driveway, it's Merv Bull who ambles up beside the car. He leans in, shading his eyes against the sun.

'G'day Loretta.' He taps on the glass of the back window. 'G'day mate,' he says to Jake.

Jake scrambles to get out of the car so fast he nearly knocks Merv over with the car door. I try to emerge in a more seemly manner. Melissa gets out of the car on her side and looks hard at Merv, then shouts across the car roof to me.

'I'll check the letter box and see if Dad's sent a card. Remember Dad? Your husband?'

I smile brightly at Merv Bull. 'I used to be married. Kids can't let things go, can they?'

He laughs. Jake is welded to his left leg, gazing up adoringly. I think about how strange it is that he didn't react this way with his own father.

'Mr Bull, can I pleeeeeeese look at the yellow machine?'

'Sure, mate.'

Melissa pushes the mail at me and storms inside. I watch as Merv lifts Jake on to the seat of the bulldozer and lets him try to move the gear levers. Jake's so excited he's laughing like a hyena. I hope he didn't get that laugh from me.

When we all get inside and sit down at the table for tea and cordial and biscuits, Merv tells Jake about the different types of bulldozer he's worked on. He turns to Melissa, who has been sipping her cordial and nibbling her biscuits with her face turned aside, as though even the sight of Merv Bull could ruin her appetite.

'I met your dad. Worked on his car. He seemed like a great bloke,' Merv says.

It's as if he has turned on the sun.

'Yeah, my dad's great.' Melissa nods vigorously. 'Even though some people don't think so.' She glares at me. I glare back. I know she's putting this on for Merv. She's as disappointed in her father as I am. The other night she took the post-card off her bedroom wall and put it in her secret box in the wardrobe. It made me sad when I found it.

'Anyway, I did want to have a word with your mum about some stuff,' Merv says pointedly.

Now she's been appeased, Melissa gets up and herds her brother off to his room before settling into her room to do her homework.

'So,' Merv says when the kitchen is quiet. 'I wanted to say I'm sorry about Norm. He was a champion. I know I haven't been in town that long, but it was clear from the get-go that Norm was a bloke you could rely on.'

I have to wrinkle up my face to keep the tears from coming.

'He did a couple of favours for me and I won't forget that,' Merv goes on. 'Which is why I'm here.'

'Oh?'

'That Unsightly Property Notice business was out of line. Everyone knew it was dodgy.'

'It was Samantha Patterson. I heard this morning. I don't know how she's involved with that development, but I'm going to find out.'

'I might be able to help. I'm not allowed to talk about the development, because I signed that confidentiality agreement. But I can talk about some other things I've noticed.'

This is so exciting I feel a hyena laugh coming on. 'Such as?'

'Such as the 'dozer I'm towing into town today. Do you know where it's going?'

I shrug, still trying to keep the hyena laugh inside.

'It's going to the house of John Ponty,' Merv says triumphantly. 'The heavy-equipment moving firm that does a lot of work for the place I'm not allowed to talk about was supposed to pick it up and deliver it, but they had a breakdown and I said I'd do it instead. Then I found out where it was going.'

'John Ponty? The name sounds familiar.'

'Council officer? Planning Department? Currently having major renovations done on his house?'

'Ah.'

'And commonly known to be bonking a certain married female councillor.'

'No!' How come I never know any of the real gossip in this town? 'You mean Samantha Patterson?'

'Oh, yes. And here's the icing on the cake. I know my machines, right. I often work on them myself, don't only leave them to the apprentices. And I can tell you that someone has been swapping plates around on the 'dozers and the trenchers and the other machines. We note it all down, of course, for our records. Plate number and engine number on the repair sheet. And back when they started the shire swimming pool renos, I saw this very 'dozer on that site. Different plate, same 'dozer.'

'I don't get it. What's the swimming pool got to do with it?'

'I'm no wiser than you. I can only tell you what I've seen. But those machines belong to a big company with fingers in a lot of different pies, and I've seen them on jobs that shouldn't be connected.'

How can I start to figure this out? It's so

complicated. No wonder they've been getting away with it, whatever it is.

'Thanks, Merv. I really didn't know anything much, so this is a great start.'

'Happy to help, Loretta.'

We teeter into a sudden awkward silence. I can hear Jake singing to himself in his room, and the tapping and beeps of Melissa on the computer. Terror and Panic clatter up the steps of the back veranda and peer in the back window. They must be hungry.

'Liss,' I call. 'Did you feed Terror and Panic?'

Merv raises his eyebrows when I say Terror and Panic, then looks behind him and jumps when he sees the two long bearded faces in the window.

'Lawnmowers from Norm,' I explain.

'Maaaaaaa, maaaaaa,' Terror calls. It works far better than my call and Melissa trots through the kitchen and out to the veranda in the automatic manner of a mother summoned by her baby's cry.

'Suppose I'd better deliver this 'dozer,' Merv says, standing and stretching.

I follow him out to the truck.

'Thanks again, Merv.' I'm getting that same feeling I had when I went to his garage ages ago. Something hanging in the air. His gaze resting a moment too long on the footpath, then the horizon.

He stands beside the door of the truck. Brushes his hand through his straight shiny brown hair. Turns to the truck and turns back again.

'I'm heading to Halstead for a drink and some dinner on Saturday. Don't suppose you'd like to come?'

He speaks so fast I want to ask him to say it again. Slowly. I think he asked me on a date.

'Halstead? Saturday?' I mumble. A thought occurs to me. 'Aren't you . . .? Isn't . . .? Maxine . . .?'

'Maxine's great,' he says. 'She's a good mate. Kind of turned out that way.'

I open my mouth and wait for the yes to come out, but it doesn't. The silence becomes uncomfortable. I should say yes. I'm being asked on a date. But as I keep failing to answer, the realization dawns on me. He's not what I want.

'If you're busy,' Merv says. He reaches for the truck handle.

'It's a bit hard to find babysitters. You know.'

'Yeah, sure. It must be a problem. Well, maybe another time.'

'Yep. Maybe another time,' I reply. My heart is beating fast. If I tell Helen about this she'll kill me.

He climbs into the truck and starts the engine, which shakes and grunts as it strains away from the kerb, pulling the 'dozer on its trailer. His arm reaches out and waves from the cabin of the truck, and I feel a small twinge of regret.

But I could never go for a man who drives a Bedford.

CHAPTER 32

The mail Melissa brought in is fatter than usual. I sit back down at the kitchen table and open an envelope from the council. Inside is a letter and a wad of paper.

In response to your Freedom of Information Application No. 2/84/556, please find enclosed council documents relating to the Forest Springs Leisure Resort area rezoning and building application.

Please note that the protection of the public interest and private and business affairs may cause some information to be exempted from access.

It's signed by Bree Howarth, another girl who used to babysit my kids while she was at school. I didn't know she was an admin assistant at the council now. How handy.

The wad of paper is thick. I think about putting it aside until after tea, but I can't wait so I start to leaf through, which is when I find out what they mean by 'some information to be exempted from access'. About two-thirds of every page is blacked out. They've left phrases like 'from the zoning regulations' and 'pertaining to the regulatory framework' and 'in the' and 'with reference to'.

This makes me madder than ever.

Next afternoon I leave the Neighbourhood House at lunchtime, jump in the car and race to Halstead. After a quick appointment at the legal aid office about my assault charge, I scoot over to the park across the road from the shire offices in Halstead to eat my sandwich. Around me a few pigeons burble. The fountain sits dry and empty in the centre of the park, shut down by water restrictions. The plants are struggling and the grass is brown, but people still sit here in the dappled shade of the gum trees, eating and chatting and reading newspapers. At half-past one, Bree trots down the council steps and heads in the direction of the shops.

'Hi Bree,' I say chirpily as I hurry up beside her. I hope I haven't got curried egg on my face. It wouldn't be the first time.

'Oh, Mrs Boskovic.' She looks at me in shock and starts to walk faster. I have to trot to keep up. Kids these days have beanpole legs. She's probably also heard that I'm a maniac who goes around assaulting people.

'Got your letter, thanks, Bree.'

'Oh?' she says. She's starting to breathe faster

now with the exertion of running away from me. The shops are within sight. 'I send out so many letters. They're not really from me, they're from the bosses.'

'Ah, I see. So you weren't the one who blacked out everything.'

'I do what I'm told, Mrs Boskovic. The documents come to me marked up by hand and I do it on the computer. I don't read anything.'

'All I need to know is who gave you the marked-up documents.'

'I don't know if I should say, Mrs Boskovic. Isn't council business private?'

'No, Bree, it's not. The council is supposed to be working for us. It's our business.'

We're outside the fish and chip shop. The coloured straps of the fly curtain are flapping in the breeze. Three young men in blue overalls lean against the walls inside the shop, leafing through car mags as they wait for their orders.

'Who did the blacking out? You will never be mentioned, Bree. Not one word. You can trust me.'

'I do trust you, Mrs B, but . . .'

'If there's corruption in the council you have to make sure no one can accuse you of being involved, Bree. When it comes out, I can only back you up if you've been honest with me.' I don't want to frighten her, but this is urgent.

Bree begins to sniffle. 'I don't want to get into trouble. That horrible John Ponty made me do it and he's not even my boss! He's always telling me to do things and not to mention it to anyone. It makes me feel like I'm doing something wrong.'

'No one will know you told me, Bree, unless you need me to stand by you when it comes out. I promise.'

It's starting to fit together. I need to sit down and work it out properly, and I need space to concentrate. Child-free space. Helen's busy minding the Tim Tams. Brianna already has Kyleen's little girl because Kyleen's working in Halstead. In the past I would have had Norm as my emergency babysitter. After I've dabbed away the tears that welled up at the thought of Norm, I decide to call Justin.

'You don't need to do anything,' I tell him. 'If you come over and sit with the kids in the lounge to watch TV and I can have some time to myself, that'll do the trick. Two hours maximum.' I nod at the phone encouragingly, as if he can see me. 'Or three or four,' I add, realizing how many years it is since I attempted sustained intelligent thought.

'I don't know anything about children,' he warns me. 'I've spent the last fourteen years living in close quarters with violent damaged men.'

'Well, this will obviously be a bit more of a challenge, but I'm sure you're up to it.'

He arrives bearing lollipops and a teen fashion magazine. He's a natural. I usher him into the lounge room where the zombie children are watching a cartoon, and when he sits down on the couch Jake scoots across and snuggles up against him exactly the way he used to with Norm.

Next day after work, I hop in the car and race over to Vaughan's shop in Halstead. These trips are costing me a fortune in petrol. I wait until the customer in the shop leaves with a kettle under her arm, then wander in, peeling a banana. The shelves are stacked with the kind of labour-saving devices and luxury electrical goods people buy as presents for Mother's Day that end up in the back of the cupboard until they're discovered, twenty years later, by a grandchild who thinks they're fabulous and retro.

A young salesman comes to offer assistance, but Vaughan has seen me and he sends the salesman away.

'Need a word with you, Vaughan.'

I've never seen Vaughan angry. He's a good mayor because he doesn't get riled up. He sits like a Buddha through the stormy meetings where councillors are throwing accusations at each other, and when they've worn themselves out, he stops patting his stomach and starts negotiating.

Today, I am seeing the mayor angry. He's a gorgeous pinky orange, the same colour as a cocktail I had once called a Tequila Sunset, and he's patting his poor stomach so fast it's like watching the flitter of butterfly wings.

'No food in the shop, Loretta. And I'm not sure

I should be talking to you. Aren't you being charged with assault?'

I wrap the banana back in its skin and drop it into my handbag. 'I've been to legal aid. They're going to try to get me a bond.'

'Yes, well, don't start on me now, Loretta. You've already ruined my reputation with that article. I have never taken an inappropriate trip. I haven't had time to take a bloody trip at all since I've been mayor, except to Melbourne in the car.'

'I didn't give the information to the newspaper, Vaughan. It was Norm.'

He shrugs. 'What does it matter who did it? It made me look like a fool. Anyway, we've had an investigation and it's all been explained. So you can get off your high horse. The report will be out next month.'

'Who investigated?'

'Leave it alone, Loretta. Why are you always stirring up trouble?'

'The whole thing stinks, Vaughan, and you know it. Why would you approve a development in beautiful local bushland that takes drinking water out of the ground to use in a bloody spa?'

He's patting his stomach so fast now it looks like he's got a motorized hand. The gorgeous pink has faded. He's dead white. I hope he isn't getting pains in his chest. I had to take a first aid course when I started work at the Neighbourhood House, but the dummy was half the size of Vaughan. I don't think I'd even be able to turn him on his side.

'I didn't approve it. It didn't need to come to council because it met all the requirements of the code, so it was automatically approved in the shire offices. You don't know what you're talking about, Loretta.'

'Let's sit down in your office.' I'm really worried. He's about to keel over.

He swings around and stumbles to his glassed-in office. I call the salesman and ask him for water.

'You're killing me, Loretta.' Vaughan collapses into his office chair, which creaks and sinks an inch.

Once he's taken a sip of water and his colour is back to normal, I pull out the diagram I sketched last night. At school I did a subject we called vegie maths, for the less mathematically endowed, and I excelled at these diagrams. They are pretty, and easy to understand. Overlapping coloured bubbles show things that are connected. There are bubbles inside bubbles. Bubbles inside other bubbles connected to different bubbles. A great big bubble picture like soapsuds mixing up in the wash.

'What's this?' Vaughan says crossly, glancing over my carefully drawn and coloured-in bubbles.

'See this bubble? This is Samantha Patterson. She is touching every other bubble in some way.'

'Bubbles?'

'It's a Venn diagram, Vaughan.'

He stares at it for a moment. 'Why is the John Ponty bubble sitting almost on top of the Samantha Patterson bubble?' he asks.

'Don't make me say it, Vaughan.' I'm glad I'm not the only one who didn't know.

'You're sure?'

'I've heard that if you drive to the motel at the Bendigo turn-off on a Thursday afternoon you can see for yourself.'

'Jesus.' He looks off to the side. 'So I am a fool.' He looks again at the diagram. 'Who told you this? And what's the swimming pool got to do with it?'

'See the crosshatching of the linking bubbles here, here and here?' I'm so proud of this diagram. It took me hours. 'Same equipment used to do all these works. Equipment owned by the development company building the resort. No bets taken that John Ponty's renovations are gratis and that the tender for the pool renovations went to a favoured tenderer with a parent company based in Western Australia.'

'And that Samantha has some interest somewhere in this company or its development.' Vaughan lets out a resigned sigh. 'I'm an idiot. I didn't see any of this.'

'Norm thought she was too smart to have shares or anything obvious like that. But she's involved. It's clear from the diagram.'

'How could I have been such a fool? I didn't have a clue.'

'You couldn't have known. John Ponty must have made sure none of it ever reached a council meeting by approving it at staff level.'

'I hate it that you're right, Loretta.'

'It wasn't me, Vaughan. It was Norm. He knew something was up when he got the Unsightly Property Notice.'

Vaughan nods. 'I was a bit surprised by that myself. But I thought it was a genuine complaint.'

'Will you do something now, Vaughan? We can't let this go on. Samantha Patterson called Norm a filthy old junk man. And anyway, you'll look good because you'll be the one who exposes the corruption in the shire council.'

'Oh, hell.' Vaughan presses his hand against his belly and burps. 'I get it now. Samantha's husband told me they'd bought into some new businesses. The one I can remember was aromatherapy oils and soaps and cosmetics.'

CHAPTER 33

At six thirty, the Gunapan pub, once called the Criterion, now renamed the Toad and Bucket Bar and Grill for reasons no one can explain, is filling up. Jake, dressed in an over-sized black suit we found at the Halstead op shop yesterday, and Melissa, wearing her halter-neck dress and a splendid amount of pink eyeshadow, are welcoming people to the auction and handing them tickets for the door prize. Every now and then Jake tells someone that Norm is decomposing at the cemetery. I see them flinch when he does it.

We've been talking for weeks about what being 'dead' means. I think Jake still expects Norm to drop in one day soon, so I have been trying gently to introduce the concept of 'gone forever'. If his father hadn't turned up for that week it would have been a lot easier.

I had hoped Jake would be satisfied with the 'Norm's gone to heaven' idea, but Jake likes bugs and tennis balls and things he can touch. He's not interested in heaven or life and death or abstract ideas. He was particularly intrigued when he heard that Norm is buried at the cemetery. 'What will happen to him in the ground?' Jake asked and I foolishly answered.

A small stage has been erected at the front of the pub lounge. A microphone and gavel sit on a podium on the stage. We borrowed them from the local stock auctioneer, who is also a part-time barman here at the pub. Waiting to be hoisted above the stage is the banner Helen and I made last night.

Norm Stevens Snr Memorial Auction and SOS Eveni

We hadn't realized how long the title would be. It was ten o'clock when we got to 'i' and there was no way I was going back to Brenda to ask her for more of that roll of beige silk she'd bought at a fire sale just in case one day she learned to sew. She did offer it in the first place, like everyone else who came out of nowhere after Norm died. They apologized for missing SOS meetings and promised to donate time and stuff for the auction. Hell, they pretty much offered me their first-born children. I have enough trouble with my own to want more.

'We know how much Norm meant to you,' Kyleen said. 'He was like a husband, kind of. Oh, except he didn't . . .'

'No, he didn't. He certainly did not. He was like a father to me.'

'Yeah, that's what I meant.'

It's been so long for most of the single mothers in this town we've forgotten what husbands do to make us mothers in the first place.

Helen holds the sign up, admiring the finely wrought lettering. 'They'll get what it means. When we hang it we'll let the end drape, as if the last letters are hidden in the folds.'

Justin is kneeling at the front of the room fixing the microphone lead to the floor with gaffer tape. He was the one who insisted we go ahead with the auction. He said Norm had been excited about it, had been working hard on restoring the stationary engine and was even talking about buying a new shirt for the occasion.

He would have needed that shirt. The auction and dinner is a classy event. Ninety-four people have paid twenty dollars for adults – or five for children – for a set menu with a choice of chicken or beef. Mario Morelli's daughter is a vegetarian, due to the trauma of a summer job at the abattoir when she was fourteen, but she's only getting roast vegetables because the pub's cook is hysterical at the thought of cooking for more than ten people at a time. I've already made a quiet call to the Halstead pizza shop as a backup measure.

By eight thirty, the main meals – which ended

up being a weight-loss version of a pub meal: two slices of beef or chicken, a carrot, a potato and a teaspoon of gravy – have been served and thirty pizzas delivered and divided among the crowd. Mario's daughter was thrilled to get a vegetarian pizza to herself. The desserts are OK because the cook made the pavlovas and cheesecakes yesterday using a very reliable brand of packet mix. His kids are in the kitchen whipping cream and chopping strawberries and passionfruit as if they are getting paid for it.

With the beer and wine and whisky flowing, the auction is about to start. Or so I thought. I'm waiting for the auctioneer to come out from behind the bar when the lights go out and everyone looks up at the screen that normally shows the footy or the racing channel.

'Ladies and gentlemen,' a voice issues from the speakers around the ceiling of the pub. I think that voice belongs to Vaughan.

Sure enough, he appears on the screen dressed in his rather tight-fitting scarlet robes and chain. In the real world he's sitting at the table next to ours, staring up at the screen. I can hear his wife murmuring, 'See, you've lost some of that chub around the tummy already.' She's very much the proud wife now Vaughan is the honest mayor who exposed Samantha Patterson and John Ponty's schemes. She even nodded hello to me the other day.

'Norm Stevens Senior was a pillar of our

community. He took part in many of our town-building activities, was a member of the Save Our School Committee—'

'That's my mum on that committee!' Jake screams. He's had three glasses of lemonade, it's past his bedtime, and if he has one more sip from that glass I think his head will start spinning like the girl in *The Exorcist*.

'Sssh.' I quickly switch his lemonade for water while he stares up at the screen. Melissa's on the other side of Jake. She's gazing in the opposite direction to the screen. It's still school holidays and Kyleen's sister's kids are staying with her. One of them is a boy of fifteen, which is where Melissa's adoring gaze is directed. I think Helen's influence is starting to show. I notice Mersiha's girl is looking in the same direction. A couple of weeks ago we got Mersiha's children and my children together and they apologized to each other. If they'd done it with any less grace, baseball bats and chains would have been involved, but once it was done I did think I felt the tension in the air ease a little. Mersiha and I have been working together on a plan for the revitalization of the Neighbourhood House and a few days ago I finally got up the courage to ask about her husband. She thanked me, and she cried as she told me about his work during the war, transporting artworks and religious relics under cover of darkness out of their beseiged town. One day he risked a run in the heavy fog of a winter morning. He was driving a truck loaded with illustrated manuscripts when the mist cleared long enough for a sniper to take him. I thought then about how we don't have much here in Gunapan, but at least we are safe.

'—donated countless hours of labour as well as goods to community projects, was always around when a man needed an ear, offered excellent racing tips and could be relied upon, with adequate notice, to source almost any spare part for any kind of mechanical device you could imagine. If he couldn't find it he'd make it. Given time, that is. Plenty of time.'

The screen mayor pauses and the real-life mayor claps, looking around the room. Everyone joins in. I wish they'd hurry up. I hate these things. I hope they don't start with the soppy music and misty pictures of Norm as a baby through to old age. As much as I hate that sort of stuff, if they put it on the big screen now I'm sure it would undo me.

Across the room, Kylcen's on her feet with her two little fingers to her mouth. She lets out a piercing whistle and calls out, 'We love Norm!' and the crowd cheers.

'Now,' on-screen mayor says, 'on with Norm's Auction. But keep your eye on the screen because you'll find out something about Norm during the night that probably very few of you knew. In fact, it was a secret held by a government department that even I only found out about last week. Enjoy!'

The barman edges out from behind the bar and pulls off his apron, leaving the publican serving drinks. Under the apron he's in tails. He leaps on to the stage and bows deeply. Beside him, the headmaster, Justin and Mario Morelli pull the red velvet covering off the table with the goods to be auctioned. We stand up and peer at the table, but it's hard to see what's what because everything is piled up higgledy-piggledy.

A picture of a multi-coloured flower is on the screen. I wonder what that's got to do with Norm, or if it's a test pattern. I can't read the tiny text at the bottom of the screen.

'Without further ado,' the auctioneer calls, 'let the auction begin. Lot One. A stationary engine, part-repaired by the magic hands of the good man himself, wanting only a flat-top piston, gudgeon pin and ring set. Do I have one hundred dollars?'

Silence. I knew this wouldn't work. Across the room I can see Brenda leaning across her table, probably saying to her kids, 'I knew this wouldn't work.'

Justin stands behind the stationary engine, his arm resting on it.

'Do I hear fifty dollars?' the auctioneer calls.

Nothing.

'One hundred dollars!' a voice calls out. It's a very familiar voice. It's Melissa's voice. I almost fall out of my seat.

'One hundred and twenty,' a voice calls from the back.

Everyone turns. It's Bowden with his new girl-friend, a hairdresser from Halstead. She's given him a haircut that, together with his ultra-thin pencil moustache, makes him look as though he's come to sell you the Sydney Harbour Bridge.

'One hundred and fifty,' Melissa responds.

'One hundred and fifty from the little lady at the front table, and we'll have to get your mother's OK on the bidding, darling. How about it, Mum?'

How about it? I'm wondering why I didn't drop those children off at the orphanage when I had the chance. As if I can say no when it's an auction to raise money for SOS and it's the engine Norm was fixing for us. I nod at the auctioneer even as I rack my brain for a punishment large and long enough to make up for this.

'One thousand dollars!' Jake screams.

'No!' I call out quick smart and everyone in the pub lounge laughs, including the auctioneer.

'OK, we're at one hundred and fifty from the lovely Melissa. Any more bids?'

The heat of Melissa's blush almost sets fire to the tablecloth.

'One sixty.'

'One eighty.'

'Two hundred.'

'This is more like it. Come on ladies and gents, let's have some more bids for Norm Stevens' very own stationary engine. Remember, it's for a good cause – the education of our kids.'

In a few seconds the bidding shoots up to four hundred and twenty dollars.

'Sold! To number twenty-six. Thank you, Gabrielle and Geoffrey. I'm sure you'll have many hours of pleasure from the putt-putting of this fine engine.'

Amazingly, it's Gabrielle from the Neighbourhood House Committee who has bought the engine. I wave to her and she nods.

The auction continues while more images flash up on the screen: what could be a model of the Gunapan town square fountain, although it's missing the bunch of schoolkids who usually sit there from four till five daring each other to shoplift something, anything, from the milk bar; an outline of a pig that looks like it's done in mosaic. In fact, all the pictures look like mosaic.

'Did Norm do mosaic?' I ask Helen.

'How would I know? Mosaic doesn't sound very Norm.'

When the donations for the auction first came in, it seemed as if everyone in Gunapan thought that bikes with broken chains, Scrabble sets with missing letters, one-armed action figures and dolls with their hair cut off that their own kids wouldn't play with would be a real treat for someone else's kids. Ditto for adults with broken tools and electrical appliances, clothes covered in stains, three-legged chairs, books that had been dropped in the bath, dented bumper bars, cracked plastic containers of every shape and size. I could imagine Norm telling me to take them and dump them back in the yards of the idiots who'd dropped them off.

Instead I filled the Gunapan tip – luckily, tip fees were waived for the special occasion. They'll have to dig a new hole in the ground for the rest of Gunapan's rubbish. It's incredible how this town can generate so much landfill from so little income.

We're up to Lot 24. The auctioneer has knocked down two of the big-ticket items: Norm's engine and a side of beef from Mario. The mayor won the donation from Leonora, our entrepreneurial witch.

'What's it to be, Vaughan?' the auctioneer asked. 'Hex or charm?'

'If I say it's for a certain ex-councillor, can you guess?' Vaughan called back and the crowd cheered and whistled.

Helen, with the grade-three teacher egging her on, won the weekend for two at the alpaca homestay farm – I wonder if a demonstration of the rutting alpacas is part of the package? I paid ten dollars for a newish white dinner set that the op shop couldn't sell. A picture of Kung Fu Jesus donated by a member of the Church of Goodwill has been bought by another member of the Church of Goodwill. A motor mower and brush cutter set from the local hardware shop got knocked down to Brianna whose yard does a fair imitation of a Peruvian jungle. And dinner for two at the pub has been passed in unsold.

By nine o'clock Jake's asleep on my lap and Melissa is yawning. Justin, Mario and the head-master, who started the evening lifting the goods above their heads and parading them around the room as they were auctioned, are now pointing to the next item on the table like lazy game-show hosts. Only two things are left: Tina's hand-sewn quilt, and a packet of vacuum cleaner bags for an unknown brand and size of vacuum cleaner.

I love that quilt. I've seen the ones Tina made on commission for the Neighbourhood House Committee members. They're thick and soft and made with gorgeous materials in patterns that could send you into a state of meditation.

'Now you can bid,' I whisper to Melissa. 'Up to two hundred and three dollars, then stop, OK?'

The bidding starts and, like a pro, Melissa waits till the bid reaches a hundred before she jumps in and tries to knock out the competition with a jump to one fifty.

I look at the screen again. The shots that were on before are repeating, but linking photographs have been inserted between them. It's like a stop-motion film where the pieces are moved around between takes to create movement. I watch with my mouth open as I begin to understand.

The quilt sells to another House Committee member for four hundred and ten dollars. I barely hear the applause for the end of the auction as the film speeds up and repeats one more time. The mayor hurries to the podium and waves his arm at the screen.

'Did anyone guess what it was?' he asks.

'We got it!' several tables call out.

The mayor points a remote control to freeze the screen. He thanks me, the auctioneer, the pub, Justin and the headmaster, everyone who donated goods, the Save Our School Committee and the audience. When he's finished his mayoral duties, he turns back to the screen.

'We always knew Norm was a bit crazy. Here's the proof, courtesy of the Department of Lands aerial surveying team and their shots taken over twelve years.'

The final cycle of the photos shows the outline of the flower morph into the outline of a car, a Christmas tree, the town fountain, an aeroplane, a head with a Roman nose, a star, a tree, an arrow, a cat and, lastly, the three letters SOS. If I peer very hard at the screen I can make out the shape of the individual mosaic pieces. There are tractor bodies and harvester parts, old engines, palettes of bricks, corrugated iron, doors and windows.

It's Norm's yard from the air.

CHAPTER 34

Norm Stevens Junior (aka Justin) says I'll never sell my Holden. He says it's too old. Someone will come to test-drive the thing, and as they power down the highway at maximum speed, eighty clicks, bits of the car will fall away until the driver is sitting in a chassis with wheels and not a lot else.

'Leave it to me. I'll sell it for scrap. Send it to the compactor where it belongs.' He looks around the yard. 'Half the junk in this place should be sent to the compactor.'

'It's more than junk, Justin. It's a memorial. It's an icon. It's the art of junk. And it's where people come to get things off their chest.'

'Too right they do. I have no idea how Dad made a living. No one ever buys anything. All they want to do is stare at broken machinery and talk for hours.'

'I don't think he did make a living here.' As executor of the will, I received the paperwork for Norm's telephone betting account yesterday. It's got sixty thousand dollars in it. And that's apart from the money in his bank accounts. 'That's what

I'm here to tell you, Justin. Norm made quite a bit of money on the track.'

Justin leans so far back in his chair I'm worried he's going to topple over. When Norm's will was read we found out he had left the yard to Justin. Any cash was to be divided three ways between Justin, Marg, and me and the kids. We thought he might have a bit put away because he hardly spent anything. The man could build a working machine out of tin foil, a ribbon and lemon peel. So I guessed I might get a few thousand dollars.

The minute I heard that money was coming, I drove straight to Merv Bull's Motor and Machinery Maintenance and Repairs, and asked Merv to find me a car for five thousand dollars. Norm's money might not come through for some time, but I still have the money from Mum.

'What kind of car?' Merv asked.

'Small, but with four doors. Automatic. Yes, automatic. And with a little cupholder that flips out of the dashboard.'

'Engine size? Performance and handling? Warranty?'

'No, I just want a cupholder.'

'Colour?'

'A black or grey cupholder would be fine.' I can't count the number of hours I've spent trying to get the morning school run coffee stains out of my clothes.

'Right,' Merv said.

He's going to call me when he's found a good

one. Meanwhile, I'm thrashing this brute of a Holden like it deserves. Melissa and Jake have cinched their seatbelts very tight and occasionally hold hands when we take a corner.

Justin drops his chair back to vertical and picks up another spanner from the table to work at the rusty nut and bolt he's fiddling with.

'What do you mean by quite a bit of money?' He's not looking at me. That's Justin's way. He manages to have entire conversations while gazing at a rock or a tree or a camshaft.

'Seventy-seven thousand four hundred and twenty-nine dollars and eleven cents.' I can't help laughing. 'The sly bugger. He'd be cracking up at the idiot looks on our faces.' My breath does a quick intake of its own accord, a kind of hiccup. 'I miss him.'

Justin nods. He leans back in his chair again to flick on the kettle.

'Cup of tea?'

I sniff a yes and watch the steam fog up the shed window while Justin makes the tea.

'Milk?' He lifts the opened carton of milk, but I shake my head.

I take the cup he passes me and sip the strong brew. Outside in the yard, the rusted tractors and car bodies, the harvester combs and the sheets of corrugated iron, the motors and trays and wheel rims and cyclone wire and steel drums and sheep skulls and windows and metal lockers and a single broken vending machine crack and sigh as the morning sun evaporates the dew from their hides.

'By the way.' I've suddenly remembered. 'Did you know Samantha Patterson was bonking that council officer?'

'Of course.'

'But you've only been here half a minute! How come you knew and I didn't?'

'Dad told me. So, what will happen with the development now?'

'They have to resubmit the application to council because, of course, it broke every regulation in the planning book. There's some court case going on. Not sure what will happen. I hope I don't have to start painting placards again. I've still got marine paint on my shirt.'

I take another sip of tea. This is my life, I think. My ordinary life with tea and company and two unruly children. I don't need a Merc or an Audi, or even a Harley.

'When's the court date?'

Everyone's been asking me this. The SOS supporters have threatened to hire a bus and travel to Halstead Magistrates' Court. They said it's for support, but I'm fairly certain it's for the entertainment value. I told them we still need to save the school, so to stop playing around and start thinking about how to use the money we raised at the auction. The words 'party' and 'beach holiday' did come up, but in the end we decided on a media campaign. Whatever that is.

'Two weeks. The legal aid lawyer says I'll probably get off with a bond.'

Melissa appears at the door of the shed, dragging her brother behind her. 'I'm not looking after him anymore. He won't listen to me. He put an old paint tin on his head and I can't get it off.'

She swings Jake in through the shed door. His tin head bangs against the doorjamb.

'Ow,' Jake says from inside the tin.

'What are you doing, Jake?' I shout so he can hear me.

'I'm Ned Kelly.'

'Hold your breath, Ned.' When I give the paint tin a quick firm twist, Jake is too surprised to scream. He squeaks, then rubs his ears.

'This is a nice blue.' I wonder how the kitchen would look painted this colour.

'When are we going home?' Jake says.

I don't know why I put up with these children. Apparently there's still a white slave trade in the Middle East. I wonder how much I'd get for two.

'In a minute. Go and get some lemons and we'll head off.'

They race to the tree in the middle of the yard and jump up and down, trying to grab the lemons off the high branches. I stand and stretch.

'Thanks for the tea.' I put the cup on the table.

'I'm glad you knew my dad. I'm glad you're still here.' Justin's voice is soft as he continues examining the thread on the bolt before placing it carefully on the bench. He stands up.

341

I hesitate before I say, 'Actually, we're having sausages for dinner tonight. Top quality from the supermarket. You're welcome to come.' I am almost fifty per cent sure I didn't leave them sitting on the car seat in the sun.

He looks down at me and smiles. It's a rare thing, a Justin smile. He has beautiful teeth. Natural ones.

'That'd be great.'

'See you at six, then.' I might even put on the new green jersey dress I got from the op shop last week.

As the kids hare off to the car with lemons aproned in their shirts, I take a long look over Norm Stevens Junior's yard.

The art of junk.